Love Me Not

Edited by NiceGirlNaughtyEdits
Edited by Beth Hudson
Cover Designer Fine's Fine Designs
Formatting Caelan Fine

Love Me Not

Copyright © 2023 Shayna Astor

From the Author

Love Me Not is a full-length, stand alone that features strong language, mature situations, explicit sexual scenes, mentions of Alzheimer's, and death of a loved one. This book is intended for readers age 18 and up.

Thank you so much for reading my novel! I hope you enjoy reading it, as much as I enjoyed writing it!

Other Books by Shayna Astor

Hot & Cold

Shattered Pieces

Own Me (A dark romance)

Off Limits (Book 1 in the Limits Series)

Faking Perfection: A Brighton High Reunion (Coming June 2023)

Unknown Suitor: The Holidates Series (Coming December 2023)

Stay tuned for The Baker Sibling Series. Coming Fall 2023.

Dedication

To those who have crossed the fine line that exists between love and hate.

Chapter 1

Everybody has that one person in their life who makes their day less enjoyable. The one who you have to psych yourself up to be around. Who, once they leave, you find yourself working the kink out of your specially constructed armor. The bane of your very existence.

I work with mine. Which means I see him at least five days a week, every so often a full seven. It certainly makes life difficult. But I'm nothing if not professional, able to lock away my emotions and keep my hatred to a taunting level of banter. I do my best to avoid him at all costs beyond that.

Chase Andrews and I have been working at the same law firm for five years. We've been competitors since day one. We've hated each other since day two.

It was all well and cute until we worked our first case together and spent more time arguing than going over our depositions, arguments, and witness statements. We won the case, but only by the skin of our teeth.

After that, we haven't had to work closely again. Sure, we always have some interaction, some crossover.

We're the two top attorneys at our practice, outside of the partners, that is.

Last night, news broke about a big celebrity couple from our small area. They're the wealthiest people in town and he's some sort of music star. Apparently, he's been cheating for several years, and the wife just found out. I'm sure the partners are drooling over it, and it'd be a case that could make my career, so I can't help but be excited too.

Which means so is Chase.

It's a Tuesday in mid-April, and to prep myself for another day of Chase, I blare a Sevendust song before getting out of the car and looking up at our building.

Walking in, I can already tell the day is nothing like normal. People are milling about everywhere, buzzing chatter filling the air, and all secretaries have phones pressed to their ears, including mine.

"Nance, what's going on?" I lean down and whisper to her before opening the door to my office.

"Didn't you see the news last night?" Of course, I had. The Douglas split. It'd be impossible to miss. Not to mention, it was on every radio station. But that doesn't explain the chaos.

My knit-together brows and lost eyes must be enough for her. "They called here, and we took the case. Word is, you and Chase are on it."

Now my brows shoot sky high, eyes bulging. We cannot work together. Nope, not possible.

"Prescott!" If I wasn't so used to my name being bellowed in the surly voice of Mr. Lions, I would have jumped. As it is, this happens about three times a week.

Setting my bag and coat against the side of Nancy's desk, I smooth my blouse and skirt and take a deep breath before walking over to Mr. Lions' office, a peppy, albeit fake, smile plastered on my face.

"Good morning, sir."

"In my office. Now."

He stays in his spot against the doorframe, forcing me to walk past so I'm ahead of him—so he can stare at my ass, no doubt—and I take the added steps until I reach his office. I hate that he looks at me in such an objective way, but I'm the only female at my level, and it's an unfortunate reality of the world I live in. At least here. Would it be different elsewhere? I have wondered.

My veins fill with icy sludge before I'm even through the door. It's the very second I see the smug smirk sitting on Chase's face.

"Sit, Elizabeth." Mr. Lions' voice tears me from my spot, causing me to take the chair next to Chase with hasty but reluctant steps.

Angling myself into the corner farthest from him, I rest my chin on my hand and take another deep breath to ease the anxious fluttering in my chest. I'm sure whatever Mr. Lions wants has to do with the news from last night, but I still get that child-in-the-principal's-office feeling every time I'm sitting across from him.

Unbuttoning his coat, he sits in his wingback chair behind his large mahogany desk. "I'm sure you both heard the news last night about the Douglases' very public split. Mr. Douglas was caught cheating by both Mrs. Douglas and a private investigator. It was a public confrontation, and Mrs. Douglas reacted once she got home."

We know better than to interrupt him while he's giving the brief, but I adjust in my chair to lean forward slightly. It's like I won't believe the news of Chase and I working together until I hear it right from his mouth. And I'm hoping beyond hope I don't.

"This morning, we received a call from Mrs. Douglas that she would like *us* to represent her. It's going to be a high-profile case as they're our very own 'celebrity' couple in town. Everything about their lives is very public in case you didn't already know. There will be many front-page articles, both about the split, the publicity of it all and, of course, the impending divorce."

He pauses, standing with his hands splayed on his desk, and gets down to what I've been dreading. What I had a feeling was coming the second I walked in and saw my arch nemesis.

"You two are the best we have here. You both pull more in solo than any of the other senior associates combined, and you're both our top requested attorneys. But you know this; this isn't news." Giving a throat clear, his eyes dash between us. "What is news is that we're asking you to work together on this one. It's just that big, that important. It doesn't matter how much we've done in the past. We fuck up this one, we lose all credibility."

He looks between the two of us for a very heated minute when neither of us respond. "I know you two have your issues with each other."

"No, sir, we just—"

"Shut it, Andrews. Us partners may mostly be a figurehead, but we're not blind or stupid. You're able to keep it professional, we see that. We both recognize and appreciate it, but you don't get along. You don't like each other. That's fine, nobody has to be friends here. But you will need to figure out how to work together closely and pull late nights together for this case, regardless."

My stomach twists as I take in my reality, saying nothing. Looking from me to Chase and back again, I can tell he's waiting for something. Not sure what it is, I grit my teeth and glance over at Chase. While I'm sitting ramrod straight in my chair, my hands folded in my lap, Chase is slouching and has his long legs stretched out in front of him, crossed at the ankles. I can almost imagine him having his feet right on Mr. Lions' desk. He's so full of arrogance, I wouldn't put it past him.

When his eyes meet mine and he has that cocky smile plastered to his face, irritation creeps through me. I always have to fight the urge to smack it right off him.

"As you both know, and have been working toward, there's a promotion on the line. To become partner. We'll be watching this case closely. The three of us will be checking in, assisting, and showing up when the client is here. We'll be deciding after the trial who gets the promotion. It's between the two of you only. Not that that should be very surprising to either of you."

No, none of that is surprising. I've been up against Chase since the day I started working here. We were hired the same week, and both hit the ground running. That doesn't make it any easier to know that I'll be working closely and for very long hours with Chase, for months.

But I don't have a choice. This is coming down from the top; there's no room for argument or discussion.

"Is that something the two of you can handle?"

"Yes, sir." My voice is strong despite the rising of bile in my throat.

"Andrews?"

"Of course, sir."

"Good. Now get out of my office."

With that dismissal, I rise and quickly make my way out, heading straight into my own office after grabbing my things from Nancy's desk.

Flopping into my chair with a heavy sigh, I slink down, staring up at the ceiling.

On some level, I feel like I'm being punished. I can barely stand to be in the same room with Chase. And when he opens his mouth? It just makes it that much harder.

But the promotion is on the line. The one I've been gunning for, for over a year. I think part of me knew it would always come to something like this.

A knock at my door pulls my attention from the lines I'm counting in the ceiling.

"Everything okay?" Nancy asks as she slowly enters, closing the door behind her. She's a good secretary, a decent friend, though strictly at the office.

"I guess."

"You have to work with Mr. Andrews, don't you." Her voice says it more like a statement, and I'm sure she already knows. This office is rife with gossip.

"I do."

"It won't be so bad. You can handle it."

"It's more *him* I'm worried about handling." He's cocky and known to overstep when working with a partner. I don't need him showboating in front of me or putting it on for the client. While he's good at what he does, so am I, and we need to let the other shine too.

"When do you start?"

"I'm not sure. Probably today. This is going to be a big case. I'll have to go through and check on where my other clients stand at the moment because this will likely take my full focus."

"Oh, I'm happy to help with that." She flips her long auburn locks over shoulder and looks in the direction of Chase's office. "At least he's nice to look at, though. If you'll be stuck in a room together so much."

"Nance. Please tell me you haven't slept with him." Chase has quite the reputation of being a ladies' man. And while he's kept it out of the office as far as I know, you never *really* know with him.

"Of course not. I'm just saying…I wouldn't kick him out of bed." A devilish grin spreads across her face, her amber eyes swirling with lust.

"I'm not sure there's anything he can do that would make up for his personality." I don't go for the cocky frat boy thing anymore. That ended once I was in college, and even then, I barely entertained guys like that. Chase thinks he's God's gift to women, and I don't appreciate that kind of attitude.

"I don't know. Those eyes…"

Rolling mine at the mention of Chase's, I try my hardest not to gag. "Nance. Come on."

Smirking, she gives me a pointed look. "He may be a grade-A asshole, but he's hot. You have to be able to admit that."

A smile spreads across my face. "Never."

"You're infuriating. I'll help you with those files when you're ready."

"Thanks, Nance."

She taps the doorframe on her way out, and I exhale a heavy breath, slouching down in my chair again.

I need to spruce myself up and get ready for this. The music in the car is no longer holding out for me, and I've deflated like a cold balloon.

With a deep breath, I put on my big girl panties and start pulling files for all my current clients to double check the status of their divorces. Sometimes there's a bit of a waiting game while paperwork is drawn up and calls are made back and forth. Sometimes one party needs to think over some details or come back with their own offer. And then waiting on judges can take time.

It's the first step in prepping for working with Chase.

While working with him may be the very last thing I want to do, I can be professional, because this promotion means that much to me.

So, I won't just work with him, I'll crush him.

Chapter 2

"You wanted to see me, Elizabeth?" Chase pokes his head into my office. I called his secretary two hours ago, asking for him to come in so we can get started.

At this point, it's nearing four-thirty, and work's almost done for the day.

"Yes, thank you for showing up at some point this year." I wave my hands out to the side with a flourish, as though he's done me a huge favor.

"I'm sorry, Princess. Am I not early enough for you? I do have other clients that require my undivided and unique attention." I loathe the fact that he calls me Princess. I have no idea where the nickname came from, but it's been around since early on and has not gone anywhere.

"I'd like for us to come up with some sort of game plan for this case. Lions is right, it's going to be huge, and I don't want us looking like fools in front of the press or town. Or the partners."

"Aw, you should know by now that I can never look like a fool. Even if I were to fall flat on my face in court one day—which would never happen, but let's pretend—I still would never look like a fool." And there's the cocky attitude I can't stand.

My teeth grind together as I open and close my fists.

"For just one second, could you drop the act? Could you be an actual human being?"

"What act? This is me, Princess. I'm good at what I do, I'm a good-looking guy, and I'm confident. What's so wrong with that?" He shoves his hands into his pockets and leans against the doorframe, his suit jacket pulling to the side to reveal his tapered waistline.

He is fit, I'll give him that. I know he takes care of his body, as it's one of the many things he likes to brag about.

While he may not dip into the pool of ladies at work, it doesn't stop them from gossiping about him and his looks. I don't get it. Yes, he keeps himself put together with his styled blond hair and stubble that's clearly intentional and not from lack of shaving. But how can they see past the assholery?

"Just keep your confidence to yourself because it's not doing anything to impress me. Got it?"

That smirk I hate so much spreads across his face. "Sure thing, Princess. Is there any other reason you called me in? Or just to insult me a little."

"Listen here, Evil Spawn." I use my lovely nickname for him. I don't break it out often in the office, but desperate times. "We have to find a way to work together, and I can't do it if you're going to act like I should be thankful for you, because I'm not. We're *both* good at what we do. Understood?"

All he does is roll his eyes at me as he closes the door and strides over to my desk, placing his hands on it and leaning forward.

"Here's the deal, Elizabeth. You're right, we are both good at what we do, which means I don't *need* your help on this case, and you probably think you don't need mine. But that's not up to us. The partners put us together for a reason and we have to both respect and accept that. I don't want to be forced to work with you any more than you want to work with me." He pauses for a second, and I open my mouth to speak, but he holds up one finger and wiggles it.

"I know you hate me. And guess what, Princess? I'm not so fond of you either. Not only have we been competition since day one, but you've been a royal thorn in my side since then too. For the duration of this case, we have to work together, but let's find a way to make it as painless as possible. I'll do my best to hold back on what may seem overly cocky if you stop being such a fucking bitch all the time."

My mouth pops open at the last sentence, but I quickly regain my composure. Of course he'd think I'm a bitch. So, I stand and extend my hand. With a quick look, he straightens and takes my delicate hand in his large one and shakes it.

"Now then, what did you have in mind about this?"

"There's a chance it will go to trial, so we need to be prepared for that. Not just because it's high profile, but there's a lot of money involved. I'd like to start collecting witness statements as soon as possible. People who saw Mr. Douglas with his mistress."

"You don't think we might want to make sure their statements are factual first? Mrs. Douglas could certainly pay them off, or they'll side with her since she's wealthy and the one who was cheated on."

"Is there a prenup?" Flopping back into my chair, I start rifling through files on my desk.

"If we're going to work together, you need to clean this sty up first. How can you find anything?" His lip curls up in disgust. Chase is impeccably tidy. His office is always kept very neat and organized.

"I was just going through all my cases to check statuses. They'll be put away by the morning." Finally, I find the right file. He's right; my desk is a disaster right now, though I hate to admit he could be right about anything at all.

Flipping through, I find the right paper.

"Yes, it looks like there is a prenup. So, we should have Mrs. Douglas in as soon as possible."

"I know. She's coming in tomorrow."

"I'm sorry, what?" Confusion and anger war within me.

"I already called and spoke with her. Lovely woman. Very distraught. She'll be in tomorrow." He turns on his heel and starts to stride away.

Jumping out of my chair, I slam my hands on my desk. "Chase! Were you even going to tell me about this meeting that we should both be in on?"

"Eventually."

"I thought you were going to stop being an asshole." I practically shout it after him as he crosses the threshold of my office door.

"I'll start tomorrow." With one hand raised, he waves me off, but doesn't turn around, and I can practically hear that he has that damn smirk on his face.

"Asshole," I mumble under my breath.

It hasn't even been a full day of working with him and I already want to rip my hair out. This is not going to go well.

Chapter 3

W ell, Chase was right about one thing. Colleen Douglas is lovely and quite distraught. She's young and beautiful, a former model who still has her figure despite being in her forties and having had four kids.

The only part of our meeting that irked me is that she cried the whole time. It's not unusual in this line of work for one of the parties to cry—sometimes both do—but I never quite know how to respond.

I quietly handed her tissues, for which she thanked me every time, but each new question brought on another onslaught, and a few times, Chase and I made eye contact in abject horror because we just didn't know what to do with the blubbering mess in front of us.

A quick bathroom break for Mrs. Douglas to "refresh herself" as she put it, gave us a quick chance to think about having her come another day, but it seemed to us that it wouldn't matter once she returned. Her emotions would be the same regardless.

"I knew Seth was doing something wrong, but I never thought he'd actually *cheat on me.* "It's probably the tenth time she's said it in the three hours she's been here.

"What are some of the things that made you think he was doing something?" I try to prod her gently, wanting to avoid another round of hysterics.

"He was almost never home anymore. Which is unusual if he's not recording or on tour. And we basically stopped having sex, which is not at all like Seth. I figured he was working on something new and wasn't ready to tell me yet or was trying to snag somebody for a duet."

"Is some of this behavior not unusual?" Chase and I tag team the questions to avoid her getting the feeling that one of us is in charge. It was one thing we agreed to before Colleen came in today.

"He's made surprise records in the past. Around our fifth wedding anniversary, he recorded three special songs just for me. It was a lot of the same behavior because he was busy and keeping it a secret."

"What made you decide to hire Mr. Turpin, your private investigator?"

"When Seth started getting cagey and defensive about my questions on his whereabouts. He'd missed dinner for the fourth time in a week. It's one of the only times we all get together peacefully as a family. It's hectic with four kids who all want to do different things. We don't have enough parents to split amongst them, so they all get undivided attention. But at dinner, we all get what we need. He's always said it's one of his favorite times, so for him to miss that many is a big deal. I knew something more was going on and couldn't wait to find out what anymore." She sniffs and dabs at her nose before silent tears stream down her cheeks.

"Can we switch gears and talk about the prenup? It appears you both had your own individual funds that were to be kept separate in the event of a divorce?"

"As a former model, my images are still used sometimes so I still get paid for those. I also had a good savings that I haven't touched since we mostly lived off of what Seth made. Why? Is there a problem with it?" Her eyes widen, and she looks terrified as she glances between us.

"No, we just like to know the reasons behind it and get as much information about it as possible. What the reasons for the parameters are, that sort of thing. It's something his lawyer may try to fight, but since he cheated on you, you have the upper hand because of what was written in yours."

Colleen nods like she understands, but I know she doesn't. It's a lot for anyone to take in.

Resting my hand on her forearm, I get her attention. "Trust us, Mrs. Douglas. We're very good at what we do. The best, in fact. That's why the partners have entrusted your case to us. While many things sound confusing and the terminology can be hard to follow, *we* understand it and have a strong handle on how to utilize our tools. You're in good hands."

She nods again as her eyes well.

"Why don't we call it a day? Sound good to everybody?" Chase's hands are clasped in front of his chest as he asks.

With a quick hug for each of us and a handful of tissues, Mrs. Douglas leaves the conference room.

Chase flops into the nearest chair with a huff. "That was exhausting."

"Quite. And I still feel like we didn't get much out of her except that she was surprised it happened."

"We can run with that, though. Make it seem like he was a real family man, use the dinners to play up that he was usually around, and this new behavior was unwarranted. You know that they're going to play the neglect role."

"I'm wondering if they may make it easy so we can avoid the spotlight. Just have discussions about the kids and property. It doesn't seem like either of them will need any funds."

"Don't be delusional. It's a huge thing *because* they love the spotlight. If not, they wouldn't have made it the spectacle it already is. This is probably going to court, and we should prepare for that. Mentally and with the job." He gives me a pointed look, like I'm not ready.

"I'm well aware, Chase. Just a thought."

"A stupid one."

"Hey. Asshole alert. Maybe we should get you an asshole jar. Every time you open your damn mouth, you'll have to put a dollar in."

"Only if you have to when you're a bitch." He raises an eyebrow, his lips quirking as he looks at me in challenge. "And it was a stupid thought. This is big for a reason. It's going to go beyond kids and property and finances. I bet the kids will be the biggie." They usually are, so it wouldn't be any shock for custody to be the biggest hurdle we face.

"Ugh. I hate working with you almost as much as I hate you." I gather my files angrily and stand to leave.

"Back at you, Princess." Chase beats me to the door, and we both storm toward our offices.

This is going to be the longest case of my life.

Chapter 4

It's been four weeks of the Douglas case and things are still awful between Chase and me. We almost never see eye to eye on anything or the right way to go through this process.

I don't remember it being this hard to work with him last time, but it was ages ago. Somehow, I'd forgotten why we stopped working together besides just our mutual hatred of one another.

We haven't had too many late nights, but tonight will be since we both had to take time to prioritize other clients.

Some custody agreements came back as well as conditions for vacating a house that one of my clients was bought out on. I had to make call after call and set up meetings before I could focus on the Douglas case. I have no idea what Chase had to do and didn't bother to ask.

Right now, we're in his office, at seven-thirty, eating some Chinese food out of white cartons with chopsticks. It's us and one intern who was assigned to help, and today that means staying as late as we do.

Being stuck here with asshole one and asshole two is the last thing I want to be doing with my night, but I have no choice.

The guys are currently going back and forth about the process of divorce and whether getting married at all is worth it. I have to refrain from rolling my eyes.

Chase is in his late twenties, like I am, but Devon is a young one, only twenty-two. What does he know about life and marriage?

Still, the way Chase is talking, you'd think he's just frustrated because he doesn't have that yet. Maybe he thinks he never will. Which I can understand, since how would he find somebody to put up with such assholery on a daily basis?

"The wife, the kids, I don't know, man, I enjoy bachelorhood." Devon leans back in his chair and pops a piece of chicken into his mouth.

"You may not feel the same way when you're old like me."

"Sounds like you're jealous of something you don't have." It's my turn to participate in this ridiculous conversation.

"I can't be jealous of something I don't want." Chase looks at me with a furrowed brow.

Shock hits my system. While I may hate him, Chase and I have known each other for years and not once have I ever heard him say he doesn't want a family. I guess I just assume most people do. "You don't want kids?"

"You do? Liz, you really want this? Putting kids through this shit?"

"Not every marriage ends in divorce."

"Enough do. It's our job to know numbers, statistics. You know how prevalent divorce is, how messy things can become. Not for me. No, thank you. I'll enjoy my fun." He scoops some rice onto his chopsticks and skillfully eats it without dropping any.

I stare into my container, twirling a few pieces of lo mein on my chopsticks, but not really seeing them. I have to shake this away; I can't let him see the tears flooding my eyes.

It's not even so much a want for that right now. Yes, I want kids someday, but now is not the time. It's more the way he looks down on things, the way he talks about it. I don't need him giving me a hard time for it. He has enough ammo against me to make me feel bad if he wants to.

Working together daily, I'm sure I'm giving him more, even if unintentionally. It takes one instance to slip up for him to have something else to use against me any time he feels like it.

And having this one thing that makes me a bit emotional, because I feel my biological clock tick-tick-ticking away while there are no prospects of even a boyfriend on the horizon, is a weakness around Chase. One he'll exploit if I let it be known.

So instead, I straighten up, clear my throat, and shove it deep down where I tend to keep it. Because if I let myself really face the wants in my life and how far I am from those, then I'll surely burst into tears.

It's harder with Mom since her Alzheimer's diagnosis. She's drifting further and further every day, so having her at my wedding, meeting my children, it seems like a distant dream at this point. One that will never come to be. Half the time, she barely remembers me, and it's hard to imagine finding somebody I love enough to marry and have children with before her memory is gone for good.

Nobody at work knows about Mom. I've kept this secret to myself and my best friend Lydia. She's been through so much with me. We've been friends since high school and have never left each other's side, never wavered in support of one another.

She's my go-to when I need a moment to cry or share a good laugh. And she helped me find the place for Mom and Dad when it was clear Mom's memory problems weren't minor and Dad was still recovering from his heart attack. Talk about overwhelming. Feeling like you're about to lose two parents at once is enough to make you realize how much you *do* want the family.

For a long time, it was something I was certain I'd never need. This job was enough. It was the love of my life.

Then Dad almost died, and Mom started getting lost in places she's been going to for forty years.

It changed my perspective.

By the time I focus back on the conversation, the boys have moved on and are now talking about the cars that the Douglases have in their possession and how to appropriately split them. Mrs. Douglas has asked for the SUVs, as she plans to have primary custody. They have an Acura, BMW, and Suburban. Why you need three different third-row vehicles is beyond me, but I guess when money is no object it doesn't matter.

"You ever see him around town in the Corvette? It's sweet looking." Of course Devon would be easily impressed by a sports car.

But it's not him I'm focused on. It's this strange look in Chase's eye, like he can tell something bothered me, but isn't quite sure what it is or what to do with it.

Great. Now I've made it easier for him to give me a hard time.

It just means I'll have to listen and pay more attention to see what comes up as a weakness for him.

The problem with that? Chase is confident and happy with his life. He likes being single, at least I'd assume so with as much as he brags about it.

And he drives a Mercedes, which he claims is his dream car. Apparently, he also has a pickup truck, but it's never what he drives to the office.

No, Chase has few weak spots, and the one I know about, I would never exploit, because it hits just a little too close to home.

Chapter 5

As the case progresses, Chase and I have to spend more full days and long nights working together. We've gained a steady diet of takeout food since we barely make it home before nine most nights.

Tonight is just another night. While Chase chowed down on pizza, I opted for a salad from the local pizzeria instead. While I adore a good slice, I've been feeling off with the terrible meal choices lately.

We're in his office, and it's just the two of us. The testimonials of friends, family, the nanny, even the private investigator are what's on tap tonight. And we're both utterly exhausted going over them.

With a heavy sigh, he looks pointedly in my direction. "Elizabeth, we have to do this one first to show a history of this behavior."

"I don't think we do. I think we can start with the private investigator so it's fresh in the mind that he's already done it and back it up with the history and testimonials from the other people stating what they've seen or experienced." It came to light during some of our questions to friends, family, and former workers of the family that Mr. Douglas had cheated before. He just happened to get caught this time.

He drops his head into his hand and rubs along his forehead, stopping his pacing as he does so. "Sometimes I wonder how you even practice law. Let alone are good at it."

"Why, because I disagree with your method and the process you want to take? Is it really so impossible that *my* way might be right and beneficial?"

"In this case, yes. It's totally crazy to think that you're right. Why would we start with the person who found him guilty?"

"Because then the rest is just gravy. It's reinforcing what we already know."

"So why not start with those and build up to the guilt? It shows that he's been doing it for years and only this time got caught because Colleen was finally suspicious enough to do something about it." His hands are out, palms up, and moving from side to side. His tone only increases in desperation.

I cross my arms tight against my chest. "I don't think it's the right way to go about this. And you won't change my mind."

"You are so incredibly frustrating to work with."

"Back at you, Chase. You think this has been some grand adventure for me? I'm sure you think I'm lucky to get to work with a lawyer of your amazing caliber." I take a step toward him. "But you're an asshole and utterly impossible to work with because everything so far has been your way or the highway. I'm standing my ground on this one." I don't realize I'm still moving closer until there are only a few steps separating us.

Though he remains silent, his green irises are simmering as they lock onto mine. The look he's searing me with isn't one of anger, though, and it has my stomach flipping with uncertainty.

"I'm just as qualified an attorney as you are, Chase. Maybe more so. And just so we're clear, all this makes me hate you even more."

And that makes the fire ignite. With a growl, he moves toward me. Every step forward he takes pushes me backward until I'm against the desk, my chest heaving, heart racing, panties wetting beyond my control. He's standing so close that every intake of air makes my breasts brush against him.

We're silent for a few minutes staring at each other, breathing heavily, standing impossibly close yet unable to leave this spot. I have no idea what's happening, but I can't make myself move away. I find myself melting in the tension between us, ready for it to snap.

I don't know who moves first, but suddenly hands are flying, and mouths are crashing. His lips are forceful against mine, almost punishing, as I twist my fingers into his hair and tug, not exactly gently.

Teeth gnash and nip at lips. Our movements are frenzied, like we're afraid any second this will all crash around us.

I never realized how hot the clichéd clearing of the desk really is until he does it. Strong hands on my waist lift me to the edge as he hikes up my pencil skirt. I fumble with his belt buckle as his hand slides up my thigh, shifting my panties to the side so he can feel me.

"Next time you tell me you hate me, you might want to tell your pussy. I don't think it got the interoffice memo. You're fucking soaked for me."

"Don't flatter yourself. It's been a while and my body's just excited. You have nothing to do with it."

His hand twists into my hair, pulling backwards as he licks up my throat, nipping at my chin as he slides two fingers into me.

A moan escapes before I can stop it. *God, why does it have to feel so damn good?*

"I think we both know that's not true, Elizabeth."

I don't care what is or isn't true at the moment. I may hate Chase with a deep-seated fiery passion, but it's hard to deny what he's doing to my body. Or how it's responding.

My hand wraps to the back of his neck as he hooks his fingers inside me, causing me to arch toward him as my head tips back. I'd abandoned my mission of undoing his pants the second his fingers entered me. Releasing my hair from his grasp, he finishes the job, freeing himself.

Tilting forward, I give a quick glance and immediately look up at the ceiling, swallowing hard as I grip the back of his neck tighter. Of course he'd be well endowed. Why wouldn't he be? He thinks he excels at everything anyway.

With hurried strokes, he brings me over the edge as I cry out.

Removing his fingers from me, he puts his hands on my hips and tugs me closer to the edge of the desk.

"Don't say I never gave you anything," he murmurs against my ear as he eases into me.

His breath hitches as he gets deeper, stopping once he's all the way inside me, resting his head in the crook of my neck.

Of all the situations I thought I'd find myself in with Chase, this was not even on the list. If somebody had asked me if I thought we'd kill each other or fuck each other, kill would have definitely been my answer.

But when he starts moving inside me, I take it all back. I still hate him, it's pouring off of me in waves, albeit mingled with 'fuck me.' He must feel it rolling toward him because he starts thrusting harder and faster, as though he's punishing me for such cruel thoughts.

"Fuck, Chase." I hate the way his name feels in my mouth, but good God, I don't hate a single other thing going on right now. My nails dig into his neck as a moan rises in my chest.

"Not going to call me Evil Spawn? I'm disappointed." His words are pointed, but he's breathless. I don't even have to look at him to know that he has that smirk on his face.

"Evil Spawn." It's unconvincing as it comes out on a breath as I twist my fingers into his hair.

"Fuck, Princess. You're a better lay than I ever could have imagined." Of course he'd imagined it. He would. This asshole. I can't even believe I'm letting him fuck me right now. But the way it feels, I'm sort of regretting never having done it before.

Because as wrong as it is, it feels fucking fantastic.

The pressure in my pelvis builds again as I start whining with each hard thrust.

"You gonna come again for me, Liz? Wow, you must really be into me."

"Keep your mouth shut and fuck me, asshole." Before I know what's happening, he pulls out, yanks me from the desk and flips me around, then presses between my shoulder blades so my chest is against the desk as he slides back into me.

A few hard thrusts and he wraps my hair around his hand and tugs so I'm leaning on my hands.

"Care to say that again, Liz?" His breath is hot in my ear, sending a shudder through me.

I'm never one to back down from a challenge. Especially against Chase. Smirk on my face, I repeat myself. "I said, keep your mouth shut and fuck me. *Asshole.*"

Grunting, he releases my hair and moves his hand to wrap around my throat, pulling me against him. I've never appreciated his height before, but right now my head rests against his collarbone. It's perfect.

The hand not squeezing around my throat slides down my stomach and settles between my legs, swirling around my clit.

My head tips back more at the sensation, pressing into him as I moan loudly. His mouth finds the side of my neck, and I wrap an arm up to cup the back of his head.

Inside me, my hate for him is warring with how much I'm enjoying every single second of this. It's a good thing I didn't go into this neutral because I swear, he'd make me fall in love with him just by how well he uses his dick. But there's no way that could ever happen.

"Chase." I sigh his name as the pressure builds.

"Come for me, Liz." His mouth is right against my ear, pulling my earlobe gently between his teeth. When he bites down, it sets off my orgasm and I scream, tightening around him as my body shudders against his. A grunt and a low 'fuck' mixed with his leg trembles tell me he's coming too.

He keeps me pressed against him as we come down from the post orgasm high and our bodies regain the ability to be still. Releasing my neck, he trails his hand down my chest before taking a step back.

Immediately, he tucks himself away and runs a hand through his tousled hair. I'm sure mine doesn't look much better, and I smooth what I can as I right my skirt and adjust my shirt.

Confusion slams into me. What the fuck just happened? I'd like to say I feel even a modicum of guilt, but after two outstanding orgasms, that's just not possible.

"I still hate you," I mumble as I look at him.

"Not as much as I hate you."

"One-time thing."

"Absolutely."

We're both breathless, swallowing harshly. If only he'd been bad, horrible, atrocious. I'd even settle for tiny. Unfortunately for me, he's none of those things. And I let him know exactly how much I enjoyed every single second.

Clearing his throat, he smoothes his tie. "We can probably finish going through these briefs tomorrow."

"Fine with me."

"Listen, we can't let this get weird. We're two adults who happened to have a consensual and mind-blowing fuck. That's it." He thought it was mind blowing? Hm, interesting. And very good to know.

"And it's never happening again."

"If you say so." Wait, didn't he just agree to that?

"I do. What, you disagree? We can hardly stand to be in the same room with each other."

"I just don't think you'll be able to stay away after that." God, I hate that stupid smirk. I wonder what he'd do if I smacked it off his face. *Maybe he'd spank me.* Fuck. No.

"Keep dreaming, Evil Spawn. You caught me at a moment of weakness." Or the longest dry spell of my life. It's been at least eight months since I'd last had sex until tonight.

When you're gunning for a promotion, you have little time for much else. Like a social life. Or a sexual one.

Lydia will be so pleased to hear. Lydia's going to have my head on a platter. For all she's heard me complain about Chase, and now I'm going to tell her I broke my dry spell with a hate fuck in his office while working late on a trial?

She's going to lose her mind.

Chapter 6

"**I** had sex with him, Lyd. What the hell is wrong with me?" My head falls into my hand as I pace relentlessly up and down the hallway of my apartment.

I got home approximately three minutes ago and immediately called Lydia, starting with that sentence.

"Okay, first of all, how was it?" She doesn't need to ask who. She knows since he's the only person I ever call her to complain about.

"Really? That's your first question?" I stop my pacing.

"Yeah. I'm curious."

"It was amazing." I sigh heavily as I admit it, even to myself. "But it never should have happened." Ever. In a million years. And certainly not again, even though I'm already distracted by memories of it. On the way home, I sat at a green light for an extra beat while my mind was distracted, replaying the scenes in my head. The thought of his hand wrapped around my throat has my panties soaking all over again.

"Amazing how?"

"Ugh, you're not going to let this go, are you?" I walk into my room and rip open my panty drawer, lowering the ones I have on, right along with my skirt, and shimmy on a new pair while my phone is trapped between my ear and my shoulder.

"Nope." She pops the 'p' extra hard.

"It was...aggressive. Almost punishing in a way. It was a hate fuck in every sense of the word. We hate each other, it showed in the way we attacked each other and pulled at each other and the way he...thrusted. And all that made it the best sex I've had in ages. Possibly ever. And I'm not okay with that."

"Why not?"

"Really? Why would I be okay with my arch nemesis being the best sex I've ever had?" Maybe she's lost her mind.

"Arch nemesis feels a bit strong, Lizzie. I can understand why you hate him at work, but you don't really know him outside of that, do you?"

"No, but I don't need to. It's his general demeanor and disposition. I don't do assholes who think they're the greatest thing ever." I flop onto the edge of my bed, and Cheshire, my tabby cat, jumps up purring, ready for his evening pets.

"Okay, no offense, because you know I love you, but you have a little of that yourself. I think you have to, to be good at what you do, which you and Chase both are. But you're a lovely human being outside of that. Maybe he is too." Yup. She's definitely lost it.

"It's not possible, Lyd. I show a side of being a pleasant person at work. The only time I've known him to be anything even close to a normal human being is when his mom died. And that's something anybody would be emotional about. But outside of that, he's never appeared even close to a regular person. Just a cocky asshole. Evil Spawn."

"Alright. Well, what are you going to do about it?"

"Nothing. I'm going to pretend like it never happened." How, I have no idea, because it's still plaguing my mind, but I'll have to get it out of my system one way or another.

A round of laughter erupts in my ear and I have to pull the phone away with a scowl. "Good luck with that."

"It was a one-time thing. We both agreed. And it's going to stay a one-time thing. Mark my words."

Chapter 7

And it was a one-time thing.

Until a few days later when he follows me into the supply closet, locking the door behind him before he flips me around to face him and lifts me as he pushes me against the wall.

Hiking my skirt up, his hand grazes along my ass before settling between us. Wordlessly, his thumb swirls my clit through my panties. My body immediately responds to him, remembering the first time.

I hate to admit that I've thought about it several times since then. A handful of times with my vibrator.

"God, I fucking hate you and that stupid smirk." It's like it permanently resides on his face. At least in my presence.

"Really? Doesn't feel like it, Princess."

"Misunderstanding between my brain and other parts of my body."

Pressing his pelvis against mine, his hand closes around my throat, and he pulls my earlobe between his teeth. "No more talking, Liz. The only sounds I want to hear coming from that filthy mouth are the sounds of you falling apart around my dick."

A shudder runs through me at his words, which elicits a low laugh from Chase. My body is getting all sorts of confused. While my mind despises him beyond measure, the rest of me craves his touch. After only one time, which sends a trace of fear snaking through me.

"Now be a good girl and undo my pants for me."

"And if I don't?" I will, I absolutely will. Because as much as I don't want to admit it, my desire for him in this moment outweighs my hate.

One side of his mouth ticks up with a slight huff as his fingers push their way inside me, immediately hooking and moving furiously. At the same time, he loses his hand in my hair, tugging at the roots, forcing my head back as he licks up my neck. Closing his mouth around mine, he only needs to wait a second for a moan to ease from my chest to plunge his tongue in to explore my mouth.

Before I can even think about the type of kiss we just shared, he pulls my lip between his teeth and slides his mouth to my ear. "Undo my pants, Liz. It's not a request."

The shudder that runs through me sets off my orgasm as I buck against his hand and wrap my hands to meet at the back of his head.

Once I've come back to reality, I hastily tear at his belt and shove his pants down.

"Good girl." God, why is that such a turn on coming out of his mouth?

He doesn't hesitate to press inside me once he's free of his pants. One of his hands rests against the wall, near my ear, while the other is fully cupping my ass cheek.

When he's all the way inside me, my head tips back against the wall, one hand tangling into his hair while the other wraps around his tie.

The fact that we're mussing our clothes, tousling our hair, and just all around ruining our professional appearance for the day doesn't matter in the slightest. The fact that I'm apparently having the best sex of my life with the person I hate most in this world, now *that* is a problem.

I tighten my legs around his waist as he starts thrusting hard and fast, his other hand joining the first, supporting me.

"Fuck, why does this have to feel so good?" Shit, I just said that out loud, didn't I?

"Revealing your hand, Princess? I'm surprised at you."

"Stop calling me princess, Evil Spawn." There's so little conviction behind our name calling, it's disappointing.

"You first. *Fuck.* I swear your pussy's going to bring me to my knees."

"I'll take you on your knees any time."

"You first, Liz."

The problem with having sex at work, in a supply closet, no less, is that noise tends to travel, and when you're having really good sex, you want to be a little louder. Or at least I do. The first time it didn't matter, as we were alone in the office. But right now, we would assuredly draw attention.

Chase must be thinking the same thing as he presses a hand to my mouth, his eyes locking on mine. I hold his gaze as long as I can, refusing to back down in what feels like some sort of challenge, but I can't anymore as the pressure peaks, and I tighten around him, moaning loudly against his hand.

Slowing to move with me as I ride out the aftershocks, he shushes me gently, as if he's consoling a crying child. I'd be irritated if I wasn't so blissed out.

The second I'm still, he releases my mouth and puts both hands on my hips, holding me steady as he slams into me. I have to pull my lips between my teeth to keep from screaming as his thick cock rubs against all the right places.

With a choke of a breath, he leans his forehead in the crook of my shoulder. "Fuck."

We stay in that weird sort of embrace for a moment before reality seems to come back to both of us, and then we scramble away from each other.

He clears his throat and looks around as we both fix our clothes.

Though our gazes meet in a heated stare, neither of us says anything.

"I'll, uh, see you back out there, I guess." Chase turns on his heel and leaves before I can answer him.

With a deep breath, I run my fingers through my blonde curls and smooth down my shirt before turning to the shelves and finding a box of the pens I like.

Somehow, we manage to go through the rest of the day like nothing at all happened between us.

Chapter 8

"Hello, Miss Prescott." The warm greeting from the front desk never ceases to amaze me. There are over two hundred residents here, on various floors, but the front desk always remembers my name, even though I'm sure I'm here far less than most other families.

"Hi, Pete. How are you?" He's a regular at the front desk when I'm here, so it's easy for *me* to remember *his* name.

"Hanging in. How are you?"

"Oh, you know, same old same old." Except I'm fucking my mortal enemy slash coworker on an almost daily basis. But I can't tell anybody that.

"Well, I'll let you get to it."

Nodding, I head toward the elevator bay, but am stopped before I hit the button. "Oh, Miss Prescott? They're out on the patio today."

"Thank you!" I walk straight through the foyer and out to the large, paved patio. My parents live in the main building, this one containing the memory ward. There're sprawling grounds for walks and the whole thing is gated, just in case somebody starts to wander. It was the safest and highest-rated place I could find.

I spot my father immediately, and every ounce of tension seeps from my body, warmth like sunshine spreading through my extremities as a smile spans my face.

It only grows when he spots me, standing from his chair, his eyes twinkling and his own lips parting to show still perfectly straight teeth, albeit a bit yellower.

"Lilla Bean!"

"Hi, Daddy." I take three steps toward him as he does the same, and we meet in the middle. He's a frailer version of the man that used to twirl me around in the backyard, but he still gives me the same calming sensation, the one that makes me feel protected and loved.

Pulling me over to the spot he recently vacated, we sit in wrought-iron chairs, looking out at the residents milling about. The weather is starting to warm, and it's a beautiful day.

"How's my bean?" He pats my hand where it rests on the arm of the chair.

"I'm good, Daddy." My tone is gentle and light. I could tell him a bit about the troubles at work, and have as far as the case is concerned, but Chase is entirely off limits.

"It's been a while since you've been here."

"I know, I'm sorry." While I call several times a week, getting myself here is far more difficult.

"Don't worry, sweetheart. I love to tell all of my friends about my big-shot lawyer daughter. I'm proud of you."

"Well, I'm glad, because it's what's been keeping me away."

"I'd be lying if I said I wasn't a little disappointed that there's not a man keeping you away."

"Daddy!" The heat that creeps to my face is almost unbearable. I don't want him to see through me.

While being with Chase hasn't necessarily kept me away, it has taken our time from working on the case, which pushes us back a little bit each and every time. Though neither of us seem to care enough to stop fucking every chance we get.

"I'm sorry if I want my only daughter to settle down and have children before I miss it. I'm not getting any younger, you know."

"Don't talk like that. You're still a young, sprightly man." His heart attack scared the crap out of me. He's my rock, and I'd be utterly lost without him.

"In spirit maybe, but not in body."

Concern wraps around my consciousness and suddenly all I can think about is the phone call from the ambulance. "Are you feeling okay?"

Dad takes my hand in his. "I'm fine, sweetheart. But I'm old. I have to face the facts. I won't be here forever. And I just want to make sure you're loved before that happens. I don't know where I'd be if I didn't have your mother. She made all those years the happiest of my life. And gave me the very best gift of all. You."

I don't know what to say when Dad becomes introspective like this. That doesn't stop a mist from overtaking my eyes.

Sniffling and shaking it away, I turn out to the yard, searching for the head of full brown curls, filled with streaks of gray. When I do, I find Mom, sitting at a table painting with another resident.

"How is she today?"

"It's not the best day. Not the worst. This morning was rougher than the afternoon has been."

Every so often, Mom has full days where she doesn't even remember my father. Those are his most heartbreaking days. They've been married for more than half their lives. The doctors say it's because he's so much older than the version she sees in her mind, the one she remembers. Since she doesn't see herself, she doesn't have the same reaction.

Those are the days that tear my heart in two, because they're the ones where she doesn't recognize *me*, her only child.

"What are my chances?" I ask with a sharp swallow.

"I'd say seventy-five, twenty-five split in your favor."

Swallowing around the lump in my throat, I stand. Those aren't the greatest odds with Mom, and Dad's been wrong before.

He gives my hand a final squeeze as I slowly walk toward the table where Mom's painting.

I plant a smile on my face when I'm within a foot. That's when Mom looks up. At first, her blue eyes are hesitant, distant, but I see the moment they focus on me.

Her whole face blooms with excitement. "Elizabeth. Oh, my darling girl, come over here and give your mother a hug."

Glancing at the sky quickly, I try to push away the sting behind my eyes. "Hi, Mom." I wrap my arms around her frail shoulders. Her eating habits aren't the greatest in the past few years. It's not that she forgets to eat, because Dad and the staff make sure she doesn't. It's that she has little appetite.

Pulling back, she sits with a slothful glide, a light groan easing from her lips. I take a moment to truly look at her, and my heart bottoms out, falling to my feet as a shiver races up from where it lands.

My poor mother. *She looks so different, so weak, so small.* Mom had always seemed larger than life to me. As a child, I thought she could do anything. She always gave me one hundred percent of her attention, always stayed engaged. We baked cookies on snowy days, built forts, picked flowers in the spring, planted gardens. She always explained everything. When I was older, I realized it was because she had fought so hard to have children, to have me. But that just made her even more amazing to me. That she put so much into wanting me, it was almost like she willed it into existence. It felt like a superpower.

Dad appeared behind mom while I was focused on my memories. His lips turn down at the corners, surely matching my own face. But when Mom turns her face up to look at him, a broad smile stretching her weathered face, one dances across Dad's as well. The adoration they have for one another is unparalleled, and it makes an ache claw at my heart.

I want that. I want that devotion, that undying love. To have somebody I love and who loves me so much they would live in a place like this just to be near each other.

But the facts are what they are. I'm not getting any younger, and my job prevents me from meeting people in a normal manner. The only prospect I even have right now is Chase, and he's not exactly interested in any sort of real relationship. Not to mention, he's made his thoughts on things like marriage and children very well known. Plus, I despise him more than I can calculate.

"So, sweetheart, tell me about what's going on with you. Any special men in your life?" It's like she can read my thoughts. Just another one of her superpowers.

"Not really, Mom. I'm so busy with work. It doesn't lend to dating or having a relationship, since I can't really put the time into it."

"That boy at work still giving you trouble?" Dad's voice has such a protective edge to it, I'm immediately thrown back to being a teenager sitting in my mother's arms in tears over my first heartbreak. He was ready to hunt the poor boy down and give him a taste of fatherly words for breaking up with me a week before the dance.

I swallow the bile rising in my throat and stiffen my spine. Almost daily orgasms for five weeks isn't exactly trouble.

"No, Daddy, everything's fine. This case is putting us in close proximity every day, but we're making the most of it." Not a lie, since we are in fact making the most of it. Most days we wait until everybody leaves, and he's inside me once the office door is shut. His office or mine, doesn't make much of a difference. Then there are the days we can't wait and end up in a closet or the storage room in the basement where ancient case files collect dust.

Anytime we end up down there I leave the room sneezing, which is always to Chase's great enjoyment.

"I'm not sure you're telling me the truth, Lilla Bean, since your cheeks tell a different story." *Crap.*

"It's not that, I promise. He's better than usual. We're both on our best behavior. The partners made it very clear we were to work together and amicably or there would be consequences. So, we're doing just that." With a few added perks.

I hate that just thinking about it has me adjusting in my seat. And it's Saturday, which means I'm on my own until at least Monday. There is no part of me that is willing to call Chase for some relief on the weekend.

That would cross a line.

In fact, a few days ago, after a fairly intense session in the basement, he laid out some ground rules.

"This is just a work thing, Elizabeth. And only while we're working on this case. After it's done, we go back to just two coworkers who hate each other. Maybe we fuck now and again, but mostly just hate each other. And there's no going back to the other's place or sleepovers or dinners. No falling in love here, just sex. Agreed?"

"Absolutely one hundred percent. So, try your best not to fall in love with me." I had patted his cheek as I walked past him to leave the basement.

But he caught up and squeezed my ass, shoving me into the wall and sticking his tongue down my throat. "Back at you, Princess."

With a sneeze, I watched as he walked away.

"How is the case going, darling? Any progress?" The fact that Mom remembers I'm a lawyer is a good thing.

"It's going well for us. Being high profile, I can't give too much information about the case, but I think we're in a good spot. The other lawyers—"

"Oh! You're a lawyer? How lovely. I'm pretty sure my Elizabeth will be a lawyer when she grows up. She just loves to argue."

My heart plummets, and all the blood drains from my body. She was just here with me, and now she's gone.

"I'm sorry, who are you?"

I plaster a fake smile on my face, even though it hurts to wear it. "Just a friend. I'm sorry, I'll go now."

"Lilla Bean." Dad tries to stop me, but he can't. Not this time. She was with me, she remembered. Even though the odds were in my favor, they don't always go that way. And this time they did and then she was just...gone.

But Dad catches up to me and grabs my shoulder. "You know she can't control it. And you know she loves you."

"I know, Daddy, but I can't be here. Not right now. I love you, and I promise I won't go so long without a visit again. Next time she's lucid, tell her I love her." With a quick kiss on his cheek, I make a beeline for my car, feeling a need to lose myself in Chase.

Chapter 9

"I know this goes against our verbal agreement, but I want you to come back to my house tonight." When I stare at him blankly, he continues. "Before you build your counterargument, remember that verbal agreements don't hold up in court." He gives me a smirk, like he's joking, but I'm not sure he is.

"It's not that. Chase, it's, we're..." Why am I suddenly tongue tied in front of him? This has never happened to me before. I am always poised on my feet, with my words, with my arguments.

Coming to stand in front of me, Chase cups my cheek, running his thumb over my lower lip and pulling it down slowly. "I just want to see what it's like to fuck you in a bed. And on a couch. Maybe in a shower."

For all our talk of stopping, we certainly seem to be heading in the opposite direction. If I were to go home with him, what does that say? Is it really just for sex? But if I don't, will he pull the plug on this?

It's not even that I haven't thought about it. I'd like to say things are getting stale in the office. But I'd be a liar.

No, it's not the location. It's certainly not the sex itself, which is no less stellar than it has been.

No, the problem, that I have to be honest with myself about, is that I find myself hating Chase less and less. Sometimes not at all.

I'm afraid if I go home with him, I'll find some redeeming quality that will make it harder to hate him. Worse, maybe I'll find a lot.

"Please, Liz? Just this once. If you really hate it, you can leave." Is he really asking me with a hint of desperation? That's very unlike the Chase I know.

Taking a deep breath, I search his face for any sign of...well...anything to make me think he's not being sincere. But I don't find it.

"Okay." The smile that nearly splits his face sends my pulse skyrocketing.

That's how an hour later, I find myself standing in front of an impressive modern style house with more windows than any one house really needs. It must be so bright in there in the morning. It's the only thought I have as I step out of my car, eyes wide.

"You live here?"

His brow furrows as he looks at me and then back up at the house, hands sliding into his pockets as he approaches me. "Yeah? I mean, we are at my house."

"It's just not what I expected." My eyes flutter closed as I realize I didn't want to have said that.

That cocky half grin plants itself on his face. "You've thought about where I live?" And that's exactly why I didn't want to have said it out loud.

"Not intentionally. Don't flatter yourself."

"Well, now that you're here, maybe you'll change your mind." Jutting his head toward the house, we start walking to the front door. Turning to look at me, he has one eyebrow cocked. "What exactly did you imagine?"

"I don't know. A coffin, maybe? The underworld."

One corner of his mouth pulls down. Which not only draws my attention to his lips, making mine tingle, but makes guilt wrap around my ribs and start squeezing.

"I think it's all the windows that are throwing me. I just didn't expect you to live somewhere so...bright."

Rubbing his fingers along his lower lip, he stops and looks up at the house, as if just considering it for the first time. Then he shrugs and puts his hand back in his pocket. "I like natural light."

When we get to the door, he digs his keys out of his pocket and turns to look at me before opening it. He gives me a quick once over and hesitates.

"What?" I lean back as he continues to look at me.

"Nothing, this was just not something I *ever* expected."

"Same here. Now open the door before I change my mind and leave."

He scoffs as he throws the door open and leans against the frame. "Like you could. Sorry, Princess, but you haven't hidden how far my hooks have dug in."

Rolling my eyes, I turn to look at him. "Oh, please. I think it's the opposite, I'm the one who's hooked you. We're at your house, by your invitation. Not the other way around."

Pushing off the frame, he steps right next to me, one hand resting the slightest bit against my lower back as he talks low in my ear. "And look who didn't put up a fight to come here."

A shiver runs through me as I turn my face toward his, taking a second to settle my staccato heart and erratic breathing. "I put up some fight."

As expected, it's not exactly convincing.

That stupid half smirk settles on his face again. "Not enough." Pressing his hand firmly to my back, he leads me over the threshold and closes the door behind us.

Looking around, I'm no less awestruck by the house. Honey-colored hardwood floors as far as the eye can see, large lighting fixtures with simplistic designs in every room, and dark furniture greet me.

We enter into the living room where there's a dark leather couch and matching recliner. Not surprisingly, I find a bar cart against one wall and the largest flat-screen TV that could possibly fit on the wall. The other thing I notice is that it's spotless.

I can't see the kitchen, but I'm sure it's just as astounding. I'd be jealous if I didn't refuse to be impressed by more things about Chase.

"It's very nice here."

"Thank you. Honestly, I paid a designer to do most of it. But I liked all the windows; it's what sold me on the house. The back is very private, no neighbors." He shrugs like it's no big deal. "It's a good enough place to sleep and eat."

I turn to look up at him. "You're not here much?"

"I mean, you get it, we're both at the office a ton. But otherwise, I don't know, not really. It's kind of big and lonely."

"Oh please, like you don't have your share of ladies filing in and out."

"Here? No. I don't bring women here. Or anybody, really. The only people who come in this house are myself, my brother, and my cleaning lady." Well, that explains the cleanliness. Though his office is neat and tidy, keeping a whole house clean is another story. And this is immaculate.

"Why'd you bring me here then?" My heart is fluttering, and when his eyes shift to my neck, I know he can tell.

Running a hand through his hair, he opens his mouth to speak and hesitates. "I, uh, I just did." He's lost the bravado he had earlier. Dropping his hand to his side, he opens his arms toward the center of the house. "I figured I'd make some dinner. Don't look at me like that."

It takes me a second to realize my eyes have grown to the size of saucers, and I have to bite my cheek to make sure my mouth stays closed.

"Elizabeth, this doesn't have to be more than it is. But we're working together, long days, long hours, and having some of the best sex I've ever had. We can still hate each other but be pleasant here and there."

"Best sex you've ever had?" I ask as I follow him down the hall, my heels clicking. It opens into a large kitchen with dark granite counters, complete with a massive island that has an eat-in bar.

"Don't let it go to your head, okay? Besides, you've already let that little fact slip." Opening the fridge, he starts rifling through and piling things in his arms. "And I wasn't lying when I said the purpose was to invite you over for various other sex locations. I just need some fuel first."

Slamming the door shut, that smirk is plastered on his face again, and his eyebrows dance up and down.

"Do you even know how to cook?"

He throws a hand against his chest in true overdramatic Chase fashion. "How the hell do you think I eat, Princess? Of course I can cook."

Honestly, I'd assumed he either ate out or had a meal delivery service.

Sliding onto a barstool at the island, I rest my elbows on the cool surface and settle in.

When he cuffs his sleeves, a pulse echoes through my body and settles in my clit. I've been so mesmerized by the house and distracted by the situation that I'd all but forgotten that we'd come from work and are still in our dress clothes. The ache in my feet returns, and I kick off my shoes.

Chase's eyes flick up to mine with a light smile on his face. "Feel better?"

"Huh?"

"You just moaned."

"I did not." Did I?

"Okay, Liz, whatever you say." He shakes his head as he says it. "Make yourself comfortable. If you want to change, my bedroom is upstairs. Feel free to go pick out a shirt and pants or something." He points the knife he's using to cut up chicken toward the stairs.

"I don't know how I feel about that."

"Elizabeth. If I can fuck you every day, you can put some of my clothes on to be more comfortable. You don't have to. I'm just letting you know you're welcome to."

"You haven't even changed."

"I'm going to as soon I get dinner in the oven." It occurs to me I've never seen Chase in anything besides a suit. Even at the few functions we've attended out of the office together, we're both always dressed for work. This is getting weirder and weirder. It's making my head spin.

I stay in my seat, but as soon as Chase walks out of the kitchen and up the stairs without a word, I hop off my barstool and follow him, leaving my heels on the floor.

Quietly, I make my way up the stairs. I may be following him like a lost puppy, but he doesn't need to know that. Yet.

I find the master en suite, as well as two smaller bedrooms and a hall bath on my way and walk in without knocking. The first thing I notice is the wall of windows that look out over the backyard. Chase isn't in the room, but I hear water running in the bathroom.

Walking over to the windows, my breath stalls in my chest. It's an absolutely stunning view. Looking in either direction, I can't see anything but trees. No neighbors, no road. It's not just private, it's serene. Fire and ice race each other through my body as Chase appears behind me, brushing his fingers down my arm. It's what I've come to find is his predatory stance. He towers over me, hand just barely laying claim to my body, standing so close I can feel his warmth but not his body. It's incredibly dizzying.

The hand grazing my arm slides to my hip, running across my stomach and dipping between my legs above my skirt. It's too tight to have much give, which results in a frustrated growl from behind me. Gliding his hand up my body, he closes it around my throat and pulls me flush against his chest, taking a small step closer to the window.

Leaning forward, he murmurs against my ear. "I'm going to fuck you in front of this window."

The tiny whimper that escapes me makes Chase smile against my ear and pull my sensitive skin between his teeth.

I always figured Chase would be dominant in the bedroom, the very few times it briefly flashed into my mind before I wanted to take a scrubby brush to it. But the last thing I ever expected was that he'd do it with me, and more so, that I'd like it.

"Soon, Princess." Trailing his fingers to the top button of my shirt, he starts undoing them. When my hand flies up to stop him, he grabs it with the one not working on undressing me and holds it tightly in his grasp. "Now, now, Elizabeth. I'm helping you."

I haven't even had a chance to see what he looks like in street clothes. But I get my opportunity after he finishes with my shirt, unzipping my skirt, leaving the clothes on me as he spins me to face him.

Part of me feels like I expected him to look different, misplaced. Instead, it's the opposite. He's wearing simple drawstring pants, hung low to reveal a deep V in his hips. There are muscles in his chest so perfect I want to run my tongue along them. Without even realizing what I'm doing, my fingers are trailing gently over their ridges.

The pad of his thumb brushes my lower lip, pulling down gently and causing me to begrudgingly pull my gaze from his chest to meet his eyes. Fire and lust dance in his irises.

"Drooling, Princess? That seems beneath you." I'm sure I wasn't drooling. Actually, that's not true, I'm not entirely sure. But it was likely just a tease. Probably.

"Shut up. I've never actually seen you without a shirt on. I can admit it's impressive. And you know how much I hate to compliment you. How do you even have time to maintain yourself?"

"I have a gym in the basement. I'm up at five every day." My eyes grow wide, and he laughs. "Too early for you, Princess?"

"Do you even sleep? I mean, we're at the office until eleven some nights. It took a half hour to get here. Then I'm sure there are nights you partake in your fair share of fun."

Another noncommittal rise of his shoulder. He seems to favor the right. "I get what I need. Why, do you care?"

"Of course not. I'm just curious. If you fall asleep in court one day, it only makes me look better."

Rolling his eyes and shaking his head, he takes a step back, and I have to fight a pout that he's taking away my new toy. "I put a shirt in the bathroom and some pants. They'll be big, but you can roll them. Or wear just the shirt. Whatever you want. There's some frou-frou bath shit that my cleaning lady keeps replacing every time I throw it out."

When I stare at him with large eyes and nonstop blinks, he sighs and rubs his hand down his face, letting out a frustrated sound. "Elizabeth, just change. You can put your dress clothes back on after dinner if it will make you more comfortable. I'm not playing any game here or anything. I'm not trying to make you fall in love with me. I'm trying to be a decent human being to my coworker who I happen to be fucking daily."

Without hesitating, I step away from him and slip out of my clothes, intentionally doing it in his presence so he can get a full shot of my black bra and matching thong. The groan behind me brings a smile to my face as I head into the bathroom, adding a little extra sway to my hips on the way.

The bathroom is almost all tile. There's a huge multi-head shower, a jet tub, and a double vanity made of a light gray granite. It's just as stunning as the rest of the house. Near the tub is a vase filled with bath bombs. I fight back a laugh as I think of Chase soaking in the tub with a bath bomb. He just does not at all strike me as the type.

Taking a few minutes, not feeling at all self-conscious or awkward about being practically naked in Chase Andrews' bathroom, I look around a little more, examining bottles and labels and his medicine cabinet. Pulling the cap off his cologne, I take a sniff, a warmth filling through my body and a heaviness settling in my clit. That was a mistake.

Putting it back, I jump and nearly drop the bottle. Chase is standing against the doorframe, arms crossed tight against his chest. He's since put a shirt on, which fills me with disappointment.

"How long have you been standing there?"

"Long enough to see you going through all my shit and wriggle at the smell of my cologne. Find anything exciting?"

"Bath bombs?" One of my eyebrows arches towards my hairline.

"Is that what those stupid things are?" A corner of my mouth tips down. Even though I was pretty sure Chase didn't use them, I guess some part of me had hoped I caught some dirty secret he had. "Whatever, I'm going back downstairs. Join me when you're ready."

Having already had my fun of looking around, I pull the shirt over my head and slip the pants on. They're huge, as to be expected. Even rolling them a few times, they won't stay up.

I slink downstairs in just a t-shirt to the most heavenly smells. Chase doesn't look up from the stove as I sit back on the barstool, where I'd set up camp earlier. He must hear me though, because he turns and slides a glass of wine across the counter, lifting his own glass in a sense of 'cheers.'

"About five more minutes."

"Sounds good."

"Don't feel like you have to sit here. Feel free to explore. There are bookcases in the office." He extends his arm down the hall.

"Can this come?" I raise my wineglass.

"Sure. Just don't dump it on anything."

Hopping to the floor, I roll my eyes at him. I do make sure to glance back to get a peek at his face when he realizes I'm in just a t-shirt. It doesn't disappoint.

There's a small hallway I hadn't seen from the front door that leads to the side of the house. I pass a half bathroom and a door that I assume is a closet or stairs and find the office.

When I open the door, my jaw drops. Two full walls are floor-to-ceiling bookcases. I can immediately pick out the one that has the law books. I have many of the same on my shelf. Strolling by the other cases, I trail my finger along the solid wood, stopping every so often to examine a title more closely.

I'm finding myself surprised by some of the authors I'm finding. I wouldn't expect him to have the Bronte sisters, Jane Austen, Louisa May Alcott. He has a rather large collection of classics, which is extremely respectable. Moving along, I'm finding more modern and contemporary reads, including a few of my favorite titles.

Sipping and walking along the two walls, I see there are more books and editions than I could have ever imagined he'd own, a library that rivals my own very extensive one, and I lose all sense of time and self.

"I had a feeling I'd find you here." I nearly shriek as I jump at the sound of Chase's voice.

"You're lucky this was empty, or I would have spilled all over your floor."

"Hardwood. Easy to clean. Come on. Dinner's ready."

Sliding back the book I was examining, I skip behind him to catch up.

"You have a lot of books."

"Yes."

"Have you read them all?" Every one of his strides takes at least two of mine.

"Most of them. Some were to complete a collection."

"The Bronte sisters?"

"Read." He doesn't look at me as he answers, continuing whatever he was doing.

"Jane Austen?"

"Also read."

Well, color me surprised. "You don't seem like the type to enjoy that sort of novel."

"Oh, I didn't say I enjoyed them. Just that I read them."

"Why do you keep them if you didn't enjoy them?"

"Why not? Don't you have things on your shelf that you didn't enjoy, but keep anyway?" With a pointed look, he reaches down to pull dinner out of the oven.

He has me there. I have a hard time parting with books, liked or not.

"Sit." He points to a small round glass table, already set with silverware and napkins.

Doing as I'm told, which is still strange, I plop into a chair.

Chase carries over two plates, the wine bottle tucked under his arm. I take my dish and the bottle before he drops something. He refills both wineglasses as his eyes dash over to mine with one corner of his mouth upturned.

The look is what I've come to read as mischievous. It means he's planning something for me. This isn't a new discovery; it's something I learned years ago when we went through a stint of pranking each other. The day we got caught was the only time I was ever worried about my job. I'm sure the plans for tonight involve me being naked.

"This looks and smells delicious. What is it?" I hold my curls back as I lean forward and take a big whiff, making my mouth water.

"Chicken cordon bleu, broccoli, and roasted carrots."

I have to stop myself from letting my mouth hang open. "You actually made all this?"

"You watched me in the kitchen. So yes, I did."

"Where did you learn to cook like this?" Cutting into my chicken, the knife slides through easily. Through the smoky tendrils that rise from the cutlet, I catch Chase watching me intently.

"My mom." Clearing his throat, he takes a sip of wine.

I look up at him through my eyelashes as I take a small nibble. I have to bite back a moan. It doesn't feel appropriate.

Chase's Mom died a few years ago. I don't know much about the situation, but it seemed they were close. He took two weeks off. I don't think I'd seen him take a day before that, and I don't think he's taken one since.

"I'm sorry. I didn't mean to bring up anything. It's really good. Thank you."

"Don't worry about it. And you're welcome."

We eat in silence for a while, the only sounds of silverware scraping and clanking and the setting down of our wineglasses. The tension is palpable. Maybe coming here was a mistake.

"Sorry, I know this a little awkward. We don't exactly like each other, but we're having dinner together and not takeout on the floor of somebody's office. And really, all I can think about are all the different things I want to do to you tonight."

I nearly choke on my wine, sputtering as I set it down and pull my napkin to my mouth. Once I've calmed from my spasm, I meet his eyes, and they're nothing but devilish. Swallowing roughly, I consider the options. I've eaten most of what's on my plate, and I have a relatively significant buzz going.

"I'm ready when you are."

For a second, I'm worried he's about to flip the table to get to me sooner. Hastily setting his wineglass down, it tips and falls to the table. It doesn't break, but it does spill what's left.

I move to dry it when Chase grabs my wrist. "Leave it." The gravel in his voice makes me instantly wet. It's like Pavlov's dog. I hear that low, husky voice, so often used during sex, and my body reacts to the stimulus.

As he stands, he pulls me to stand with him, immediately yanking me against him. "I never thought I'd like having you pressed up against me, Liz, but I gotta tell ya, it's certainly not a bad feeling."

I squeeze myself closer to him, rubbing slightly against his erection as he groans.

"Are you going to lose your mind if I kiss you?" He's not even looking at me. Instead, his eyes are closed, his face pointing toward the ceiling as I keep grinding myself against him.

"You've kissed me before, Chase."

"Yeah, but not the way I want to kiss you right now."

Ice quickly sprawls through my body, freezing everything in its path. I start to step backward, but Chase wraps his arm around my waist and pulls me back to him. Now his eyes are open, and he looks right at me.

"If you don't want me to, say no. Communication, Liz, we have the skills in spades. Let's use them. I want to kiss you. I wouldn't say tenderly, but not quite as viciously. I also want to taste you. I want you to have your perfect mouth around my hard cock."

The ice immediately melts, pooling right between my legs, as fire tears through my body at his confession.

Instead of communicating with words, I speak with my body, pressing up on my toes to latch my lips to his.

Within a second, his mouth starts moving against mine, pushing it open as his tongue curls in. I see what he means by different. He's forceful and hurried, but there's no anger behind it, no aggressiveness. It's more...*claiming.*

Almost like he's telling me that my body is his to do with what he pleases. And while I give it willingly, I'm happy he wants me as much as I want him. Because I'd be lying if I wasn't desperate for his body, his cock, his warmth.

The hatred that used to boil within me at the mere mention of his name is now no more than a slight simmer. Possibly even just tepid water.

It's slightly disarming, going from hating someone so much for so long to not. And it's not that I like him now, because I definitely don't have feelings like that for him. It's almost as though the constant fucking has made him tolerable.

Though I'm having the best sex of my life, I think I liked it better when he was just the object of my absolute disgust and hatred. Because now the lines are blurred. Add in the pleasure he brings me while he's deep inside me, and I can't tell the shades of gray from the black and white.

Is it wrong to fuck your enemy? Maybe. Is it wrong that it feels so damn good? Absolutely. But do I want it to stop?

Not a chance in hell.

Chapter 10

C hase keeps kissing me as his hands slide up and down my body, exploring with measured movements.

We've never really had an opportunity to take it slow, and I can tell he's savoring every second, getting a feel for my body in a way he hasn't ever been able to before.

"Can I take you upstairs?" His voice is filled with grit, and I know he's trying to not just throw me over his shoulder. I can practically feel him vibrating as he restrains himself.

When I nod, he takes my hand in his and pulls me up the stairs.

Once in his room, he turns me to face him, and I wonder if he's going to fuck me against the window right now. But he starts kissing down my neck and across my shoulder, his hands making a trail down my body, over my breasts and farther down.

His mouth follows. Quickly, his shirt is lifted over my head and thrown over his shoulder.

My hands hold on to the back of his head to help me keep my balance as he lowers to his knees, pulling my panties down.

"Of all the pussies that could bring me to my knees, I never thought it would be yours," he says against my thigh before laying a line of kisses along my skin and settling his face between my legs. Giving a tentative lap of his tongue along my slit, he moans, wrapping his hands to my ass and digging in.

When he starts licking, tongue swirling around my heavy clit, I tangle my hands in his hair as my breath catches.

Adjusting his stance so he's on his feet instead of his knees, he hooks my legs over his shoulders and stands up, keeping his face between my thighs, as he carries me to the bed. It's the sexiest damn thing he's done so far.

As he lays me down, he starts using his tongue in earnest. Licking, swirling, piercing me. Fuck, why does he have to be good at everything? I'm moaning and tugging his hair without reservation. When he closes his lips around my clit and sucks, I nearly levitate off the bed as I scream.

"*Fuck*. Chase." It hasn't become less strange to say his name while in such a vulnerable state. I never expected to say it laced with ecstasy. But it no longer feels dirty. It can't possibly.

Giving a final tug at his hair, I start bucking against him, chasing his tongue, as my whole body quakes. His hands run calmly and smoothly up my thighs as he slows his pace, giving a few long slides of his tongue up my pussy, lapping me up.

As I calm to a tremble, he kisses the inside of my thighs and along my lower belly before resting on his elbow, hovering over me.

"You taste better than I ever could have imagined, Princess."

My eyelids are fluttering as my whole body tingles.

"Still regretting staying?"

"Nope, not even a little." I shake my head to go along with my words. I shift with his laughter, his moan rumbling through me.

"Are you good now? Because I swear if I don't get inside you soon, I'm going to burst."

"Since when do you ask?" Raising one eyebrow, I pop an eye open and glance at him.

"Don't say it like that, Elizabeth," he grumbles as his brow pulls together, and if I didn't know better, I'd think he was offended.

"Like what?"

"Like I force you. This is the first time we've done more than just fuck."

"You always make me come before hand." This conversation should feel awkward, since he's lying on top of me and we're naked and I just stopped trembling from one of the most incredible orgasms I've ever had. But like so much with Chase, nothing is quite as it should be.

"Chase, I'm sorry. I was teasing. Listen, you and I have known each other a long time and while we've spent most of that time giving each other shit, you know I stand up for myself when needed. It's not needed. This has shocked the hell out of me, for sure. It's the last thing I ever would have expected, but I'm certainly not complaining."

Shifting slightly, he blows lightly over my nipple until it pebbles. "Good," he murmurs against my skin before pulling the hardened flesh into his mouth. My back arches, and I wrap my arms around his head as he swirls his tongue expertly.

This isn't the first time he's done this, but it's the first time it hasn't been hurried and sloppy. While that certainly has its place, this is far better.

Gliding a hand between us, he circles my clit before sliding his fingers into me, his moan vibrating through my body. Using both his tongue and fingers in tandem, I'm panting and writhing beneath him in minutes. When I start bucking against his hand, kisses across my chest and up my body until he rests against my ear.

"That's it, Liz. I want you to come for me. You're so close, aren't you, Princess?"

All I can do is nod in response, a small whine escaping my lips.

"You're going to come, and then I'm going to ease inside you. I'm going to go so slow at first. I'm going to move so agonizingly slow you'll be begging for more because you just can't stand it anymore. And then I'll plow into you until you scream for me." One thing I can admit is that his dirty talk is top notch. Though that really doesn't come as much of a surprise. As he said earlier, we have good conversation skills.

"Fuck, Chase." I'm screaming *now*, my hands wrapping to his shoulders and digging in as his muscles work beneath my fingers.

He doesn't hesitate to slide into me once my second orgasm leaves me panting.

But the slow approach lasts for only a few minutes before he's groaning against my neck. "Forget this."

Pushing away from me, but staying deep inside me, he rests my feet against his chest, running his hands down my legs to wrap around my hips.

"I'll deny this until the end, Elizabeth, but your body is perfection."

"You're not so bad yourself." I've gawked at him more than once tonight. Any other time, we've been almost completely dressed.

A small smirk splays across his face as he starts thrusting into me. I've given up even trying to dislike what he feels like inside me. It's just not possible.

As he leans forward slightly, my knees press to my chest and while the angle feels amazing, I'm not the most flexible person. Seeming to know what I'm thinking, Chase adjusts, taking my legs and looping them over his shoulders. It's new and different and perfect and just…"Fuck."

And then it's over, and he's gone. I whine at the loss of him, ready to bite out a complaint when he flips me over. "On your knees, Liz. Chest stays down, or I'll keep it down myself."

Pulling my knees in, I leave my chest flat against the mattress. He stops once he's all the way inside me, running his hands down my back, trailing his tongue along my spine. "Perfection."

It is. Every single slide in and out is absolute perfection. It doesn't take long with his hands wrapped around my hips as he pounds into me until I'm whimpering and fisting the sheets.

I scream out his name as I tighten around him. It sneaks up on me, taking me by surprise, which only heightens the sensation as waves of euphoria roll through me. He doesn't stop or slow, picking up his momentum for a few more hurried thrusts until he groans, and I feel his dick pulsate inside me.

Lying next to each other, chests heaving, I finally turn to look at him. He has one arm flung over his forehead but turns to meet my gaze.

A smile spreads across his face. "Definitely better in a bed."

Rolling my eyes, I can't help but laugh. "I guess it has its benefits." Chewing the inside of my lip and looking away, I'm not sure what to do. I pull the sheet between my fingers and start to formulate how to leave without it being more awkward than it already is.

Before I can figure out more than getting out of bed and getting dressed, Chase puts his hands on my hips and rolls me to my side, curling around me, chest pressed firmly to my back and arm thrown over my waist.

Startling and trying to move away, he tightens his hold on me and pulls me flush against him. "What are you doing, Chase?"

"Cuddling."

"We hate each other."

His shoulder lifts lightly. I'm starting to notice how much he does that, brushes things off like they're nothing. "I like to cuddle after sex."

My eyebrows shoot skyward as I crane my neck to look at him, spinning slightly in his arms. "Seriously?"

He cracks an eye open. "Yes, seriously. What's so crazy about that?"

"You just never struck me as the type. And especially with me."

"Well, it's been a while since I've cuddled with anybody. We may not be each other's number one fans, but we know each other pretty well. It's nice to just be with somebody who knows more than my name and the size of my cock. And not for money, because you make at least as much as I do."

Swallowing heavily, I start to say something, but don't know where to start. I'd be lying if I said I didn't like the feeling of his arms around me. It feels like a puzzle piece clicked into place, but one I didn't know I was missing from the picture I'd started.

"Elizabeth. Relax. If you're that uncomfortable with it, you can leave. I'm not going to start whispering sweet nothings in your ear. We both work, a lot. I know because we both usually leave at the same time, even before this case. It's just nice to have some real human interaction that lasts beyond putting the pants back on."

"The first sweet nothing, I leave."

"If I whisper a sweet nothing, *I'll* leave. I don't think I've ever done that with anybody. If I were to do it with *you* of all people, well, something would be very wrong with me."

On some level, I should be offended by the way he said "you", but I can't be because up until now, we've had nothing but hatred for each other. And while I'm not exactly sure what is going on, it doesn't feel so much like hatred anymore.

I wouldn't say it's as far as like, or even mutual admiration. I'd say at most it's acceptance of the other's existence. Instead of being coworkers who hate each other, we're coworkers who tolerate each other and fuck.

Taking a deep breath, I allow the tension to ease from my shoulders as I sink into the pillow. His bed is annoyingly comfortable, soft and plush in all the right places. The cedarwood scent that had always made my teeth collide doesn't bring the tension it used to. Instead, it makes my body throb, especially between my legs. I could never tell him, but the other day at work, he leaned over me, and when his cologne wafted into my nose, I was instantly wet. He doesn't know what happened earlier, he just thinks he does.

"So, you're staying?"

"Yeah, I guess I am."

"Turn over." I do as I'm told, something I can't quite get over that I do so easily with him. His arm tightens against my stomach, and he nuzzles against the back of my neck, his nose settling into my hair.

My eyes are darting all around the room, not quite sure what to do. I'm so out of my depth here, I don't know how to cope. In the courtroom, I can trounce anybody, even Chase if I had to, though I'm often thankful he's on my team as his cross examination is pretty impressive.

"Close your eyes, Elizabeth." His tone is forceful.

"You want me to *sleep* here?" Shock coils up my spine. I figured this was just a one-night thing. Come over, have some sex, go home. Sure, he wants to cuddle now, okay. But I assumed it'd be short lived, and then I'd leave. Not that he'd ask me to actually sleep. Or maybe even stay.

"I want you to take a fucking chill pill and relax a little. Sleep, don't sleep, I don't care. But I can feel your unease. We've been working fourteen-hour days for weeks now. If you fall asleep, you fall asleep. You can wake up in the middle of the night and slip out, and it won't affect me at all. I won't be hurt and broken and avoid you on Monday. I'll still come in, do my job, give you shit when it's needed, and fuck you when the mood arises."

"Fine."

"Good girl." Well, hot damn if he doesn't just make me hot and bothered every single time he says that. I can't let him know; I can't even fidget or rub my thighs to try to relieve some of the pressure that's now sitting in my clit. If I do, he'll absolutely use it against me in court, leaning over and whispering it in my ear so I'm uncomfortable and thinking about sex in the middle of the trial. The whispering alone would be enough to disarm me.

Resettling myself into bed, easing into the pillows, I adjust a little, rubbing my ass right against Chase's groin, which results in a pulsation of his dick. I get a slight thrill at knowing I have such an effect on him that just the slightest graze causes a reaction.

Looking out the wall of windows in front of me, the sky twinkles and shimmers. It's peaceful. Chase mentioned earlier that he owns the land for a few acres farther back and plans to keep it private. The mass of trees helps keep the ground light to a minimum.

Soon, my lids are too heavy to keep open, and I give over the fight to sleep.

Chapter 11

Waking up in the morning, I find myself more refreshed than I've been in weeks. There's a lightness in my chest. It's replaced with lead, though, when I roll over to an empty and cold bed.

I don't know why it bothers me so much that I'm waking up alone. We're not a couple, we're not dating. We're just fucking.

So why do I have to keep telling myself that?

I'm in his house. It's not like he could have gone far. Sitting up and wrapping the duvet around my chest, I worry my lip between my teeth. I have two options. The first is to throw on a shirt and pad downstairs and hope he's there. The second is to get dressed and leave.

Before I can land on either, I decide to brush my teeth with the extra toothbrush Chase handed me last night, taking the time to help me reach a conclusion.

As it turns out, the decision has been made for me. Looking everywhere, I can't find my clothes, but there's a fresh crisp button-down shirt taunting me on the hook in the bathroom.

Slipping it from the hanger, I slide it on, buttoning it most of the way. The sleeves are far too big, and the shirt hangs to almost mid-thigh. But it's comfy and smells like Chase, which is a scent I immediately equate with sex, so now I'm turned on and uncomfortable.

Giving my hair a quick refresh and shake, I huff and head down the stairs. Chase is leaning against the counter, coffee in one hand, newspaper in the other. He has on just a pair of drawstring pants that hang low on his hips. I pull my bottom lip between my teeth as I take a minute to stare.

I shouldn't be enjoying his body. I shouldn't be here. But since I am, I may as well take a little added enjoyment in it.

As he puts the paper down and finds me walking toward him, his eyes widen and a smile pulls at his lips.

"My clothes are gone."

"I know. I took them."

My eyes bulge out of my head. "You did what now?"

"I took them."

"So, you're holding me captive now?"

"No. You can leave whenever you want. Just say the word. I knew that you'd wake up alone, think I was a dick, and plan your escape. Hard to do with no clothes."

It makes my skin prickle that he knows me so well. Working closely with somebody for years will do that, even if you hate each other most of that time. I guess part of me expected it, though I am surprised that he's going to such lengths because he *wants* me to be here.

Running my tongue along my teeth, I move farther into the kitchen. "Coffee?"

A smile spreads across his face as he fills a mug and slides it across the island.

"So, are you always up this early, or just out of habit?" I slide into the same seat I occupied at the counter last night. My heels are still where I left them.

He shrugs as he leans back against the counter. "I'm a morning person." I crinkle my nose in detest. "Not you, I take it?"

"No. I mean, I'm up and going for work, of course, but I sleep in on the weekends."

"I see that."

Glancing around him at the stove clock, I see it's only eight-thirty. "It's not that late. I've been known to sleep until ten on the weekend."

His eyes narrow at me, but there's still a smirk on his face. "How old are you again? Just making sure this is all legal."

I look for something, anything, to throw at him and settle on the cork from last night. It hits him in the chest with a low thud as he laughs.

"Just because I'm twenty-eight doesn't mean I can't sleep in every now and then. We work hard all week, up early those days and burning the midnight oil. I'm a night owl to start with, but it's different when I'm working than when I'm relaxing."

"You don't have to explain yourself to me, Elizabeth. I'm not judging, I was teasing." Something he does best.

"I'm not, I'm just..." I take a look at his down-turned lips and crossed arms. "Okay, you're right. I don't know call it the lawyer in me needing to build a defense to a questionable behavior."

"It's not questionable. You're right, we do work hard and late and are up early. If you want to sleep in, sleep in. Who cares how old you are. You

don't have other responsibilities to worry about. Wait, you don't have a
secret love child, do you?" One eyebrow quirks up as a smirk spans his
face.

"Ha ha, asshole. I've been a little focused on my career to have a child.
Not that that's the way I'd do it. Though, maybe now..." I'm getting
into territory I don't want to get into. Especially not with Chase. He
doesn't need to know that I'm starting to worry about my age and
finding somebody who can handle my schedule enough to stick around
to even fall in love, let alone get married and have children.

Waving a hand through the air while gripping my mug with the other,
I focus on the almond shaded liquid inside. "Either way, I only have a
cat. He'll be fine until later."

"Cheshire, right?"

My eyes flick up to his in an instant as my heart races. "How'd you
know that?"

"I listen. It's part of being a lawyer. I'm sure you know random tidbits
about me you'd never expect."

Thinking about it, I probably do. I know his mug likely has cream, no
sugar, much like mine—another thing I'm realizing I didn't mention but
he just knew. He doesn't have pets because he's more of a dog person and
doesn't want one to be alone all day. I know he's a dog person because
he talks about the one he had growing up, Jenson, pretty regularly, how
hard it was on him when the dog died his senior year of high school.

"Yeah, I guess I do." Our eyes meet for what feels like an eternity before
I have to turn away as heat starts to tingle up my spine.

Whatever this is between us, it's morphing, it's changing. For me, at
least. I'm not sure what to make of it, what to do with it. I'd been so
comfortable in my blind hatred for him for so many years that I kind of
just expected it to last forever. He was my nemesis; he'd always be my

nemesis. I found comfort in the stability of it, the knowingness of where my enemy was. Now things feel...messier. Those lines are blurring even more.

"So, breakfast. Eggs?"

"Sure. I don't usually eat breakfast."

"You're going to eat with me, Elizabeth. So, if you don't want eggs, I suggest you tell me now."

"Eggs are fine." This bossy side of him is nothing new to me. It comes out in the courtroom, with a client, in the bedroom. But I have to admit, I don't mind it so much in day-to-day life either.

Crossing my legs, I rest my forearms on the granite as both hands wrap around my mug.

"So, today. Is this like a 'thanks for a nice fuck, here's some fuel to start your day' breakfast? And then I leave?" Is he the type that will cook you breakfast the next morning so you can't claim he's a complete asshole?

But no, that can't be it. He doesn't have girls here. So, what, exactly, is this?

Without turning from the stove, one shoulder ticks up in response. "Let's just see where the day goes."

Where could the day possibly go? I'm either staying or leaving.

Sighing and putting his hands on either side of the counter, he pushes backward slightly, bending at the waist. "Listen. It's the anniversary of my mom's passing. I don't...I'd prefer not to be alone. If you want to leave, if it will really be that terrible for you to be here, I understand."

My stomach drops to the floor and takes all the blood from my body with it. I feel like that's something I should have known. The whole company went to the funeral five years ago.

"I'm sorry, I should have remembered."

"Why? We're not exactly friends."

Heat rushes to the apples of my cheeks.

"I mean, we're coworkers, who up until a few weeks ago have basically despised each other, with or without reason, I can't tell anymore. It's not something I'd expect you to remember." Chase still doesn't turn around to look at me, but he does tilt slightly in my direction.

"I can stay."

"Don't do me any favors, Liz. If you don't want to be here, then don't be." I understand his sentiment. It's about pity. He doesn't want mine, just like I wouldn't want his.

The hardest thing to admit to myself is that part of me does want to be here. And not just for the sex.

"When have I ever done you a favor, Chase? I don't even make a copy of something for you." And I still won't.

He keeps his back to me, taut through the shoulders for another beat before straightening and flipping the eggs in the pan like no words had been spoken between us.

Not knowing what to say, we remain in silence, aside from the sound of sizzling bacon. Kicking my leg, I look around the house a little more. There's not a touch of personality anywhere besides the office. No pictures, no art, nothing decorative. It's very...plain.

I startle at feeling of his warm hand on my back, turning around to notice a plate in front of me. When did he finish cooking? I must have been so engrossed in dissecting his house that I missed him setting the food down.

"What's wrong?" he asks as he slides into his seat.

"Nothing. What do you mean?"

"Your face. It's all scrunched up and sad looking." A quick stab of his fork and he picks up a piece of egg, shoveling it into his mouth.

"There's no personality here."

"Personality?" He arches his brow.

"Yeah. Like photos or art or anything that represents you or who you are. It's blank walls and furniture. The only place I got any sense of you was when I was in the office last night." And that was mostly the law books and his choices of authors. There was one frame on his desk that I didn't look at but would assume is somebody of importance.

He glances around his space with his brow furrowed, almost like it's the first time he's seeing it. Then he shrugs. "I guess I never really saw a need for that stuff."

"Not even a picture of your mom?"

Starting at his jaw and rippling downward, his whole body stiffens. "I have one in the office." His voice is low and clipped, and it immediately makes the color drain from my face.

"I'm sorry, it's not my place, I shouldn't have said—" I'm quieted by Chase's hand closing over mine.

"It's fine, Liz. Stop worrying and eat."

"I'm not worrying," I mumble before scooping a forkful of eggs into my mouth.

"Well, you certainly seem to be trying hard not to hurt my feelings."

"Ha. For one, like I care. For two, we both know you don't have feelings. Or a heart. It's just, I know your mom meant a lot to you, is all." My voice steadily drops.

"If I don't have a heart, how can she have meant a lot to me? Wouldn't I have to have some sort of capacity for feelings and emotions for that to be the case?"

"Parents fall under their own special set of circumstances. I mean, shit, I bought a house out in the country for my dad. He never got to live in it." My appetite has vacated my body and now my fork swirls around my plate, not actually picking anything up.

"Hold up, you live out in the country?" He turns his upper body to look at me while leaning backward, fork dangling between his fingers.

"No. I have an apartment in town. And own a house in the country."

"Wait a minute. You live in an apartment? How have I not known this?"

"Like you said, we're not exactly friends, Chase."

"No, but we see each other five days a week. And as of six weeks ago, we've been screwing on the regular. I should know where you live." There's a hint of protectiveness and ownership coating his words.

"Okay. Well, I can show it to you at some point if you like." It's not really that big of a deal, it's just a house that I don't use or live in.

"Why an apartment? You can afford a house."

"I have a house."

"That you don't live in."

Taking a deep breath and releasing it forcefully, I realize I'm going to have to get into the story. "When I was a kid, there was this farmhouse my dad always used to talk about. He'd show it to me any time we were within twenty minutes of it. It was that classic style with the wraparound porch, painted red. He'd always say, 'that's the house, Lilla Bean.'" I freeze, my eyes growing wide as I turn so quickly in my chair toward Chase, I almost fall out of it.

"You are *never*, under any circumstance, allowed to repeat that name. I mean it, Chase." A pointed finger is merely inches from his face.

"Elizabeth. It's clearly important to you. I wouldn't do that."

Shaking my head, I face forward again, taking a sip of my coffee, needing to use two hands, thanks to the shake that's set in.

"Anyway. He'd say, 'that's the house, Lilla Bean. *The* house. The one I've always wanted, will always want. If I could own any house in the world, it would be that one.' I never really understood it as a kid. It seemed like just another house to me. But as I grew older, and especially as I became an adult, I saw the beauty in it, the rarity. It's not like any of the other farmhouse style houses in the area. It's rustic and sophisticated at the same time. There're over four acres of land that it sits right in the middle of." My voice trails off as I look off into nothingness, the image of my property popping into my mind.

"So, about two years ago, after that big case with that couple from Lake Fern, I noticed the house was for sale. I'd check up on it every so often, just keeping tabs, maybe wanting to take a look at it again without taking the drive. I bought it sight unseen. I didn't even hesitate. My dad was over the moon when I told him. But as you know, he had the heart attack and lives in a facility now." My voice trails off and my eyes drop to my plate. It's hard for me to talk about the big dreams I had versus my reality.

"How are your folks doing there?"

"Okay, I guess. I don't see them as much as I'd like, but it's hard when it's a two-hour drive with the hours we work. I try to make sure I call at least twice a week, but it's not the same."

"That sounds tough."

I shrug in response. It's easier than words, which will be difficult to produce around the lump that's settled in my throat. "Part of the problem when you have older parents."

"Well, if you'd be willing to show me, I'd like to see it sometime." His voice is filled with sincerity, and I can tell he means it, though I'm not sure why.

"It's a two-hour drive each direction."

"Okay. I'd still like to see it."

"Why?" Is there some sort of ulterior motive here? Is he going to try to buy me out of Dad's dream home? No, he wouldn't do that, but it has to be something.

"I'm curious about this house you speak so highly of. The house your dad just had to own."

Is that a boyfriend thing? It feels very much like a boyfriend thing.

"Yeah, maybe sometime."

"You don't have to, Elizabeth. I'm just curious about your life. You're here in my house, you slept in my bed last night. I'd like to know a little more about you, including where you live. It doesn't have to *mean* something."

"How do you do that?"

"Do what?"

"Answer the questions in my head, know when something's bothering me." It's a little uncanny and a lot scary. I've dated people who understood me less than Chase seems to.

"You're easy to read."

"I am not."

He raises one shoulder. "For me you are."

"You have an unfair advantage." Of being a lawyer, for starters. He's used to reading people and having to figure out if that person is off or not.

"Or maybe I've just paid attention for years."

"You already to—"

"I know. I told you that already. I'm saying it again." His eyes lock on mine in a heated stare that makes everything slow down.

Without another word, he runs his tongue along his teeth and looks back at his plate. We eat the rest of our breakfast in silence before he takes the plates and puts them in the sink.

Chapter 12

Somehow, we end up on the couch to watch a movie. It's not the weirdest thing that could happen, spending the weekend at somebody's house. It is a bit odd that it's happening between myself and Chase.

There's really only so much you can do when stuck in a small space with one another.

I'd happily read, since there's a book in my work bag I'm dying to get back to, but Chase mentioned a movie, and I feel like I can't say no. This isn't my house, and this is still...well, I don't really know what it is.

So instead, we're sitting awkwardly on the couch, next to each other but not quite touching while some random comedy he picked drones on in the background. I'm too distracted by his presence to focus on it because he's sitting as still as a statue. And I'm acutely aware that I'm doing the same.

It's been ages since I've watched a movie with a guy I'm dating. At that point, we'd usually snuggle up on the couch to watch together.

But Chase and I aren't dating. We're fucking regularly, and I'm at his house despite my better instincts against it, but here we are.

"This is crazy." I startle as he breaks the silence.

"What is?" I don't know why I ask when, clearly, we're thinking the same thing.

"The way we're acting. We can be comfortable. I've been inside you every day for weeks now. Why can we not be comfortable together on the couch to watch a movie?" The way he asks makes me feel foolish, like I'm the only one who's acting strangely here, but he is too, which is surely why he's saying it in the manner he is, with a hint of incredulity.

"Because it feels different. More intimate."

"It's a fucking movie. We're not watching anything romantic. It's supposed to be a comedy, though for the life of me, I couldn't tell you why since it's not that funny."

"You can focus on it enough to be able to tell?"

He turns his head to look at me, and I'm struck still by those intense green eyes. They stop me in my tracks far more often than I'd care to admit. "You can't?"

"No. I'm distracted by you sitting like a statue. And my own stance."

"This doesn't have to be awkward, Elizabeth. We're just watching a movie together. We sit closer and more comfortable at work when we're going over things with Colleen. We should be able to do that here, in privacy."

He's right. At work, we're both looser and more animated and sit right next to each other all the time. We even touch from time to time in completely platonic ways, like a brush of our fingers or him touching my lower back as he ushers me into the conference room.

That's all outside of the office fucking.

But now, I'm pretty sure if he touched me at all, I'd jump out of my skin and burst into flames simultaneously.

"You're right. I just don't know what to make of this."

"Why does it have to be something? Can't it just be what it is, which is two coworkers fucking daily, spending the weekend together? You can even say that I don't want to be alone and would appreciate your company because of the anniversary of my mom's passing if you need to give it a reason beyond just us spending time together."

While he's right, that it doesn't need to be *something*, I don't know how to act with it. I've never done the free and simple, no strings attached, sleeping around. I know he has, but that's never been my style. If I'm sleeping with somebody, we're in a relationship. This is the first time I've ever had carefree sex.

Which brings a thought to the forefront of my mind.

"I'm not sure why it matters...maybe it doesn't, I don't know. But when was the last time you slept with somebody?" I barely turn to look at him, trying to feign disinterest.

"You know a few months back I worked that case with the wife whose husband cheated on her with her sister?"

"Yeah." I drag the word out a bit, not sure I like where this is going.

"I slept with the sister." He rubs his hand along his jaw as he says it. If I didn't know better, I'd say he was embarrassed. But Chase has no shame. It doesn't surprise me, not in the least, but it does make me itch under my skin. "How about you?"

"Oh, uh, it's been...a while."

"A while?" One eyebrow arches as he tries to interpret my meaning. But I won't give him that much fuel.

"Yeah. Let's just leave it at that." He doesn't need to know it's been almost a year. I'm thankful he doesn't push it or argue.

I turn to the side and scratch the spot behind my ear as though I'm not turning away in shame. There's nothing wrong with going so long without sex. The problem is that had Chase and I not gotten started, that streak would have continued for who knows how long.

"Okay, so we're each other's only partner in a while. That's nothing to be ashamed of. We're busy people." His 'a while' and mine are very different, but that's okay because he's right.

With a heavy sigh, he throws his arm over the back of the couch, right near my head, and starts twisting a curl.

All the air stalls in my lungs, and my eyes widen, but I quickly shake off the feeling and allow myself to relax into the couch and lean in his general direction. Not against him, not even brushing his body, but enough that I'm not going to have a crick in my neck from sitting so straight.

Now that I'm actually relaxed, I allow myself to watch the movie and giggle a few times. Chase is right, it's not truly funny, but there are some comical parts and now that I've loosened up, it's allowing me to focus and enjoy what we're watching.

I try to ignore the tiny voice in the back of my head, wondering what the hell is going on here. The one that's telling me this is more than just two coworkers having sex. Though maybe it's not. He wanted some company this weekend and surely to be able to distract himself from the thoughts of his mother. What better way to do that than losing yourself in somebody else?

No, this is nothing more than just two people wanting to get lost in each other for the weekend.

Chapter 13

"**S**how me what these stupid bath balls are all about." He's standing right behind me, his chest pressed against my back.

I've been here all day, and we've ended up in the bathroom. I told him I wanted to shower and asked if he had a clean towel and a new shirt for me. Instead of telling me where to find one, he followed me in and now is standing so close I can feel his warmth.

"Bath bombs." My voice is low and quiet, almost a whisper. It's a weird situation to be in with Chase. This whole weekend is strange, and I don't know what to make of it. But I'm taking advantage of every second because I don't have nearly as nice of a bathroom.

"What?" He sounds completely confused.

"Bath bombs. You called it a bath ball. It's a bath *bomb*."

"Whatever. What's the excitement behind them?"

"I don't know. They're kind of fun and relaxing. Some have prizes inside." I don't really use them myself. I've never quite seen the appeal either, but they do smell nice and make your skin soft.

"So, you get a new toy for taking a bath?"

"Kind of."

"They sound stupid."

"Just try it. Maybe you'll love it."

With one hand on my hip, he reaches over and turns the tub on.

"What, right now?"

"Sure. Why not?"

He turns the water off before it's full.

"Why are you stopping it already? There's room for more water."

"For one person sure, but not two."

"You want me to take a bath with you?" My brows shoot sky high as shock makes my heart rate climb.

"Is that so crazy?"

Is it? I can't decide. I've accepted I don't hate him. But taking a bath together feels too romantic. Still, it looks so warm and inviting. I doubt he'd take a bath by himself and then let me take one by myself.

"It is, but my whole body is sore, so I guess it's worth it." Twisting my hair up to keep it out of the water, I unbutton my shirt but leave it on so it's covering my breasts and leaving my middle exposed. "Okay, now for the fun part."

"No, Princess, the fun part will be when I slide that shirt off of you and lick you and tease you a little before taking you into the tub and rubbing down your slick skin." The deepness of his voice in my ear sends shivers racing from the nape of my neck to my toes.

"Just watch." I unwrap the bath bomb and gently toss it into the water. The fizzing begins immediately as the water starts to change from translucent to a light purple. Chase is standing right behind me, his chest continuing to brush my back with every breath. His finger grazes down my neck, resting an extra second at the place where my pulse is fluttering rapidly. Turning toward him, I jerk my head to the bath. "Watch."

"I'm not interested in that, Elizabeth." Sliding his hands under the hem of my shirt, he moves them up my sides, wrapping to the front to cup my breasts. He breathes gently against my neck. Every so often, I wonder if he'll kiss me across the tract of sensitive skin, but he never does. I'm thankful for that, it would feel too intimate. The less kissing, the better.

All the same, his hands massage, adjusting to take my pebbled nipples between his fingers, and as his breath caresses my neck, my head tips back to rest against his chest. "Chase." I say his name breathlessly. It rolls off the tongue far easier than it should and laced with more desire than I ever could have thought possible.

His hands leave my chest and move to my shoulders, ever so gently sliding off the shirt as his fingers graze my down my arms. The garment falls to floor and his fingers hook under the hem of my panties, kneeling as he lowers them. Lifting one foot at a time, he carefully eases them from my ankles.

Gliding his palms up my legs, he cups my ass and kneads gently. I shriek at the loud clap from his open hand hitting my butt cheek. I don't need to look at him to know there's a smirk on his face, especially because one is spread on mine as well.

There's a warm wetness on my skin as he licks from my ankle up to the crease where the swell of my ass and thigh meet. Trailing his tongue along that line, he rests his hands firmly on my waist as he spins me around. His eyes hold mine as he lays kisses along my lower belly before settling between my thighs.

The second his tongue touches me, my head tips back, eyes shut, and fingers twist into his hair. He keeps his grip on me as he starts laving me with long glides and quick flicks around my heavy clit. My chest is heaving as he works me over, but once he slides two fingers inside, I tighten my grip in his hair, demanding his closeness.

As he hooks them, I buck against him, whimpers rising in my chest. A few more hurried strokes and he closes his mouth around my clit, sucking and teasing with the tip of his tongue. The hand not in his hair grabs at his shoulder, trying to find traction on bare skin. Starting to tremble, I feel unsteady, but Chase wraps his free arm around my waist to keep me upright and hold me as I scream, my voice echoing off the tiles.

Pulling away but keeping his arm around me as I come down from the high, Chase stands in front of me, looking down at me. Once I've stilled, he releases me, sliding off his pants and climbing into the tub. Silently, he holds out a hand for me to take, and I join him.

Settling against one of the backrests, I sit opposite him. The water is purple and soft around us. I look at him with raised eyebrows.

"Well?"

His eyebrows are scrunched together, and one corner of his mouth is ticked down. He looks from side to side and swishes his hands through the opaque water. "It's purple. And smells like..."

"Lilacs. It smells like lilacs."

"I'm not seeing the appeal."

"Well, it's supposed to be relaxing. A nice light scent, the water's softer, your skin will feel amazing after."

"I'd rather feel your skin."

My cheeks burn at the suggestion. He just tasted me in an epic orgasm and is already talking about giving me more. "Okay, well, *my* skin will also feel amazing after."

"No, I mean, right now."

"Huh?" Before he answers, he grabs my wrist and pulls me toward him, water sloshing out of the tub and onto the floor. "You're getting the floor all wet." My words come out low and breathy as my body aches with need all over again and my lungs constrict at his nearness.

"It will dry." The breathlessness is in his voice too. Shifting my hands to rest against his chest, his heart hammers against my palm. Clearing his throat, he turns me around. He cups my shoulders and begins massaging gently.

My head tips forward as a low moan eases from my lips. His hands move lower, wrapping my ribs as his thumbs rub along my spine, making small circles.

"Are you always this tense?"

"Probably."

I jump as his hands slide below the water to my lower back. It's not just because my sides are ticklish, but most of tension resides at the dip in my waist.

"Hurts or ticklish?"

"Both." I'm wondering if I'll regret saying it, that he'll start tickling me immediately, but he doesn't, working his thumbs extra hard into the muscle. There's momentary pain quickly replaced with loosening muscles.

"This won't do." Releasing me, he leans forward, his chest pressing to my back as he adds hot water to the tub. It warms instantly, which eases more of the tension in my muscles and chases away the chill that had started to set in my bones. As he turns off the water, he closes an arm across my chest and pulls me against him as he leans back.

My heart starts hammering against my sternum at the intimacy. But that feeling lasts for all of a second as his hand glides down my body and rests between my thighs. He eases me open and slips along my slit, giving a few circles around my clit, applying just the right amount of pressure.

"I'm going to drain this water and fill it with fresh so I can fuck you."

My breath catches at the words murmured in my ear.

With the water draining and refilling, it's an agonizingly slow process. Chase makes it worse by running his fingertips along and between my thighs, up my sides, over my breasts, and down again. Over and over in a circuit. All the while, he's running open lips from one shoulder to the next, every so often stopping to nip at my ear or the nape of my neck.

A growl behind me that rumbles into my own chest makes my eyes snap open. The water still has a heavy purple hue.

"This is taking too long. Come on." Leaving the water both running and draining, Chase stands from the tub, taking my hand and pulling me toward the large shower.

"It's going to be freezing. You have the tub on still."

"Don't worry, it's a big enough tank."

Guiding me under the water, Chase stands behind me, chest pressed against my back as the water runs over us.

"Rinse, Elizabeth. But be fast."

I give a quick swipe of my hand over my body, moving to the side so he can rinse as well, taking in the swell of his cock. He gives himself a few rough strokes, which sends an unusual tingle through my body.

Reaching out for me, he grabs me by the waist, tugs me against him, and loses a hand in my hair, setting it free from the loosely twirled updo, as he closes his mouth over mine. Tongues clashing as they meet, he moves us so my back is pressed against the wall as a hand raises to close around my throat. He seems to like this move, not that I'm complaining. He swallows down my moan and hooks my leg around his waist as he eases into me. I pull my mouth from his as I gasp for air, my hand wrapping to the back of his neck as my fingers twist in the littlest bit of hair they can.

Thrusting hard and fast, my body is shifting against the tile, the warring sensations of cold against my back and heat everywhere else only amplifying my pleasure.

"Chase. Fuck. Why does this have to feel so damn good?"

"Are you paying me a compliment, Liz?"

"No. Yes. I don't know. Shut up and fuck me."

His hand tightens around my throat, making it hard to swallow or take a deep breath. He stops moving completely, leaving himself completely still inside me.

"Oh, Princess. Don't get things twisted. I'm in charge here. All the time, every time. Talk back again and there will be consequences."

I arch an eyebrow. "What. Kind. Of consequences." It comes out broken due to not being able to breathe fully.

Licking along my jaw to rest at my ear, he growls from deep in his chest. "Push me and you'll find out. I'll never hurt you, Elizabeth, but I will take it out on you in bed. I'm not opposed to fucking your mouth. I'm not opposed to tying you up and teasing you. That one, I'm actually looking forward to. But push me and you'll find out."

Is it bad that I'm tempted to push him? In this moment, it doesn't feel right. Instead of waiting for an answer, he releases me, pulling out and setting me flat on my feet. Turning off the water, he pulls me from the shower and guides me straight back to the bath. Surprisingly, it's still warm.

As he sits, he pulls me toward him, face to face. Wrapping his hands around my hips and setting my legs on either side of him, he raises me slightly as he brings me to him, settling himself against my entrance. Slowly, he lowers me onto him, my hands resting on his shoulders. When I try to move and wriggle, he tightens his grip.

He tsks with his teeth before sinking them into my shoulder, causing me to shriek. Before I'm even quiet, he's sliding me all the way onto his cock. For a minute, I can't even breathe.

Chase rubs small circles along my hips, keeping me still as I try to gain some semblance of composure. "You good?"

All I can do is nod. I want to wriggle. I want to grind my hips against his. I want to *move*. But Chase's grip on me is too tight and while whatever punishment he has in mind might be fun, I'm not ready to find out. This weekend is weird enough already.

Thankfully, Chase seems to hear my silent plea for movement, pushing me forward and backward on his lap. Any time I make the slightest adjustment or try to go faster, he tightens his hold on me.

Leaning forward, he closes his mouth around my nipple, curling his tongue around it while keeping the momentum of my hips going. I loop my arm around his neck to keep myself upright as my eyes start to roll back in my head, and I tip backward.

With a few more pushes and pulls and swirls, I'm moaning and tightening around him as I dig my nails into his neck. Still moving me on his lap, Chase takes a deep inhalation and releases a groan as he pulsates inside me, slowly bringing me to a stop.

I collapse against him, panting and warm, too warm. The heat of the water and exertion of our bodies a little too much. I should get out, cool down, but I can't move.

With some slight shifting, Chase unplugs the tub and gets some cooler water running.

His chest heaves against mine as he rests his head against the lip of the tub. He still has his hands around my waist and is allowing me to sit draped across his chest while he's still inside me.

Clearing his throat, he leans up. "I guess the tub wasn't the best idea. You feel alright?"

I nod but don't move from my spot. The cooler water is helping, but my head is spinning a bit.

Lifting my hips, he removes himself, sliding an arm under my legs as he adjusts and stands, lifting me out of tub. He wraps a towel around his waist while still holding me before sitting on the edge of the tub and wrapping me in one as well. I'm keeping my eyes closed to try to stop the swirling of the room. Circling my arms around his neck, he scoops me back up, carrying me to his room where he lays me gently on the bed, curling up in front of me.

"Do you need anything?"

"For the room to stop spinning."

"It's not spinning, Liz. You're okay. Do you want some water?"

I shake my head and inch closer to him. I hate that I'm seeking his comfort right now, but he's right here. A cool breath hits my skin, causing me to jump. My hand flies to splay against his chest. Wrapping his hand around mine, he holds my palm above his heart, which is beating at a steady rhythm. He keeps blowing as I try to make my heart slow to the speed of his.

Within a few minutes, my pulse has slowed, and the spinning has stopped. I take a chance and open my eyes to find everything is fine, except for the scrunched brow I see on Chase's face, with worry flashing through his eyes.

"This happen to you often?"

"No. I just got overheated. I'm okay. Sorry you had to take care of me."

"You're not a bother, Liz. You don't have to apologize for being vulnerable."

"But this"—I quickly move a finger between the two of us—"isn't supposed to be about taking care of each other."

"Says who?"

"Says the fact that we hate each other. Because...because you do still hate me. Right?"

"Of course." There's no conviction behind his words. "And you still hate me?"

"Sure." Nor is there any behind mine.

We look at each other for a minute. I'm trying to see something, anything, to help me find a solid place to land. What he's thinking, what he's feeling. I read clients and witnesses as part of my job, and I'm good at it. But I can't read him. I only hope he's struggling as much as I am.

"I'll give you a few minutes. I'm going to change."

Before I can answer, he slides away and quickly pulls on a clean pair of drawstring pants, leaving without another word or glance in my direction.

Flopping to my back, I sprawl out and stare at the ceiling. There's a pattering against the windows that I hadn't heard before, and I wonder how long it's been raining.

I'm staring at the droplets pouring down the glass, still wrapped loosely in a towel as my mind wanders when the bed dips next to me. Something cool runs up my arm, making my jump.

Turning to Chase, he's holding out a bottle of water. It must be what he ran along my skin. The look of concern that's still settled in his eyes makes my heart race.

Pushing up to sitting, I take the bottle and gulp a few sips, the cool water soothing my parched throat. A shiver sets in as the temperature reaches the rest of my body.

Chase immediately jumps up and pulls a shirt from his drawer. Sitting back down next to me, he unfolds it. "Arms up, Liz." His voice is gentle. I do as he says, letting the towel fall away from me first as he lowers the shirt over my head and arms.

"Are you okay?" Worry coats his words. I'm not sure I've ever heard it in his voice before, but it's unmistakable.

"I'm really okay. I just got too hot."

"I'm sorry. I wasn't thinking about the heat and the body temperature."

"It's okay, Chase. How could you know? It's not like a problem I run into frequently." The look on his face doesn't change much as he purses his lips. Sighing, I move to get up. "I'm going to brush my teeth."

Taking my towel with me, I make my way to the bathroom. I'd considered leaving at one point today, but it feels so far away now. The longer I stand, the more the woozy feeling starts to settle into my head and extremities again. By the time I'm walking out of the bathroom, I'm feeling a little unsteady on my feet.

Chase must see something wrong because he walks over to me, wrapping an arm around my waist, and guides me into bed. He pulls the covers up so they're around my shoulders as I curl into his chest.

I can sense his hesitation as he puts his arm around me and pulls me closer.

Resting his chin on my head, he rubs circles on my back.

I'm asleep before I can pay much attention to my feelings on how non-hate filled this all is.

Chapter 14

The first thing I do when I get home midday Sunday is dial Lydia, not even taking the time to change, as I bounce on the balls on my feet waiting for her to answer.

"Hello?"

"I spent the weekend at Chase's house." No point in pretense. It's best to just blurt the words right out.

"Well, shit. First of all, hi. Second of all, what? Are you serious?"

"Yeah. I just got home. Like, literally, *just* got home." To emphasize the point, though possibly only for myself, I pop my shoes off and set to making a pot of coffee.

"Tell me all about it."

I begin detailing the events of the weekend, starting with him inviting me back after our quick closet fuck on Friday. She oohs, aahs, and awws at various parts of the story.

"And then this morning after we woke up and had breakfast, I told him I needed to come home to get ready for work tomorrow. He still kept me for a few hours." More like four hours. Somehow, he managed to keep me for four hours, and now it's after noon, and I'm just getting home to start getting myself together.

Cheshire still hasn't shown his face, clearly angry that I left him alone all weekend. Though, his bowl is almost empty so at least I know he came out to eat while I was gone.

"How'd he do that?"

"How do you think?" Sex. Lots of it. In the shower, the bed, on the floor. The man fucks like he's going to die tomorrow and it's his dying wish.

"Sheesh, Liz, you two are ridiculous. Are you sure you hate him? You two fuck like nobody's business."

My hand tightens around my phone and my eyes dart around the room. She just called me out on my biggest fear. As far as Chase is concerned, I still hate him, but in reality, I'm not so sure.

"Liz? Are you there?"

"Yeah, I'm here."

"Holy shit. You *like* him."

"No! I don't like him. I just. I might not hate him." That's the only level I'm willing to land on. The only allowance I'm willing to make.

"Uh uh, Liz. There's more than that here."

"That's the problem, Lyd, there can't be. He hates me. I can't start having feelings for him if he still hates me. So as much as I may not loathe him and his existence, it can't be more than that. It can't be more than a neutrality at his presence."

"Liz, how often do you two screw?"

"Frequently." Daily. Sometimes more than once a day. Sometimes I wonder if it's stress induced. The harder the day we're having, the more likely we are to end up in a closet or the basement. How nobody has found out, I haven't a clue.

"With somebody you hate. Or maybe don't hate anymore, but *definitely* don't like." I don't appreciate the way she said "definitely". There was no missing the sarcasm dripping from the word.

"It's just that good, Lyd, I don't know what else to say." Because it really is just mind blowing. I don't think I'd be able to stop if I wanted to.

"I think you can say that you maybe, just maybe, like him."

"No. I can't say that. It might kill me." In fact, I'm fairly certain it would.

"Have you tried? Have you tried to admit that you could possibly like him?"

"I'm not ready to die yet, Lyd."

Her laugh makes the corner of my lip town downward. The hardest part? She may be right. And it makes my heart palpitate to even consider that I might like Chase.

And the two days spent in his never-ending presence did what I was afraid they might. I found a few redeeming qualities in him. And he made me laugh, he took care of me, he made me comfortable. It was beyond just sex.

It was beyond hating somebody but enjoying how good they feel, and he does feel incredible.

Having him inside me is like nothing I've ever experienced before. His strong chest brushing mine just adds to the sensation, and I feel safe when I'm beneath him.

Great, now I'm going to need to fuck him first thing tomorrow. This need that's settled in my clit won't go away until he's inside me again. I've tried masturbating, I've tried toys, but none of it hits the same as he does. None of it's the same as the real deal.

And Chase's cock is like something magical. Never in my life have I felt anything even remotely close, and it's a terrible feeling that it's from the person I spent the majority of my recent years loathing.

"Okay, so you don't hate him, but you don't like him. Tolerating him is still a step in the right direction."

"Right direction? What on earth are you talking about?"

"For you two to fall in love."

I practically choke on the sip of coffee I just took. "Are you insane? Chase Andrews and I will *not* be falling in love. I can't love somebody I spent so long hating, and he's not even interested in the things I am. He doesn't want what I want, Lyd. I can't fall for somebody like that. It's totally out of the question."

"Okay." The way she says it is not at all convincing.

"Alright. You're starting to frustrate me. I'm going to go take a shower and get changed into my own clothes."

"Ooo, you wore his clothes? Match made in heaven."

"*Goodbye,* Lydia!" Her laughter is the only goodbye I need in response, and I click end on the phone.

But instead of hopping into my first solo shower in two days, I flop on the edge of my bed.

While I have absolutely zero intentions of falling in love with Chase, I also had none for this to happen. And yet here we are. But I can control myself. I can make sure that it doesn't go further than some hate fucking, or at least, coworkers who don't like each other fucking.

Right?

Chapter 15

We're wrapping up for the day with Colleen, but she seems reluctant to leave. "Is this something you do often? Go over witness testimonies?"

Chase and I make brief eye contact. "Um, not exactly. It comes up from time to time when one spouse is trying to prove the other unfit. We maybe have a witness that will speak on behalf of our client, either to say they *are* fit or that the spouse is not. But no, it's not common for us to have witnesses or have to take testimonies."

While we don't need to do it, it is something that both Chase and I excel at. At one point, before we were each poached from our separate firms, we used to go head-to-head in the courtroom, for criminal law. I despised him and his cocky attitude even then.

The number of jurors we refused, as well as cross examinations that droned on and led to heated shouts of 'objection' were some of the most

infuriating times in my career. And a big part of the reason I was happy
to be poached by this high-end firm.

"Due to the nature of your relationship, your popularity in town,
doing it in the courtroom and with witnesses is more to create...um..."
How does one politely say, "a show?"

"A spectacle?" The word squeaks out from between her lips.

Chase and I lock eyes again, and he intervenes for me, clearly sensing
my struggle. "A bit, yes. It's high profile, which is why you came to us.
There's no avoiding that it's going to garner a lot of attention from the
town and media. But we can handle it, and we are very good at what we
do."

Her shoulders droop, and she nods into her lap. I can't imagine how
hard this has to be on her. Not only is her marriage ending, but her family
is being torn apart, and in a very public way.

The newest insult is that Mr. Douglas is trying to claim that Colleen
is an unfit mother when her entire life revolves around those children.
She's been a stay-at-home mom since their first, Glenda, was born. But
Mr. Douglas is claiming that the nanny was often the one caring for the
children and that Colleen has no skills to fall back on to provide the same
lifestyle for her children.

While it's true that, even with her savings and what she has from the
prenup, Colleen won't be able to provide the same lifestyle and level of
living that she and her children have become accustomed to, we have zero
doubt that she's a great mother based on what we've seen, heard from
our testimonies, and our conversations with her about her children.

I take her hand in mine in and squeeze. "Please trust us, Colleen. We
know what we're doing. We know how to win cases. It's why we're the
best not only in this firm, but in town. Mr. Douglas' lawyer is scared to
go against us. I can promise you that."

It's getting a bit cocky, and Chase's raised eyebrows says as much. But I know it's what she needs to hear right now. This whole process can be trying on a person, and she needs to keep her confidence in us because it's shattered pretty much everywhere else.

She adjusts her hand to squeeze mine back. "Thank you." Tears are welling in her eyes, and I reach over to grab the box of tissues for her. "I swear I don't usually cry this much."

"It's okay, it's a hard situation and not something you're used to. Divorce isn't easy on anybody, even those where it's mutual, even when you've been hurt. Because you didn't go into it expecting this and you have to relive the good times and bad times in this process. And it is a process. It's long and drawn out, so when you think you've moved on and are feeling better, you're back at square one."

Her head bobs up and down along with my words. "You talk like you've been through this before. Are you divorced?"

I can't help but notice how Chase turns a little toward me at the question. He should know I'm not, but we've never really discussed former relationships, so why would he know for certain?

"No. I'm not. I've just done this a few hundred times by now. And I see my clients go through it over and over. It can be hard, and heartbreaking, but we have you. Rely on us. Let us do our job. You're in the best hands."

"Thank you again. Let me get out of your hair. You have more than enough to do and worry about without me hanging around any later. It's already past seven." I hadn't realized that it got so late, but the rest of the office has cleared out.

For all Mr. Lions' talk of being in with us when Colleen is here, he's been with us maybe three times. Which is more than any other partner who all sit at zero.

As Colleen gathers her things, I stand and push in my chair. Chase puts a hand on my lower back and presses his lips to my ear. "You're about to be in very good hands."

The deep timber of his voice, so low that only I can hear, makes me hot under the collar, and I have to take a deep breath to steady myself.

"Mrs. Douglas. Let me see you out." Chase extends an arm toward the door. Following after her, he looks over his shoulder and takes a long glance down my frame, dragging his tongue along his lower lip before leaving the conference room.

I quickly clean up our papers, folders, and notepads, bringing them into his office. His is farther from the door should anybody come to the front.

Since I'm alone, I may as well prepare, and shimmy my panties off, putting them in the pocket of his sports coat which hangs over the back of his chair. They'll be a nice surprise for him to find later.

I hop onto the edge of his desk, crossing my legs at the knee, and wait for him to find me.

When he does, he's already working the belt from his pants, and I open my legs as wide as my skirt allows.

"I thought she'd never leave." He crosses the room in a few quick strides and loses a hand in my curls, pulling my mouth to his in a heated kiss, his other hand sliding up my thigh. I feel the moment it registers with him that I'm naked under the skirt. "No panties, Liz?"

"I put them somewhere as a fun surprise for you later."

"I can't wait to find them." The words are husky against my lips, and he pulls the bottom one between his teeth before sliding his hand over and thrusting his fingers into me.

With hooded eyelids, he watches as my head tips backward and my hands fist his shirt. One wraps around his tie and pulls him closer to me.

"Chase."

"Come on my fingers, Liz."

"Mmm, more."

He hooks them then, moving his thumb so it presses and swirls against my clit. I cry out in ecstasy, and he pumps his fingers harder until I explode around them.

"Such a good girl. Now you're going to come on my cock."

"Happy to."

With a strong arm around my waist, he lifts me and hikes up my skirt. The second I'm back on the desk, he slams into me with a loud whine tearing from my chest.

"Fuck, Princess. So damn good." He starts thrusting hard and fast, and it's not long before every single one rips a whine or a moan from me.

I just can't help that it doesn't take him long to get me to the finish line. I have not only one orgasm with Chase, which can be a feat to begin with, but several.

"You going to tell me how much you hate me?" He's breathless as he pounds into me, shifting me on the desk despite his strong arm around my waist.

"Mhm." Except I can't get the words to leave my mouth. Because the only thing I hate is how much I *don't* hate him. That and I can barely think right now, my mind as hazy as the room is with the scent of sex and sweat and our bodies colliding over and over.

"Chase. I'm going to...I'm going to come. Fuck. Don't stop." I grip tightly at his shirt, practically untucking it as he thrusts hard and fast until I tighten around his cock and start to tremble.

A few more pistons and he groans against my neck, pulsating inside me. It's this moment of vulnerability as we wind down, this moment when we're wrapped in each other's arms that I realize how much I truly don't hate Chase anymore.

Working with him during the day is still infuriating in many ways; he still pisses me off regularly, and I sometimes still want to wring his neck. But this closeness makes it hard to keep that up all the time.

It ends too quickly and not soon enough as Chase backs away and starts redressing, trying to smooth down his shirt. He gives up the cause when he likely realizes it doesn't matter since we're just going home.

Taking my hand, he helps me off the desk, and I shimmy my skirt back into place, twisting it a bit to make sure it's on straight.

"I'll, uh, see you tomorrow, I suppose." I never quite know what to say after these episodes. Thanks? That was a great fuck? When we go back to work, we just go our separate ways, but when it's the end of the night, I feel like it requires more.

"Good night, Elizabeth. I'll see you tomorrow. Be ready."

"I always am. Night." Without another word, I leave his office, gather my things, and walk out into the night sans panties.

Chapter 16

"Let's go out tonight."

While we've been spending more nights together, we've never gone out in public. "Like on a date?"

"Like as two coworkers having dinner." He zips his pants as he says it, which makes it even stranger. Sensing my hesitation, he puts his hands against the wall of the storage room and leans forward, boxing me in. Tilting my chin up, his eyes darken, and his cheekbones sharpen. "Say you'll have dinner with me, Elizabeth."

"What if I say no?"

Snorting, he rests his forearms against the wall so he's even closer. My whole body thrums beneath him as his pelvis presses up against mine. I have never and will never shrink to this man. But I'd be lying if I said I didn't want to give in to him.

"You won't." His voice is low and commanding, and it sends an ache ricocheting through my body.

"Fine."

Sliding his hand down the inside of my pants, he pushes aside my panties, circling my clit with the pad of his finger. My arms snake around his neck as my head tips back against the wall. Moving his hand forward, I take a sharp inhale as he slides two fingers into me, his mouth resting against my ear. "Good girl."

Hooking his fingers and moving them quickly inside me, he has me coming in minutes as I grip at his hair and shirt.

"I hate you." I'm breathless as I say it, and don't even really mean it anymore.

"Not as much as I hate you." There's no authority to his tone, no conviction.

That's how I find myself pulling up to O'Leary's Bar and Grill the very same evening. I went home and changed into jeans and a blouse before dinner. Staring up at the sign through my windshield, I'm looking at it as though it's a foreign planet instead of a bar I've been coming to for years.

Taking a deep breath and checking my hair and makeup—I want to look good after all—I turn off the car and head in. I find Chase leaning against the wall immediately as I enter. He's scrolling through his phone with a scowl on his face, one foot against the wall. He didn't change from work, and now I feel underdressed.

It irritates me to no end that he can still look so damn good in the suit he's been wearing since six in the morning. I'm not the only who thinks so either, as the hostess has clearly taken note.

Looking up, he notices me and slides his phone into his pocket, scowl staying on his face. He gives me a quick once over as a glint flashes through his eyes. "You look nice. Not sure I've ever seen you in jeans."

That would be because any time we're together outside of the office, I'm either still dressed for work or barely dressed.

"I feel underdressed, I changed. Why didn't you?"

He shrugs as he ushers me forward. "Something came up as I was about to leave. Plus, it's a little far. You look great."

We follow the waitress to our table, Chase letting me go first, and I'm sure he's checking my ass out. I wore my best ass jeans on purpose.

Once we're alone at the table, an awkwardness settles over us. Being together has become more comfortable the more we do it. But being here, at a restaurant, just feels different somehow.

"What were you looking at when I got here?"

"Huh? Oh, nothing. Well, not nothing. But not something I want to talk about right now."

When I narrow my eyes at him, he continues.

"It's something about the case. Nothing urgent, nothing life altering. Well, for us, anyway. But I don't want to talk about it right now. It can wait until Monday."

"You seemed angry."

"Am I ever not?"

"Sometimes, yeah. Or really, you're rarely angry. You're confident, an asshole sure, but rarely *angry*." In fact, I'm not sure I've seen Chase truly angry more than a handful of times. The other moods, yes, dozens, but not mad.

"Elizabeth. I don't want to talk about it tonight." The tone in his voice tells me the conversation is over. But I don't give in that easily.

"If this about the case, the one we're working together, I think I have a right to know."

Sighing, he slips his phone from his pocket, swipes a few times, and hands it to me. Skimming the message, I see it's a simple request to adjust some of the custody dates. Again.

"She's just scared, you know. She's not trying to be difficult," I say as I hand the phone back to him. Colleen has already asked to adjust these specific dates about ten times.

"I don't want to talk about it. Let's move on. No work talk tonight." His face scrunches, and he shakes his head. I can't blame him for not wanting to talk about it; it's all we do five days a week and long hours.

"Well, whatever will we talk about then?"

"I was actually thinking after we eat, maybe you'd be up for a fun little competition?" He quirks up an eyebrow in challenge.

"Think about who you're asking. I love every and any excuse to beat you at something." And anything. I'll take any challenge with Chase.

"Wishful thinking, Princess."

"So, what did you have in mind?" I let the slight go because I know I can best him at many things.

"How about we start with darts?"

Oh. He's in trouble. I used to rule the dartboard at the bar my law school friends and I frequented. "Sure. Darts sounds great."

"First rule. We both drink. Doesn't have to be a lot, but I want a beer and want a level playing field."

Even better. My shot success always increased as my alcohol consumption did. Seems backward, but somehow it worked.

Running my tongue along my teeth, I try to stop my smile from breaking through. "Sure. Been a long week anyway."

After we each order a burger and beer, I take a minute to look around the familiar restaurant. Even though I'm on what's clearly a date, it doesn't look any different just because of the circumstance.

The bar area is filling up as we get further into the night, and as we finish our meals, I worry we'll have a wait to play.

"Guinness, huh? Wouldn't have pegged you for a dark beer kind of girl." We've finished eating and are nursing our drinks before we start our game.

I shrug as I consider my glass. "A boyfriend a few years ago was big into it, guess it grew on me."

Glancing up at him, I take in his down-turned lips and dark glare at the glass in my hand. "Wait, are you jealous? Of me talking about another guy I dated, like, five years ago?"

Scoffing at me, he sits low in his chair, swirling his glass slightly, but refusing to meet my eyes. "Don't be ridiculous. What's there to be jealous of? We're just having fun here, Liz."

There's something in his tone that makes me doubt that, but I drop it anyway. "Why do you do that?"

"Do what?"

"Call me, like, three different things. You're the only person I know who can't settle on one."

He narrows his eyes at me, and I know he has no clue what I'm talking about.

"At any given time, you'll call me either Elizabeth, Liz, or *Princess.*" I count them off on my fingers as I say them.

"I don't know. I guess I don't pay much attention to it. Probably just based on what feels right in the moment. Why, does it bother you?"

Now he does meet my gaze, and it makes me squirm in my seat as desire licks at my insides like the fire flickering through his brilliant green eyes.

Clearing my throat, I shake my head slightly to clear my thoughts. "No. I was just curious."

He takes a big sip, and I watch his Adam's apple bob as he swallows. Standing, he holds his hand toward me. "Come on. Game time."

I let him lead me over the back area of the bar where all the games are. It's rowdy back here and much noisier than the restaurant section, so we have to stand closer to hear one another.

"Have you ever played darts before?"

I shrug nonchalantly. "Once or twice." I can't reveal my hand.

The first game I win, he chalks up to beginner's luck. The second game, which I also win, he says is a fluke. By the third win in a row, he's frustrated. I can't contain myself anymore and burst out laughing as I hang on his shoulder.

"You hustled me!" Though he sounds truly offended, I know he's not.

"I'm sorry. I had to."

Slipping his fingers inside my belt loops, he pulls me flush against him, his mouth right next to my ear. "You're going to pay for that."

A shudder racks my body as many possibilities run through my mind. I have to rub my thighs together a few times to try to alleviate the pressure that settles in my clit at his few simple words.

Taking my hand, Chase pulls me toward the pool table. My heart hammers against my sternum.

"Ever played before?"

I shake my head, which receives a raised eyebrow in response.

"No, really, I've never played pool before. Maybe once, but I'm telling the truth this time."

"Good. That means I'm actually likely to win. You know I hate losing."

I'm as frozen as a statue as Chase gets the balls set in the triangle, chalks the cue, and does whatever else to prepare for the game.

He sets himself up and takes a shot. The familiar sound of pool balls clinking into each other, which can be heard in the right spot in bars everywhere, fills the air around me. One sinks into the pocket. Lining up, Chase takes another shot. Then another. Then another. He sinks four before his first miss.

Looking over at me, he leans on the pool cue, smug grin on his face. Swallowing hard, I walk over to him slowly. I pick up my stick from next to the table and lean over.

"You're solids." He tilts his chin toward the table like that's supposed to help.

Standing up straight, my whole face is scrunched as I look at him. He laughs as he shakes his head. "You want to hit the white ball into the other balls. You want to get the ones that are a solid color into the pocket. Not the eight ball, not the white ball."

When I lean over the table and try to set myself up, he interrupts. "No, no. Not like that. Here." He stands next to me and acts like he's about to shoot. "See? Stand like this."

I try to do what he's showing me, but he fights a laugh. "I've never done this before! Don't laugh at me."

"I'm sorry. Here." Taking my hips in his hands, he adjusts my stance so it's wider. My breath catches, and my heart starts hammering when he presses his chest to my back, fingers tracing down my arms so his hands can cover mine. "See, like this, you're lined up much better." His warm breath in my ear sends a shiver racing down my spine.

I turn around slightly to look at him, noting exactly how close his face is. My gaze locks on his lips before raising to meet his eyes. Inching forward, he closes the gap as his lips meet mine. It's soft, gentle. A brush of skin. Simple, short, *sweet*.

There stands the problem. It was sweet. The sort of kiss a couple may give one another while playing together, before saying goodbye for the day, just a quick kiss to share an emotion. But Chase and I aren't a couple. We can't be.

Turning back to the game, heat pricks the back of my neck because as much as that kiss was not what Chase and I are, I want another one.

"You know, I'm suddenly considering getting a pool table for my basement." Chase's warm breath caressing my neck does nothing to help my heated skin, instead causing my pulse to quicken right next to his mouth.

"Oh, really? Why is that?"

"Because I want to fuck you on the felt. Bend you over the table and smack your ass with a cue. You know, a few reasons." His hands glide up my arms and down my sides, thumbs slipping into my belt loops as he presses me to his chest, digging his erection into my lower back.

A soft moan escapes my throat as my head tips back against his shoulder. One hand slides up to close around my throat, his thumb rubbing along my jaw.

Pulling me away from the table, he takes the pool cue from my hands and lays it down. He keeps me against his chest as he walks us in staggered steps toward a dark hallway at the back of the bar that contains the bathrooms and entrance to the kitchen.

Pushing me against the wall, his lips meet mine. They're hasty and sloppy and eager. I wrap one leg around his waist as we paw at each other. My need for him has grown exponentially in recent weeks. It scares the shit out of me.

As somebody comes out of the kitchen, he pulls his mouth from mine and presses tighter against me, squishing me into the wall. Once they're gone, he flips us around, leaning his head against the wall as he slouches, legs outstretched on either side of mine. His hands are resting on my hips. Brushing a thumb tenderly along an exposed tract of skin he looks at me with the oddest sentiment. "I'm realizing I don't hate you, Liz. Not even a little bit."

Swallowing around the lump in my throat, I stare at him. I've come to this realization already. And now we're both here. This isn't good. It can't be. We can't be anything more than coworkers who fuck here and there. Okay, daily, but still. What would it say about us that we started our relationship out hating each other?

But instead of saying any of these things, I find myself nodding, resting my hands on his chest to find his heart beating erratically. "Yeah, Chase. I know what you mean."

"Come home with me."

"How would that be different than any other Friday night lately?" Most Friday nights, I end up at his house or he stops over to my apartment for a quick bed or shower fuck. We typically spend the night, but just the one night. After breakfast the next morning, and usually another fuck, we go on our merry way back home. Alone. This has been going on for several weeks now.

"I want you to spend the weekend again." *Boom.* Bomb drop. The first time it had been an...accident. Of sorts. I hadn't planned on staying ahead of time; it hadn't been brought up, just sort of...happened. But this? This is planned. Well, a little. I don't have clothes. Though I'd really get by just fine without them.

I'm nodding before I even realize I'm doing it. "Okay."

Losing a hand in my hair, he pulls my mouth to his, tongue pushing my lips apart and slipping along mine. It makes my heart race, and my knees weaken. Which is bad.

Very, very bad.

Chapter 17

M y legs are wrapped tightly around Chase's waist as he holds me up against the window in his bedroom. I'm clinging to him as tightly as I can.

"Elizabeth, look at me." I meet his eyes, realizing mine are wide and frantic. "I've got you. I won't let anything happen to you."

"What if the window shatters?"

"It won't." There's such a sureness to his tone.

"How do you know?"

"Would you believe me if I told you I had them replaced and super enforced for this purpose?" One eyebrow cocks up, and I don't know if I should take him seriously or not.

"Actually, I would believe you'd do something like that. But I don't think you actually did."

The cold licks against my spine, causing me to yelp as Chase leans me against the glass and moves his hands from under my thighs to cup my cheeks. Leaning in, he closes his mouth over mine, his tongue sweeping in. It's slow, calming, tender. It makes my heart race even more than it has been and a moan rises in my chest.

Moving his lips away, he trails them along my jaw to rest at my ear. "Nothing is going to happen to you, Liz. Nothing bad, at least. I told you I was going to fuck you against this window. I haven't followed through yet, so I'm doing it now." Pulling my earlobe between his teeth, he elicits a low growl that vibrates straight down to my clit. "You're going to come, Elizabeth, at least once, right against this window."

The wriggle I make against him makes his lips tick up in one corner as he slides a hand between us. His fingers slip along my pussy. "Mm, always so wet for me, Princess." Slowly he slides two fingers inside me, and my breath catches as he starts moving them feverishly.

My head tips back onto the glass, the cold pane feeling delightful against the extreme warmth that's radiated to the top of my head. Gripping the back of his neck, I twist into the strands at his nape.

He holds his face a few inches from mine, mouth open as he takes in my reaction as he replaces his fingers with his erection. When he starts moving inside me, I forget all about the window. One of his hands holds the back of my neck while the other wraps around my hip and he pumps hard and fast into me.

"Fuck, Chase. Mm...don't stop, fuck, don't..." I can't even get my words out as my grip in his hair tightens and I cry out.

Tilting me forward so I'm against his chest and clinging to him, Chase carries me to the bed as I tremble. He lays me down gently, his eyes locked on mine for a minute. There's something in his, like he's questioning something, trying to make some sort of decision. I'm not sure what that something may be, but he leans in and brushes his lips against mine. As he starts moving slowly inside me, he opens my mouth with his, tongue sweeping in. We've kissed before while having sex, but never like this. This kiss is tender, sweet. Picking up speed, Chase keeps his lips moving against mine, swallowing my moans as one hand runs down the side of my body, continuing down my leg and wrapping my ankle to rest behind his back.

The pressure building, I pull my mouth from his to gasp for air, his lips closing on my neck and kissing across to my shoulder and back again. When my head tips back and I moan loudly, he latches onto the base of my throat, shifting to the side of my neck where my pulse flutters wildly.

As I'm still shuddering through the end of my orgasm, he thrusts harder and faster until he's groaning against my neck. "Fuck, baby."

I go completely still, my veins filling with ice.

Pushing up to look at me, there's a scowl on his face. "Shit, Liz. I didn't—I didn't mean it in a weird way. Don't look at me like that."

"I'm not looking at you any way." But I know my eyes are wide and brows are high.

"You're looking at me like I just slaughtered a whole flock's worth of lambs."

"I am not." This is a strange conversation to have as he's still inside me and hovering over me. But part of me thinks he's doing it on purpose so I can't flee, can't get away. I'm trapped.

"Liz. I just. Fuck, it just came out, okay?"

I nod enthusiastically, but my heart is trying to fly out of my chest.

Dropping his head to my shoulder, he sighs, leaving a small kiss against my collarbone, before rolling to his back.

We lay next to each other, staring at the ceiling. My hands are on my stomach, my fingers playing lightly across my skin as I chew my lip. I don't want to chance a look at Chase, but I can't help myself. He has an arm flung over his forehead and his eyes trained above him.

The problem here? I didn't hate that he called me baby. Or kissed me so tenderly. The bigger problem? I'm starting to feel like not only do I maybe like him, but that it's more than that.

When Chase releases a heavy sigh next to me, I settle my gaze on him. His eyes are narrowed like he's deep in thought. Otherwise, he hasn't moved or changed at all. While I'm still watching him, he slams his hand to the bed and rolls back on top of me, crashing his mouth to mine and pushing his tongue in.

Pulling away from a kiss that leaves me breathless, he rests on his elbows above me. "Here's the deal, Elizabeth. I don't hate you anymore, not even a little. In fact, I'm pretty sure I kind of like you. I definitely like fucking you. A lot. So, I'm going to do what I want with you, say what I want when it feels right. It's not a term of endearment. I'm certainly not going to start calling you babe or baby in conversation. But every so often, it may come out while I'm deep inside you. And I really hope you're okay with that, because I'm not planning to change this decision, and I really don't want to stop whatever it is we have."

Hesitating for a minute, he moves one of his hands to twist around one of my curls, his mouth pressed into a hard line.

I decide to give in to a desire I've had for weeks and haven't allowed myself to indulge. My fingers tingling before I even raise my hand, I lift it slightly, stalling partway in the air, before running through his hair. I've tangled my fingers in it several times; possibly every time we're together I'm tugging at his roots. But this is different, this isn't edged in anger or passion.

When his eyes lock on mine again, I freeze, my hand still lost in his hair. Keeping my curls between his fingers, he moves his hand to cup my cheek. Running his thumb across my lower lip, he pulls it down before leaning down to close his mouth over mine.

This is the first kiss that hasn't had a purpose, that hasn't been part of sex. It just is. Maybe its purpose is an exploration, maybe his intention *is* to lead to sex. Either way, I'm not complaining. It's actually kind of...nice.

Lydia was right. All those weeks ago, she was right. I'm realizing that now. And I'm also realizing that I'm completely fucked.

Chapter 18

I wake up in Chase's arms the next morning. No part of it feels weird anymore. Things are shifting, quickly. Or maybe they already have and I'm just catching up. Staring out the window, I take in the dense spread of trees, leaves wavering slightly. It's a bright, sunny day, possibly what woke me, though I don't know what time it is. Am I up early? Or did Chase sleep in?

Despite all the nights we've been spending together, this is the first time I'm waking up with him still in bed with me. Deciding to relax a little, I enjoy the peaceful time and stare out the windows, watching the birds and fast-moving clouds dance across the crystal blue sky.

As I'm zoning out, my mind completely blank, Chase tightens his arm around me and kisses the nape of my neck, working toward my shoulder. He moves his body up so his chin can rest on my shoulder.

"Nice view, isn't it?"

"It really is. A very peaceful way to wake up. Except bright. Don't you have curtains?"

"I'm usually up before the sun." He says it like it's no big deal and not one of the crazier things I've heard.

"So, I guess you slept in today?"

"Guess so." He turns his head down to me as I tilt mine up toward him. Leaning down, he closes his mouth over my own as his tongue demands entry, which is quickly granted.

Rolling in his arms, I turn into him, keeping my tongue moving against his. Pushing against me, he eases me to my back, hovering over me as he slides one hand down my body to rest between my legs. Chase is by far the most insatiable man I have *ever* been with. I'm not really complaining because I find myself wanting him as much as he wants me. It's hard not to when it's just so damn good.

Pressing two fingers into me, his thumb finds my clit and starts making smooth circles. I'm writhing against him as he hooks his fingers and kisses across my neck. When he sinks his teeth in, I scream as I buck against him and grab at his shoulders. It's almost not fair that he knows me well enough to make me come so quickly.

Without a moment of hesitation, he removes his fingers and plunges his erection into me, and all the air is stripped from my lungs as I forget how to breathe. A few slow pumps and Chase stops.

"Breathe, Elizabeth."

I draw in a deep breath, one that catches all the way down my windpipe. He fills me so much sometimes it takes a moment of adjustment.

When I'm able to take complete, smooth breaths, he starts moving inside me. As he picks up speed, he rests his forehead against mine. My eyes close at the feeling and the flutter that sets in my chest. I grip his shoulders to hold him close.

Our breaths are mingling in the slight space between us, adding something to the intimacy of this moment that I know should feel awkward but doesn't. Instead, it feels right.

When Chase tilts his face forward and closes his mouth over mine, his tongue explores my mouth, and I moan into his. My fingers twist into his hair.

As he starts moving faster, I have to tear from him as my eyes roll back in my head and my back peels off the bed.

"Chase." His name comes out on a breath as I tighten around him and drag my nails down his arms.

Kissing along my neck, he gives a few more pumps before his moan catches in his throat, creating a strangled sound as he comes.

Pushing up to look at me, his mouth is set in a hard line, and there's something I can't read floating in his eyes. I'm frozen to my spot, not quite sure what's going on. When he reaches up and brushes some hair from my face, my blood slows in my veins.

"I want you to show me your farmhouse today." He hasn't gotten off of me, or out of me.

"It's far."

"I don't care. I want to see it."

I open my mouth to rebut, but he stops me with a kiss.

"I'm not really asking, Elizabeth. Let's take the day and head out to the country to see your farmhouse, the one your dad had to have."

"Okay." If he really wants to see it, why am I going to deny him that? He seems truly interested.

"Is there furniture there?"

My head cocks to the side as my brow furrows.

"For fucking on, Elizabeth. Is there furniture I can fuck you on there?"

Heat rushes my face at both the thought and the fact that I couldn't figure that out. "Oh, um, not really."

"So, you own an empty house out in the country that you don't go see because with your job you have no time?"

"Pretty much." That really about sums it all up.

"Now I'm *very* intrigued. And if you tell me that you only keep it because of your dad, I may have to reconsider this arrangement."

"I keep it because I like it. I *bought* it because of my dad. My intention is to fix it up and live there at some point. It's a great yard for dogs and kids and—" I stop, pulling my lip between my teeth when I realize I mentioned kids. He doesn't want any, and he made that very clear. I'm not sure he knows that I do despite our disagreement months ago. Not that it matters; this isn't heading anywhere remotely close to that. I just don't need him giving me shit for it.

"Well, I'm excited to see it. Despite the lack of furniture." He narrows his eyes for a minute as if considering. "Is there hot water?"

"Of course there's hot water. There's also a toilet instead of an outhouse."

"I'm going to assume there are no towels, though. We should bring some."

"Do you think about anything other than sex?"

Rolling away from me, he sighs. "Sometimes, but it's kind of hard to do that around you. Right now, I'm thinking I'm hungry and want to make us some breakfast before we get ready to go."

"I only have the one pair of clothes, from last night." Wow, was that only last night?

"That's fine. Those pants did you all sorts of favors."

"Good, huh?" I know they are, I just want to hear him say it. I roll toward him so I can see his face as he says it.

"Don't pretend you don't know they are." Reaching around me, he smacks my right butt cheek. "You have a great ass, Liz." Standing, he pulls pants on and tosses a shirt at me. "Come down when you're ready." Once Chase is out of bed, I roll to the middle and stretch wide. His bed is far more comfortable than my own. But this aspect of it still makes me feel strange. Like it's just normal for me to be alone in his bed. Or really in it at all for more than sleep or a screw. And I'm staying again tonight. After he sees my house.

Sometimes, like at work when we're driving each other to the brink of insanity on a daily basis, it still feels like we're just coworkers who take our frustrations out on one another's bodies. But then there are times like now where it feels so much beyond that.

When I get downstairs in just his t-shirt, I find him at the stove, making what I've come to find is a specialty of his, omelets. They're utterly delicious too, which is just another thing to both love and hate about him. He's a surprisingly good cook. His talents are wasted on just himself, and he doesn't even use them often since he's so busy with work.

"Hope you don't mind another omelet." He doesn't turn around as he talks, instead pouring me a cup of coffee.

It's possible he heard me come into the room, but lately it seems more like we can sense each other instead. He doesn't have to hear me come in because he just knows that I have. It's happened to me a time or two at the office. It's the air that changes, there's a crackle to it or something I can't quite explain.

"Not at all, they're delicious."

"Seems like we're going to need to be well fueled up to go to this house in the middle of nowhere. There are restaurants nearby, correct?"

"Of course, Chase. It's not that rural. It's a farmhouse, yes, and private, but there's a town and everything with shops and restaurants within ten minutes of the house." I mean, seriously, what exactly is he expecting? He knows the general area, so how does he not get that it's not actually the middle of nowhere?

"Well, thank fuck for that."

We eat quickly, our bodies needing the fuel not for the day ahead, but from the night past. One thing I've noticed since starting up with Chase is that my appetite has increased, and not just for him.

I know his has as well because I used to see what he ate for breakfast and lunch, and now I note the difference.

We're dressed and ready to go by ten o'clock.

"We should swing by your house, get you a change of clothes." Chase makes this comment as we climb into his car.

"I thought you said these pants were good?"

"I'm thinking a skirt would be better." A devilish smirk crosses his face. It's not the same as the cocky one I've always hated, it's more sexually oriented. Or maybe it's the same and I just know the meaning behind it now.

"You really can't go a few hours without fucking me?"

"I have zero intention of finding out."

I shake my head and stare out the window, heat rushing my face.

An hour later, I'm letting us into my apartment. Cheshire greets me with a high-pitched meow before immediately making figure eights around Chase's legs. I move to grab him because Chase says he's not really a cat person, when he squats down to scratch Cheshire between the ears.

"Hi, little buddy. Thanks for letting me borrow your mommy so much." When Chase looks up at me, my mouth is hanging open. I'm stunned into a statue, unable to tear my eyes away or move. My breath has completely stalled in my chest. "What?"

"Nothing, I just didn't expect you to be so nice to him."

"I may prefer dogs, but that doesn't mean I'm an uncaring asshole. He's sweet." The few times Chase has been here at night, Cheshire has made himself scarce. This is the first time that he's even come out to see Chase in person.

"He seems to like you."

"Well, I'm a very likable person."

With a scoff, I head toward my bedroom. "Make yourself at home," I call over my shoulder as I wave a hand in his general direction.

I'm sorting through my closet, trying to find something that may work for Chase, wondering why I care and when I started taking his thoughts into consideration, when my hairs stand on end at his presence. Standing right behind me, his breath caressing my neck, he trails his fingers down my arm.

"I think you should bring some of your clothes to my house."

I freeze in his arms and try to calm my racing heart before I flip around to face him. "I'm sorry, what?"

"You can bring Cheshire too." He's just piling on to the shock he just threw at me.

"You want me to move in with you?"

"I want you to be comfortable in my house, Elizabeth. I'm having the best sex of my life, and I don't really care to go a day without it. I like having you in my bed, my shower, my kitchen."

When he pauses, I look at him for a minute, not sure if he means sexually or physically there. Until he adds, "Bent over my desk."

Rolling my eyes, I start to walk away when he grabs my wrist and pulls me close. "Just think about it, please. You don't have to, I just thought maybe you'd be more comfortable with your clothes instead of wearing my t-shirts all the time. Not that I'm complaining because I definitely prefer the barely covering shirts. And I know you'd prefer to be with Cheshire."

"I'll consider it." Sometimes I feel like I do live at Chase's. While this is only the second full weekend we're spending together, I sleep the majority of my nights in his bed.

Stepping around me, Chase pulls a navy sundress out of the closet and hands it to me. "This one."

Twenty minutes later, we're on the highway heading toward my house. We have a long drive ahead of us and I'm already squirming in my seat as my heart tries to lodge in my throat. I can't tear my eyes from the scenery already turning more desolate outside my window.

I nearly hit my head on the roof when Chase's hand rests on my thigh, just above my knee. His fingers tease below the hem of my dress, spreading warmth through my body. He makes small circles with his thumb.

Glancing over at him, he takes a peek at me quickly before turning back to the road. The whole picture seems strange. We've never been in a car together. In all these months of messing around, we've never had a reason to be in the same car. He leans back in his seat, one hand loosely at the top of the steering wheel.

"Everything's going to be fine, Liz."

I nod before turning back to the trees whizzing by. This house means a lot to me, and while Chase has changed in a lot of ways, I'm not willing to let him tear it down at all.

My lip is between my teeth when Chase starts moving his hand up and down my thigh. He tips under my dress every so many passes. When he slides all the way to my panties and makes a pass over my pussy, I clamp my legs shut, effectively yet unintentionally trapping his hand.

"What are you doing?" There's a slight panic to my voice.

"I'm trying to get you to relax, Elizabeth. I don't know why you're so nervous." So, he's trying to finger me while driving? Is an orgasm the only form of relaxation he knows?

"Can you really not have an adult conversation with me instead?"

"Is it going to relax you?"

"Maybe. This just sex thing gets a little exhausting." In a good way. I wouldn't change the constant sex. But I would like a little more depth if he's willing to give it to me.

"What do you think we're doing today, Elizabeth? I want to see your house to know you more. I asked you to put things at my house. Yes, there is the very added benefit of you being at my disposal more readily that way, but it's also having your presence. You want to have a conversation? Let's have a conversation. But you need to decide if you want to keep my hand or if you are going to give it back."

Glancing down, I see his hand is still caught between my legs. I'd forgotten it was even there. Loosening my grip, he gives a quick, pressurized swirl of my clit through my panties, eliciting a low moan, before pulling away.

"So, what exactly would you like to discuss?" There's a taunting lilt to his tone that I choose to ignore.

"I don't know, I just don't know that I like that your answer to everything is sex."

"I like sex, Liz. I *really* fucking like it with you."

"That may be so, but we can have conversations, we can communicate aside from with our bodies." Though I will say, it's our best form of communication.

"Do we not talk during the day? We talk for a living, Liz. And we have plenty of good discussion when we're together. I'm not going to apologize for being insatiable for you. Many women would find that flattering."

"If you haven't noticed, I'm not like most other women." While I do find it flattering that he wants me all the time, I find it a little insulting that he doesn't have stronger conversations with me. Sometimes it feels like he doesn't think I'm smart enough to keep up with him.

"I have, in fact. It's part of what makes you so damn attractive." He doesn't look at me as he glances in his side mirror and changes lanes smoothly.

"Tell me something about yourself. Something you don't share with other people."

"If I don't tell other people, why would I tell you?"

"Because I let you be inside me at least once a day."

"Well, I guess that's as good a reason as any. Alright. Something nobody else knows." He's quiet for a few minutes, and I'm not sure if he's avoiding the question or thinking. When he pulls his hand to rub his lips, I know he's trying to decide what to tell me. It's a look I've come to know as his decision-making one.

After a few moments of silence, he still hasn't made a peep. "Never mind, you don't have to say anything." I turn back to the window.

Linking his fingers through mine, my breath catching at the gesture, I turn to look at him, my mouth agape.

"No, it's okay. I'm just not sure what to say."

"Well, then maybe tell me about your childhood. I don't know too much about those early days except for Jenson. And that you have a brother."

A tension sets into his jaw, and he lowers himself in his seat. "I don't really talk about my childhood much."

It appears I've struck a nerve. On some level, I want to push. The old Elizabeth would have. But we're beyond the point of giving each other shit just for the hell of it or to piss the other person off. We're beyond the layers of hatred that cause us to be bad people to each other. Taking a deep breath, he gives my hand a squeeze before pulling away and putting it on the wheel. He does the slightest turn of his body away from me. It's a defense tactic, one I've come to notice when reading a client or a witness. I hate that we use these learned skills on each other, but it's become second nature to both of us.

"My brother, Justin, is a few years older than me. He actually lives out in Washington with his wife and three kids. He's not out here as much as he used to be. We're fairly close for brothers, we talk a few times a week. But he turned and left as soon as he could. Dad is...well, let's just say, if you think *I'm* an asshole, I'm a cuddly puppy compared to him. I'm a bit more...hardened than Justin.

"It doesn't help that he took the brunt of Dad's bullshit for four years before I was born. Then I fell under the protection of Mom. He wasn't physically abusive, most of the time, but his words. His words were on another level. I think that's where my desire to be a lawyer came from. A job where I could use my words just as strongly, but in a productive way. I guess it doesn't always work."

He gives me a side-long glance like he's trying to express something to me without words. It takes a minute before it clicks.

"Chase, you're making yourself out to be some evil monster."

"You did call me Evil Spawn for years."

"Okay, but you're not that person. We hated each other, it makes sense for you to be like that."

"But you hated me *because* I was an asshole." I can't argue with him there.

"Well, you're not that person anymore."

"Really? You don't think so? Not when I'm bossing you around in bed? Not when I'm bossing you around day to day? We're driving to your house right now because I said we were going. You're wearing a dress because I told you to change. Hell, I even picked it out. You sleep at my house because I tell you to. Want to rethink your stance?" Shock wraps around my ribs and tightens as I realize that he really means it and thinks he's this horrible asshole.

Yes, I thought he was an ass for years, but it was solely at work. We barely knew each other on a personal level, and I didn't want to try because of the professional attitude. But he has a right to be cocky about his work performance. As do I. And it's what made us enemies.

"No, Chase, I don't. I can tell you no. I've never had a problem standing up for myself with anybody, least of all you. Having sex hasn't changed that. I let you boss me around because I *like* it. It's possessive and domineering, but I don't hate it. If I did I wouldn't stand for it."

He smiles and lets a low laugh out. "And the aggressiveness?"

"Aggressiveness? You mean, like pulling my hair? Please. That's child's play, Chase. Like I said, if I didn't like it, I'd stop it. And for the orgasms you give me, I'd maybe reconsider some things if I *didn't* like them because it'd be well worth it. Not to mention, real assholes aren't giving in the bedroom."

Chase is one of the most giving men I've ever been with. He's always apt to please me before himself, getting right down to business and burying himself inside me before I can return any gestures. He initiates nine and half times out of ten.

"Hm, you think I'm giving?"

"Please don't get small headed on me now. You know you are. At least with me. I can't say with others, don't want to know."

"Well, maybe I have to rethink things then. Wouldn't want you thinking I'm a giving person."

I lash out and smack him in the chest. My hand connects with a thud, and he winces, though I'm sure it doesn't hurt. He's solid muscle.

"Alright, counselor, I'm pretty sure you're distracting me from the conversation at hand." A strong tactic for sure, but he's trying to get me to drop his childhood. But I want to know more. I want to know Chase, and some of his childhood may tell me what makes him tick, what makes him the way he is.

"Caught onto that, did you?" Sighing, he adjusts in his seat. "From what I know, until I was born, Dad went what would be considered easy on Justin. He was caring, loving. Or as much as he could be. Justin says it still wasn't much, but it was something. They went to the park, threw a baseball, you know kind of typical dad stuff. I guess when I was born things changed. During Mom's pregnancy, he had some business troubles, and that turned his mood worse. He didn't leave it at the door ever.

"When I was born, Mom was overwhelmed with caring for me. I mean, new babies are needy. That left Justin a little more exposed to Dad and the bad moods he'd developed. As we got older, if Dad would start to tear into me about making a mess or something that's typical kid behavior, Justin would often step in. One time I accidentally knocked over a vase of flowers Mom had picked from the garden. There was water, flowers, and glass everywhere. I was five and scared. Mom and Dad came running in, and Mom immediately set to work cleaning it up. Dad didn't like that. He thought *I* should. At five. He started screaming at me that I was a stupid, reckless kid and not going to learn how to be a real man if people always did things for me."

With a quick glance to the side, he clears his throat. I can tell by the tone and the way he's telling the story that it's difficult for him to get it out, to say what needs to be said.

"Justin walked right into the room, sneakers on his feet, and stepped in between us. He said he did it. That he was playing with a ball, and it knocked the vase. That I was just in the room, and it wasn't my fault. That was the first time he hit one of us. Mom screamed and started crying. The look in Justin's eyes, though. I haven't forgotten it to this day."

He swallows hard and closes his hand over my thigh again, squeezing tight. The gesture spreads warmth through me and makes my heart race. He's seeking comfort and finding it in me. I rest my hand over his, giving him more reassurance of my presence. When his eyes flip to mine, I offer him a small smile.

"Things continued like that for years. As Justin got older, he grew interested in things that took his time. Sports took a lot of it, since we both had a lot of talent in athletics. That let Dad sink his claws into me more. The physical wasn't often. He'd been able to put some control on himself. But the words. There's only so many times you can hear that you're worthless and never going to be anything before it starts to take its toll."

He quiets as he carefully changes lanes again. I hadn't realized we were getting close to our exit.

"That same fire I saw in Justin, I felt in myself. He had plans to get out as soon as possible, and he was hoping some sport would take him far away. It wasn't a totally thoughtless plan. By sophomore year, there were rumblings from scouts for school and minor leagues for both baseball and football. He was willing to play anywhere."

Shaking his head, he glances back over at me. I give his hand another squeeze. "Anyway, my junior year of high school was the most epic shitshow one could imagine. Dad had been caught cheating. Like, really cheating. He had a whole side family and everything. The oldest kid was ten, the youngest was four, with two in between, all his. He left screaming about how worthless we are and, of course, he started a new family and that he loves them more than us, that he only stuck around because we're all weak and somebody needs to be around to do everything for us. Despite how much he hates us, he wouldn't let us starve.

"I haven't heard from him since he walked out that day. Mom got more than half his money in the divorce, but after supporting two families and having some money troubles, though he was making six figures at the time, it wasn't much."

He stops talking and clears his throat. I want to say something, but I'm not sure what. My parents have been loving and supportive my whole life. I'm an only child, despite Mom's want for more children. Fertility problems showed it just wasn't in the cards for her.

"Anyway. Later that year, Mom got sick. When she died a few years ago, that was her cancer coming back. And it came back with a vengeance. Five years after the doctors told her she was in remission, we found out she wasn't anymore. From that moment to her death was all of six months." Removing the hand from my leg, he runs it through his hair and down his face. I know this has to be hard for him to talk about, just like it's hard for me to talk about *my* mom.

"When she'd first been sick, it basically all fell to me with Dad gone. Justin was at Notre Dame in Indiana so he was too far to be helpful, though he started coming home whenever he could. By the time I left for Princeton, she was in remission. And thank fuck for that because there's no way I would have been able to leave her otherwise."

I lift my hand and hesitate for a moment, curling my fingers inward. Straightening myself, I follow through, reaching out and running my fingers through Chase's hair. He leans his head the slightest bit into my hand as I continue to scratch my nails against his scalp.

"I'm sorry, Chase. That's a lot for one person to go through. Does Justin come out this way often?"

"Not as much as he used to. He sometimes has business out this way, extends his visit, and stays with me for a day or two, but he hasn't been here in almost a year."

"That sounds difficult. Do you miss him?"

"I'm not really sure the question computes. I'd have to have a heart to miss somebody." He turns to me with down-turned lips and a pointed look, clearly referring back to my comment from a few months ago.

"Chase, you have a heart. And I'm finding it's bigger than I thought it could be."

"And how is that?"

"Are you not sweet to me? Sometimes. I'm not going to claim all the time, I'm not that crazy. But certainly sometimes."

"Well, either way, it's different now. We're adults, I don't need my brother to protect me anymore. But yeah, his presence is missed." He split hairs a bit, but I'll give him a pass.

"I don't have any siblings, so I don't really know what that's like, but I'm sorry he's not closer for you to see more."

He shrugs briefly before pulling his hand from my leg and running his fingertips along his lower lip. The distant look in his eyes tells me he's lost in thought. While I'm sure I could interrupt to ask, I don't. I'll let him come back to me on his own.

"Where do we go from here?"

My heart races. What does he mean? Does this change things?

Jutting his chin toward the road, I swallow down the lump that lodged in my throat. "After I take the exit, what do I do?"

Shaking away the thoughts of what else he could have meant, I think for a second. It's been a while since I've been here. "Uh, take a left at the light at the end of the off ramp. We'll take that for a few miles, and then we'll hit an intersection with three gas stations. We'll go right there and drive for another several miles."

His brow furrows as he glances over at me. "Three gas stations? Is that really the marker you're using?"

"Trust me, you'll get it when you see it. This is not the populated town you're used to, Chase." Populated enough for a Starbucks, McDonalds, and a few other staples, but not for more than one of each.

"Alright. I trust you."

We're quiet for a few minutes as we take the off ramp and wait at the light. My fingers lace together in my lap. I know Chase trusts me more than just for directions and the town. He wouldn't have told me all of that if he didn't. I trust him too.

His hand reaches over to lace with mine, and when I glance toward him, he gives me a slight smile, which I return automatically.

"Did I ever tell you *why* my parents are in the care facility?" It's a conversation I haven't had with many, and even Lydia doesn't know the true extent of things. But Chase just shared a lot and I want to do the same, open up and see what comes of it.

His brow furrows as he considers, and the light turns green. He keeps his hand in mine as he turns left and continues our journey. "Your dad had a heart attack, right?"

"Yeah, but that's not really enough for him to need to be in a care facility."

"I guess I never considered that."

"Nobody knows this. Nobody except my friend Lydia. I've never told anybody else." I think some part of me always knew I'd get here with Chase. Even if we remained enemies, I knew he'd somehow find out about my parents.

"You don't have to tell me, Liz. This doesn't have to be something more than you want it to be."

"No, I want to tell you. I just...I want you to know that it's not common knowledge and that it means something that I'm telling you." He can't think this is just water cooler gossip that I tell everybody. He needs to know that it's serious that I'm telling him.

"I know, Liz. I appreciate it."

Gritting my teeth, I take a deep breath. "My parents are in a care facility because my mom can't care for my dad on her own. She can't even care for herself. She has Alzheimer's. It's pretty advanced. I'm an only child because my parents had a lot of fertility problems. I was basically a miracle. My mom was forty-two when she had me." I swallow around the lump in my throat that always places there when I talk about being an only child. I know they both wanted more kids.

"When she hit sixty, she started having some trouble remembering things. It was small at first; dates, phone numbers, things that maybe weren't such a big deal. But it started to grow quickly. She started forgetting bigger things. By the time I was at college, it was a problem that my dad refused to recognize. Until the day she ended up at the store and forgot where she was.

"He took her to the doctor the next day and they broke the news. Early onset Alzheimer's. She was almost borderline, being sixty-three at the time. But it had taken over her so fast. My dad had been taking care of her for so long and then when he had the heart attack and was in the hospital, it was too much. He realized he couldn't keep going the way he was, the way their life was going. His biggest fear was something happening to him and my mom being left alone and scared." Taking a moment, I turn to the window and wipe a stray tear.

Talking about my parents never gets easier, but Chase needs to know. He deserves to know.

"So, he and I sat down and decided it was for the best. Where they are...it's a nice place. They have it pretty decent over there compared to a lot of other places. They have their own little apartment, and they get to live together. It's really their own living space, and they have people who check in on them a few times a day and are available in case of an emergency."

I quiet for a minute, because the hardest part is what comes next. But Chase squeezes my hand, letting me know he's there for me, just like I was for him. We all have skeletons in our closet; we all have things that are hard for us to talk about, and this is mine. It's a very vulnerable state but it doesn't feel strange like I'd expect. It feels right.

"It's just. It's hard to go there. It's hard to see her like that. She doesn't usually remember where they are. It's just, it's hard. Especially knowing one day she probably won't remember me at all." The twist of pain in my chest draws my hand to it as I rub against my breastbone. My mother, the person who fought so hard to have me, who yearned to have been able to have given me a sibling won't remember me someday. The realization is something I'm rarely able to face.

Sure, there are times now she doesn't remember me, but she usually comes back to me. Or the next visit, she knows everything about me, down to the tiny details of my life. One day, there'll be no return.

"I'm sorry, Elizabeth. I had no idea."

"I didn't want anybody to know." My voice is quiet as I relace my fingers in my lap.

"That's a lot to hold on to all by yourself."

I shrug, but he's right. "It's not so bad."

"It is, Liz. Nobody should have to go through that alone."

"I'm not alone. I have Lydia." I mumble it because I know he's right. Lydia's been there every step of the way, she took me out and got me hammered the night I moved them in, but it's not the same.

"You can talk to me, Liz. It doesn't...it doesn't have to mean anything other than another person in your corner."

"I appreciate that. Truly, I do. And it's nice. You can talk to me too if you ever need to. I know your mom passed a few years ago, but I'm sure that's something that doesn't go away."

His jaw tightens as he follows the directions I laid out earlier, and he mumbles a "thanks."

When we get to the intersection with the gas stations, he turns to me and cocks an eyebrow, one hand resting against his face while the other is loosely over the wheel.

"What?"

"You weren't kidding when you gave this as a set of directions. Were you?"

"Of course not. Why would I do that?" I told him he'd see what I was talking about when we got here. Now he clearly thinks my house is in podunk nowhere.

With a heavy sigh, he mutters something incoherent and makes a right-hand turn.

We ride the last few minutes in silence before we end up at our destination. The house Dad just had to own.

Chapter 19

Dust kicks up on either side of the car as we pull up the long drive. I hadn't bothered to mention that the driveway isn't paved.

As we get out of the car, I'm immediately struck with a thickness that makes it hard to breathe. The air almost looks like it's shimmering, and cicadas are the only sound that can be heard.

"Wow, Liz. You were right, this place is pretty impressive. Very peaceful." He loops his arm around my waist as he pulls me against his side. It's not a sweet gesture. It's possessive. There's no need for it, as we're alone, but it's almost as though he likes to remind me that I'm currently his, even if only in the bedroom. Since this isn't a relationship, we've never actually discussed dating somebody else, but there's no time for either of us to be with another person.

All the same, I find myself leaning into him. If this was any sort of real relationship, this would be where he leaned in and kissed the top of my head. But I know better than to think that would ever happen with Chase.

"Yeah, that's part of what I like about it. Come on, let me show you around." Taking his hand, almost like an afterthought, I head up toward the house. Instead of going in, I walk him around it, showing off the wraparound porch that is the ultimate highlight for me.

"Nice spot to sit and read some books. Watch the dog play in the yard." Of course he'd mention a dog.

Watch my kids play. "Exactly."

Looking off around the property, Chase's eyes settle on a second building. "Stables? You like horses?"

"In theory? Yes. In practice? I'm not so sure. I haven't decided what I'm doing with a lot of the house yet. As you'll see it's pretty outdated and some parts are in a bit of disarray. Nothing's dangerous or broken, just not put together."

"How would Cheshire feel about being a barn cat?"

I snort at his suggestion. "Cheshire is far too pampered of a house cat to ever consider even stepping foot outside. No, the stables will either be converted to something or torn down. The only reason I haven't done it yet is because I don't know what I'd convert to if I went that route and don't want to be preemptive demolishing the building. It's still in good shape."

"You have a lot of nice property here, Liz. You could do a lot."

"Part of what I love about this place is that I can farm. Not like a real farm, but I've always wanted gardens. To grow my own fruits and vegetables and flowers. I used to love apple picking, back when I had the time. I've thought about planting some apple trees somewhere." I glance around the property, trying to imagine where I'd put everything in a perfect world. Some day.

"I think that sounds nice. Not sure I see you getting your hands dirty like that, but nice all the same."

"I can get dirty."

"In the bedroom, sure. But in dirt?"

"Yes, in dirt." My hands have certainly found themselves in garden beds before. I'm not really sure why he's surprised.

"Have you ever grown plants before? Can you keep a houseplant alive?"

"Well, no. But I can learn." The gardening I did was years ago, with Dad. He always appreciated having even a small garden of fresh tomatoes.

"How do you plan to do all of this, and even live out here, when you work two hours away?"

He stops walking and pulls our linked hands toward him when I keep walking and don't answer. "Elizabeth."

I can't meet his eyes.

Yanking me against him, he wraps an arm tight around my waist and tilts my chin up with the other. I'm trapped in a Chase cage. "Talk. Now."

"I don't plan to stay at the firm forever. If I get partner, well, I'll reconcile that somehow. I'm not necessarily going to leave in the next year, or even five or ten. But at some point, I will. What I do with this place until then? I don't know. Maybe I'll rent it out."

Clearing his throat, he skims over my question. "The lawn looks cut."

"I have a service come out to take care of it starting in the spring. I know there's a lot of costs with everything, even just owning it and keeping the lights and heat on, but it's worth it. I come out here every so often to check on things. One of the neighbors stops over every day when she walks her dog."

"That doesn't seem super safe, Liz." His concern for my house is somewhat touching. Sometimes I'm still surprised that he cares. But I'm finding more and more frequently that he cares a great deal. Or at least seems to.

"There's nothing inside worth stealing. And even if there was, it's probably something I'm junking anyway so they'd be doing me a favor taking it."

"Show me the inside."

Carefully, I lead him around the inside. There really isn't much to see besides peeling wallpaper, cracked paint, and crumbling walls. The carpets are old and threadbare. The house isn't meant to impress on the inside, and most of it is outdated.

But the bones of it are amazing. The kitchen is large, and there's a nice open floor plan. All it needs is a little attention and TLC.

The only words said while we walk through the house are me explaining what each room is, not giving too much more information and feeling a little dumb since he can likely figure it out.

Chase examines every room with a scowl, checking fixtures for water and light. When he's finally seen enough, he turns and walks back out without a word. And I don't ask what he thinks, because honestly, I don't care. It doesn't make a difference to me because I love this house, even if he finds a million faults with it.

The thing that's somewhat frustrating is how sexy he looks as he walks through the house and looks around. The slight mumblings he makes to himself just add to that. I don't know what it is about seeing Chase in the house, but it's like he belongs there. It's a ludicrous thought, but it makes need settle in my core.

Some of the things he mumbles as he walks through the house have to do with the fact that no place is suitable for fucking. Even the showers are old and kind of gross, not something we want to get into in the middle of the day.

But he seems to have forgotten that we have a car, and I plan to make full use of it.

He's barely closed his car door before I'm leaning over the console, my hands flying to the top of his shorts and hurriedly undoing them. When I free his cock, I smile, seeing he's already hardening.

Licking from his base to his tip, I take him slowly into my mouth, giving a swirl of my tongue around his head. His legs tense underneath me, and I taste a hint of saltiness, a low moan rising in my chest as I take him farther into my mouth.

My ass rises from my heels to be in the air. Chase's hand immediately pulls up the hem of my dress and palms my bare ass. After a few more strokes with my mouth and laps of my tongue, he twists my hair around his fists and halts me. Then he starts bucking his hips up as he fucks my mouth.

Without any indication, Chase tugs at my hair, popping me off of him. "You need to stop now, Elizabeth." His voice is low and gravelly.

"Why?" It's really one of the few times I've gotten a chance to give him a proper blow job and now he's ending it while I still want more.

"Because I want to come deep in your pussy, not down your throat. Now get over here and sit on my dick."

I hesitate for a second, wanting to finish what I started.

"I wasn't asking, Liz."

Taking my arms, he pulls me into his lap, and I go willingly. His hands hold tightly to my hips as he lowers me onto himself, my head tipping back as my breath catches and my fingers fist into his shirt.

Once I'm flush against him, he gives me a minute to get my bearings. When he knows I have them, he starts pushing me back and forth. Every so often, he'll throw in a slight lift.

Anytime I try to take over, he digs his fingers into my hips. I should know better; Chase likes to be in control.

The car is hot, the air thick. A sheen coats both of our bodies, but neither of us slows or stops.

Leaning forward, Chase runs his open mouth along the curve of my neck, blowing gently. The cool sensation against my burning skin, made stronger by the beads of sweat, sends a shiver through me, which sets off my orgasm. I tighten around him, crying out as he keeps me moving on top of him until I'm trembling. I'm still being moved forward and backward until Chase's head tips back against the seat and he bucks his hips up as he comes.

Once he stills my movements, I collapse against him, my hands barely able to hold on to his shoulders. We both breathe heavily for a moment. Chase wraps his arm tight around my shoulders, keeping me against him as he leans ups and starts the car, cranking the AC, which pours out in icy currents. He falls back against the seat, pulling me with him, reclining it slightly so I'm mostly laying on him.

Our chests heave for a few more minutes, our hearts clashing against each other. As we start to cool down, Chase brushes back the hair that's plastered to my forehead before tucking a finger under my chin and tilting up to close his mouth over mine. His lips move gently, his tongue almost soothing. When he pulls back, he cups my face, running a thumb over my cheek.

"Let's go home."

All I can do is nod as he pulls me down for another kiss. When he releases me, I climb over to my own seat.

Though there's a whole town to see, I don't care about showing it off now. He wanted to see the house, he did. If he doesn't want to see the rest of the area, then that's fine by me.

Settling in for the long drive back, I curl onto my side a bit. The heat and the sex wore me out. Chase's hand rests on my thigh and rubs small circles.

Between the soothing motions and the whir of the wheels beneath us I'm asleep by the time we hit the highway.

Chapter 20

It's been a few weeks since we went to see my farmhouse, and not a single word has been said about it again. I'm not quite sure if that's a good thing or a bad thing.

Otherwise, nothing has changed. Chase and I still fuck like rabbits and spend at least every Friday night together, though it's become most nights, including weekends. I haven't put any clothes at his house, nor have I moved Cheshire, but the thought is more appealing the longer I go. Though, to be honest, his clothes almost feel as comfortable as my own at this point.

It's Friday night, which has become somewhat of a date night, as we tend to go out before heading back to somebody's house. Chase claims it's not really dating, just two coworkers celebrating the end of another exceptionally long week.

The Douglas case has only amped up. Trial starts in a few days, and while we're prepared, our client definitely is not and came in almost every single day this week for more pep talks and for us to help her be prepared for some of the possible outcomes, especially the ones she doesn't want.

On my way back from the bathroom, I see a petite brunette standing extremely close to Chase. When her hand reaches out to rest against his chest, my blood turns to lava, and I surge forward. As I get closer, I can hear what she's saying to him in what is assuredly the most sultry voice she can conjure.

"I was hoping you'd come back to my place, give me the special treatment again. That might have been the best night of my life."

My knees suddenly can't hold me anymore as I stumble toward Chase. He seamlessly wraps an arm around my waist as he catches me before I've even begun to fall, hugging me to his side.

"Sorry, I'm with somebody." He doesn't even give her a smile despite her face dropping.

"Oh," is all she says in way of a goodbye.

Chase holds me close for a few minutes, sipping his whiskey, before he turns his body toward me. Keeping his arm around my waist, the other joins it as his fingers link behind my back and he leans against the bar, pulling me to stand between his legs. He looks at me intensely for a few minutes.

I recognize the look. It's how he looks at witnesses. He's trying to read something in me.

"Want to leave?" He jerks his chin toward the door as though I need more explanation than his words offered.

"Yeah, let's go." There's nothing left here, and I don't need to risk running into more of Chase's former sexcapades.

"What was all that?" He doesn't hesitate to ask once we're out on the street.

"I don't know what you're talking about."

"You practically fell into me, Liz."

"I tripped." I can't possibly tell him my knees went weak at the sight of him with another woman. Before he can respond, I continue. "You could have left with her, you know. I'm a big girl."

"That's not really what this is, Elizabeth. Do you not believe me when I tell you you're the best sex I've ever had? Besides, I don't really sleep with the same person more than once."

I freeze as he keeps walking. Stopping a few steps ahead, he turns to look at me, his eyebrows raised and hands in his pockets. "But...we've been sleeping together for months."

Closing the gap, he pulls me against him, brushing hair behind my ear as he wraps an arm around my waist. "Yeah, Liz, we have." His voice is quiet as he searches my eyes.

"Why?" It comes out just above a whisper. My arms stay limp at my sides.

"I have feelings for you, Liz. At first it was fun, convenient, and just that damn good. But it's morphed into something more. And if you want to tell me that this is just fun for you, I'm okay with that, because I don't want to stop, and I can push my feelings aside." Every word is full of confidence, saying everything I didn't know I wanted to hear so badly.

I can't meet his eyes anymore, focusing instead on where my fingers are fisting into his shirt. "I have feelings for you too." More than he can ever know. Pulling him down toward me, our mouths collide in a heated kiss.

If I let myself think about it, I'd have more thoughts about Chase admitting he likes me. But I can't do that right now. I refuse to. So instead, I plan to lose myself in his body and the euphoria I experience from every orgasm.

I can feel stares on us as he cups my ass and pulls my pelvis to his, his erection pressing into my thigh as his kiss turns eager.

"I have to get you home right now so I can fuck you." Brushing his lips across mine, he pulls my bottom lip in between his teeth. "God, all I've been able to think about all night is sinking deep inside you. I should go thank that girl for making you be ready to leave."

"All you had to do was say the word."

"You seemed to be enjoying yourself."

"I'll enjoy myself much more sprawled naked in your bed."

Tipping his head back, he groans as his hand tightens around my hip. "We're going. Now."

I let him pull me toward the car, almost having to run to keep up with his long, quick strides. I'm almost giggling when we reach the car until he throws me up against it and presses himself into me, claiming my mouth with his.

"I don't know that I make it home, Elizabeth." His eagerness and the huskiness in his voice paired, with his rock-hard cock pressing into me, make me stifle a moan.

Biting my lip, my head tips back against the window. Chase's hands rest on either side of my head, and I'm surrounded by him. Locking my gaze on his very lustful one, I rub my pelvis against his, causing his eyes to close as he groans.

"If you could have me any single way tonight, what would you pick?" I'm toying with him, pushing him to a place he probably can't handle going right now. And while part of me is ready to let him take me right here against his car, I'd rather make it back to his place.

"Who says I only get to pick one?"

"I do. Right now. That doesn't mean you have to follow through once home."

"Mm." He runs his thumb down my cheek, along my jaw, and skims it across my bottom lip. Somehow, every touch lights my body on fire, even though I'm fairly certain I'm already an inferno each and every time. "I have a few things in mind." Something flashes quickly in his eyes that soaks my panties even more.

Tipping up on my toes, I twist my fingers into his hair and skim my tongue along his bottom lip before shifting my mouth to his ear. "Bring me home and fuck me senseless."

Reaching behind me, he pulls the handle and opens the door the tiniest crack.

"Get in." He's telling me, not inviting me.

I scramble into my seat, ready to get back to Chase's just as much as he's ready to get me there.

Jumping into his seat, Chase gives me a hungry look as he starts the car. He practically speeds all the way back to his house, thankfully avoiding any police, because I'm not sure either one of us would be able to wait for a traffic stop.

The second my door's shut, he has a hand lost in my hair as the other wraps around my waist, jerking me against him as his mouth melds to mine.

He pushes me backward toward the door, staying pressed together, mouths moving in sync. Struggling to open the door, he lets out a frustrated grunt as he turns to unlock it, immediately returning his lips to mine as he throws open the door and pushes me through it.

But I don't anticipate the lip at the entrance and stumble backwards. Trying to catch me, but failing, I fall from Chase's grasp and down to the floor with a thunk. He didn't escape too well either, catching himself on his hands and knees just above me.

"Are you okay?"

I burst into a round of laughter.

Resting his forehead against my collarbone, Chase's shoulders start shaking with his resulting laughter. He reaches a leg out to kick the door shut.

"Elizabeth. Are you alright?"

Grabbing his collar, I pull him down to me. "No, I'm not. I have this *terrible* ache right between my thighs. Think you can help me with that?"

"Absolutely." A giant grin graces his face. As he starts to pull away, I tighten my grip on his collar and tug him back toward me.

"No, right here."

Chase doesn't hesitate to move to his knees, pressing one right between my legs, as he leans up and tears his shirt off, undoing his pants immediately after. Leaning back over me, he slides my shirt up, running his open mouth along my blazing skin as he makes his way up my chest.

As his lips glide between my breasts, his hand slides down my torso, straight under the hem of my pants and into my panties.

"Holy shit, Liz. Fuck, you're so soaked for me."

"Always, Chase."

He tears at my pants, pushing them down as he frees himself and pushes into me, hard and fast. Our breaths catch at the same time.

"*Fuck.*"

Taking one of my knees in his elbow, he starts thrusting into me. My hands grab onto his shoulders, and while I always enormously enjoy the sight of his bare chest, part of me wishes he kept his shirt on so I had a way to hold him to me.

Just as the pressure is starting to build, Chase backs away, pulling my shoes, pants, and panties off completely before standing and removing his, kicking them out of the way. Reaching down he grabs my wrist and yanks me to standing. His hands immediately fly to the hem of my shirt, lifting it and tossing it to the side. They then land on my back and my bra joins the pile.

We're stripped naked in about ten seconds flat.

He pulls me against him as he walks me backward toward the couch, where he pushes me away, and I fall to the cushions with a laugh. He's on top of me immediately, easing right back into me and resuming his hard and fast thrusts that steal my breath and cause me to make every noise possible.

"Fuck. Chase...I'm..." Before I can even finish the thought, he's pulling away again, lifting me to stand as he spins me around. Pressing himself to my back, he walks through the house, one hand cupping breast while the other is tight on my waist and his mouth is peppering kisses along my neck.

He proceeds to fuck me in various rooms, hand never leaving me. In the dining room, he let me be on top and ride him while he sat in his seat at the head of the table. Once we're in his office, he slams into me so roughly against the bookcases that books crash to the floor around us as he finally lets me come for the first time. When he has me bent over the desk, his thrusts are almost punishing, in the best way possible, as my thighs bang against the solid wood, making me come again.

We don't make it all the way upstairs before he's inside me again, laying me down on the stairs.

Eventually, we end up in bed and his movements become languid, our breathing both labored. Our bodies are both covered in a sheen of sweat, a shower would be so nice, but I'm sure we're both too tired for that.

"Fuck, Elizabeth. I could stay buried in you all damn night." He says it as he adjusts his hips, lighting me up and making me moan.

"If you keep working me the way you have been, I might let you."

"Oh, really? Am I working you good?"

"Don't play dumb. It's not attractive on you." Not even in the slightest. He knows exactly what he does to my body, and no amount of humbleness is acceptable. I want cocky Chase in the bedroom.

"I think the right answer is 'fuck me harder, Chase.'"

"Fuck me harder, Chase."

Hiking one of my legs over his shoulder, he starts driving into me. My fingers try to grip onto his slick skin but can't. The look on Chase's face, top lip ticked up slightly, his eyes hooded, sends a trill straight through me. With the next deep pump, I'm tightening around him as I scream his name and my nails drag down his back.

Three more thrusts, and Chase's breath catches with a groan in his throat as he pulsates inside me before stilling and collapsing on top of me.

"Fuck, baby. I swear to God, if I don't wake up in the morning, that was the best damn way to go out."

Chase slides off me the slightest bit, his leg still draped between mine and an arm flung across my chest.

Turning my head toward his, I find a completely sated Chase. I can say with certainty, I'm feeling the same way.

"I really want to shower, but I need to lay here for a bit." He tightens his arm around me, letting me know I can't get up either.

"You were in a certain kind of mood tonight."

"Certain words were said. It helped."

Certain words? Is he talking about the fact that we said we have feelings for each other? He couldn't possibly be. Chase doesn't talk like that. He doesn't let things like that control him. To be honest, he's lucky I didn't throw a joke at him about not having a heart or being able to express emotions.

Still, I'm not sure what else he could be talking about. One corner of my mouth ticks down as I look at him, but his eyes are shut.

Is it something I want to talk about? I'm not entirely sure because I don't know which direction it's going to go. Is he going to tell me that it's because we expressed our mutual like of one another? Or was he just in an especially fuck-happy mood tonight?

Instead of getting an answer, I close my eyes and enjoy the closeness.

Chapter 21

"**S**hit."

"What?"

I freeze with what I'm doing, hands still on my laptop as I'm in the middle of putting it into my bag to leave work for the night. "Um, I have to go home. I'm supposed to be going to my parents' tomorrow morning. Fuck." I slam my computer into the bag and put one hand on my hip, the other in my hair, and blow out a puff of air.

This thing with Chase is getting complex, but I can't let it detract from my parents.

"Liz, what's the problem?" His hands are on his hips and his face is scrunched. By his tone, he seems to think I've lost my mind.

"I thought you wanted me to come over tonight."

"Is there a reason you can't stay at my place and go see them in the morning?"

"We were going to leave right from here, so I don't have my car." After our date and the subsequent weekend, I've been spending most nights at Chase's, and we carpool to work in the morning. Neither one of us are willing to call what we have a relationship, but more and more, that's what it feels like.

Sighing, Chase closes the gap between us and loops his arm around my waist, pulling me against him. "I'll go with you, Liz."

My face snaps up to his as I try to pull back, but Chase tightens his grip on me so I can't get away. "You what?"

"If it's a choice between not seeing you and taking you to your parents tomorrow, then I'll go with you."

"But that's, that's like meeting them." Is he really willing to meet them instead of spending a night without me? That seems ludicrous.

"We're coworkers, are we not?"

"Yes."

"Do coworkers not meet each other's families?"

"Not usually, no." None of my other coworkers have met my parents, including my bosses and secretary.

"Well, then consider it me taking you hostage, which I am for the weekend, but still allowing you to do what you planned. Unless you have objections?"

"It just seems like a big boyfriend and girlfriend thing to do. And we're not that. Right?"

Chase's jaw ticks as he stares down at me. But I challenge him, refusing to break eye contact as my hands slide up his chest.

"Does it have to be a label, Elizabeth? I like you, you like me, we have really fantastic sex. Do we need more than that? Am I not allowed to meet your parents without putting a label on it?"

"No. I guess not. It's far, though." A few hours.

"Fine. What time?"

"We should leave around eight. And it's my mom's birthday, which is why I'm going. I need to grab her flowers on the way." And maybe a card, but it's hard to know if those are good or not since she sometimes doesn't remember who the giver is. Flowers are easier for her to accept.

"How hard are you going to be to wake up in the morning?" One eyebrow raises as he questions me.

"Not hard."

"Liar." Chase smiles down at me as he tucks some hair behind my ear. Every so often, Chase will be exceedingly sweet and caring. I'd say loving, but that seems beyond the realm of possibility. Despite having feelings for each other, I wouldn't go as far as to say it's more than like, or could turn into that, at least on Chase's end. And I fear getting there myself.

"I know a few tricks to wake you up, though." He runs his nose along the soft tract of skin between my shoulder and neck, then repeats the motion with a slightly parted mouth.

"Are you sure about this?" The words are breathless, and I'm ready for him to throw me up against his office door and have his way with me, but he doesn't.

Instead, he grips my hips. "Very. Come on, let's get out of here." Taking my hand, he leads me out of the office, opening the car door for me to slip inside.

Despite Chase not wanting to put labels on this, I'm okay with where things are. Yes, it still feels odd at times for us to carpool, for me to spend the majority of time at his house. Most days, we'll swing by to feed Cheshire and check in on him, spending one or two nights a week at my apartment for his sake.

I still haven't put much more thought into having some things at Chase's. I mostly just prepare a few days at a time. Whenever we go back to check on Cheshire, we plan what the next visit will be, and I grab enough work clothes. It's not hard to mix and match my professional attire either. And weekends, I spend in Chase's clothes. His shirts have become one of my favorite things.

There's just one thought that's been plaguing me. He won't put a label on it, which is fine, but eventually, we're going to get to a point of no return. As much as I try to fight it, deny it, every day I feel myself falling for him more and more. I know what he does and doesn't want, and being married is not on his to-do list in life.

I can't blame him for that, and I can't fault him either, but it *is* on mine. This has an expiration date, and I dread the day that comes. Because it's beyond just sex at this point, for both of us. He wouldn't have me at his place so often if it wasn't more for him.

Yes, he likes to say it's because I'm readily available, but he's also confessed his feelings for me. He may not be in love with me and probably never will be, but I know that I want that from somebody. There's only so long I can drag this out before I reach my breaking point and realize I need to find something, or someone, else.

Somebody who will fulfill those needs and wants. And hopefully, at a time when my parents are both still with us.

"What's in your head, Princess?" It's been a while since he's used the nickname. But now, instead of saying it with a hint of annoyance in his tone, there's a sense of endearment.

"Just thinking about tomorrow. It's not easy to go visit them."

"I can imagine. If you want, when we get home, I'll help take your mind off of it." He turns to me with that cocky half smirk on his face that I no longer hate or want to slap off him. At least not outside of the office. He's still overly cocky at work, and it drives me nuts.

"I figured you would anyway. Didn't know I needed a reason." I rest my hand on his thigh and slowly drag it higher until it rests beside his crotch.

His gaze drops down quickly to look at my hand. "A little to the left, Princess."

With a smile on my face, I shift my hand more until I'm resting over his hardening cock.

He makes a small adjustment to the way he's sitting, sinking lower in his seat and spreading his legs wider.

"You ever give road head?"

"No. And I have zero intentions of doing any such thing. It's dangerous."

He looks at me with an eyebrow cocked, the half smirk, and something in his eyes that looks like a challenge.

"No, Chase. I'm serious."

"Take my dick out, Liz."

The problem with Chase's commands is that I want to obey them. I've yet to experience the "punishment" he threatened at one point, because nothing feels like a bad thing. None of it feels like he's punishing so much as rewarding me in different ways. Some are clear rewards for him, but they benefit me too. I *like* sucking his cock, I like getting fucked senseless. Where's the bad part?

So, I do as he says, loosening his belt, a chill running up my spine at the sound of his zipper dragging down.

And as soon as he's sprung free, I pounce on him, leaning over the console and taking him in my mouth.

"Fuck." The single word is enough to make me hollow out my cheeks and take him to the back of my throat, something I've been practicing with him for some time now. There's a quick swerve of the car. "Christ, Liz. Are you trying to kill us?"

Popping off quickly, I turn to look at him, his dick tight in my hand. "I thought this was what you wanted?"

"I wanted you to give me a few licks or sucks, not deep throat me and suck me off so good I can't see straight."

"Should I stop?" I raise a single eyebrow and dart my tongue out to dance along the head of his cock as he groans.

"Fuck no."

With a smile, I put my mouth back around his amazing dick and flick the tip with my tongue, teasing him before taking him back down my throat and slowly raising to the top. I repeat the motion over and over, salty liquid hitting my tongue.

I'm about to duck down again when his hand wraps in my hair and tugs me off. "That's enough now, Elizabeth. We'll be home in two minutes."

I know he's stopping me so he can fuck me. It's not that he has a long refractory period, it's actually pretty damn quick. It's more that he prefers to come inside my pussy than anywhere else. I asked him once why he doesn't want to finish from a blow job or a hand job or even come on me like some guys' fantasies. His answer was that there's nothing better than blowing his load when buried as deep inside me as he can get.

The car is barely stopped before he's throwing it in park and jumping out, running around to my side of the car to yank open my door and pull me out. He rushes us into the house and throws me up against the closed front door, tearing my skirt from my body, effectively ripping the zipper in two.

"Hey!"

"I'll buy you a new one. I need to be inside you. Now."

And before I get a chance to say anything, he thrusts himself from head to hilt in one swift movement, causing me to grip at his shirt and scream. Slowly, he pulls out and slams back in. Over and over, he does this, my head tipping back and the door banging on its hinges with each one.

He palms my ass as he continues to pound me into the door. After a few minutes, his legs start to tremble, and he pulls me away from the door, carrying me over to the couch, where he sets me down on my feet and bends me over the back.

Before easing back into me, he kicks my feet farther apart and plunges his fingers inside me, moving them furiously while I grip the cushions and moan loudly.

"Fuck, Chase. Please."

"What do you want, baby?"

"Your cock. I want your cock." It's so much better than anything I've ever experienced.

"You going to come for me?"

"Yes." So much yes.

Without another word, he replaces his fingers with his rock-hard erection, his hands wrapping around my hips as he thrusts into me hard and fast. The sound of his balls smacking against my pussy fills the air, along with my whines and moans and my nails scratching against the leather of his sofa.

I'm about to come, and he must know, because he changes his position and starts slowly thrusting up into me so that he rubs right against my G-spot. That's all it takes for me to reach back to grip his wrist and scream his name so that my pleasure is echoing off the walls.

Adjusting his grip, he holds my wrist back as he continues his motions while I tremble in front of him and he pulsates inside me, leaning forward and biting my shoulder.

Resting over my back, we both breathe heavily for a moment. As he straightens, he pulls me up with him. "Let's go take a quick shower before dinner."

We don't bother picking up our clothes, walking half naked through his very windowed house. While there are no neighbors in the back, he does have them on either side and across the street. His house is set back from the road, but in the right lighting, I'm sure somebody walking past would see in.

But Chase is confident with his body and clearly doesn't care who sees or knows he's having astounding sex.

And I find that I don't care either.

Chapter 22

"Before we go in, my mom's memory is really bad lately. She may ask you the same question a few times." We're standing in the parking lot, looking up at the large main building.

I woke up this morning, alone in bed, with dread having taken root in my chest. It's not so much about bringing Chase to see my parents as it is about seeing them. I love them immensely, but this is hard. Every single time, it's hard.

"Oh, so no different from working with interns?"

"Very funny. I'm serious."

"I'll be fine, Elizabeth." While there's confidence to his tone, I don't know the last time he's done this and how he can possibly think it will be fine when Mom may forget what she asked five seconds ago. It can be frustrating, and he has little patience.

"Have you ever met a girlfriend's parents before? I mean, not that I'm your girlfriend or anything, but have you?" I feel the need to quickly throw on the last part. I don't want him thinking I'm giving this the label he doesn't want it to have.

He taps his chin and looks up at the sky. "Hm, I think once when I was about seventeen." My elbow to his ribs makes him huff out a breath and double over. "Yes, Elizabeth. Can you please not make this a bigger deal than it needs to be?"

"Fine. Let's go."

My parents are out on the patio, probably because it makes Mom happy. Dad stands as we approach, glancing down at Mom, who looks far away. I hope it's not a bad day. Not today.

"Hi, Daddy," I murmur as I lean to hug him. Chase's hand slides down my back, fingertips resting at my waistband.

"Hi, Lilla Bean." Dad smiles as he runs a hand down my hair, cupping my ear. He looks down at Mom, mouth tipping down and eyes sad. "I'm afraid it's not the best of days for her."

Just like that, the wind is knocked from my lungs and my posture drops, shoulders hunching. "Oh." One syllable, but it says everything.

Chase's hand tickles at my lower back, and I remember my manners, though I know he's only doing it to be supportive.

"Dad, this is Chase. Chase, my dad."

They shake hands and nod like gentlemen, but I only see it out of the corner of my eye as my gaze is glued to my mother, whose own gaze is stuck on the ground, her hands clasped in her lap. She looks tiny today.

Resting a hand on Chase's bicep, I take a step away from him, kneeling in front of her with a slight smile on my face. "Hi, Mom. Happy birthday." My voice is low and quiet, and while I try to keep all the pain out of it, I know I don't as I see Chase tense in my peripheral.

A flickering of knowledge flashes through Mom's eyes as they lock on me, and my brows lift in hope. "Elizabeth?"

A sting pricks behind my eyes as my smile widens. "Yeah, it's me."

"What are you doing here, sweetheart?"

"I came to see you for your birthday."

"Is it my birthday? Well, dear me, I must have forgotten the day." Her frail hand flutters to her chest, but her face is alight with remembrance.

"That's okay."

"You look good, sweetheart. How's your new case going? That celebrity, what's her name. Something with a D, I'm sure of it."

The tears spring free, and I cup my mouth to catch a sob. The days she can come back to me are always the best.

Dad steps forward just as I stand and turn away, immediately being pulled into Chase's warm embrace. It's best not to draw her attention to memory lapses as they only upset her more.

My hands cover my face as Chase's arms wrap tight around me, and I sob into his chest. His mouth rests against the side of my head, and he shushes close to my ear.

This is the most I've ever let him comfort me. I can't even dwell on what it means to me because I'm too focused on stopping the torrent of tears. I let him shield me so Mom doesn't see.

Taking a shaky deep breath, I swipe at my eyes and pull away. Chase lowers his hands to my lower back, quickly brushing a lock of hair behind my ear. His emerald eyes are scrunched, filled with uncertainty and concern.

"Are you okay?" His voice is low enough that only I can hear him.

Nodding, I back up a little farther. "I'm fine. Sorry about that."

"Liz, it's—"

I don't let him finish as I turn away from him and step back into my mother's warm circle. Dad eyes me warily, but I smile at him, resting my hand on his to let him know I'm alright.

This was the wrong move, though, because he quickly stands and pats Chase on the back. "Mind if we have a chat, son?"

"What? Dad, no. He just got here, and that's not—"

"Liz." Chase cuts me off with the shake of his head. "It's fine." Turning back to Dad, he nods and smiles. "Sure, Mr. Prescott. I'd be happy to."

Dad throws his arm over Chase's shoulders and starts to turn him. I focus my hearing as much as I can to hear the conversation until they're out of earshot.

"Please, call me John."

"Alright, John. Elizabeth took me to see your farmhouse. It's very nice, I can see why—"

"Dammit," I mutter under my breath. I didn't get to hear enough of their conversation.

"Language, Elizabeth."

My eyes dart back to Mom with her reprimand.

Her brows arch high. "What, you think just because you're an adult that I can't criticize you for your language? I'll always be your mother, Elizabeth, whether I'm aware of it or not."

When my chin starts to quiver, Mom takes my hands in hers.

"Sweetheart, I know this is hard on you. One of my biggest regrets in life is not being able to give you a sibling, somebody to go through all of this with. But it seems like you have a great man at your side."

"Things aren't like that with me and Chase." I shake my head emphatically, as if the number of times it goes from side to side will matter in

how much she understands that we are not together. Not like that. I'm
sure Chase is relaying the same thing to Dad right now.

"Oh, really? What are they like, then?"

"Um, we're just...friends. We work together and we started spending
some time together."

"Ah, yes. Time. Well, darling, despite the fact that I'm old, I do know
exactly what sort of *time* you're spending with one another. And I'm not
going to ridicule you for it. You're a responsible adult with her head on
straight. But you're fooling yourself if you think that's all that's going on
here. You both are, if he agrees."

Turning around, I find Chase and Dad walking the path. Chase's arms
are crossed against his broad chest, one hand picking at his lip with a wide
smile on his face while Dad talks and gestures wildly with his hands in
typical Dad fashion.

"It's just, it's not like that, Mom. And I don't know that I want it
to be. He doesn't want the same things I do. He's married to his job,
doesn't want kids, and we barely like each other." That last part may
not be entirely true, but I'm not sure how far his feelings truly do root.
Having them and having them be deep are very different. "It's temporary.
We're both aware and both okay with that." I fight the urge to pull my
lip between my teeth because I know she'd see right through me.

"Whatever you say, sweetheart. But the way he comforted you, well,
there's certainly something there. And I know there's more than you're
letting on. A mother knows these things. So be careful with your heart,
but don't shut him out entirely. I think maybe you'll be surprised at what
you discover."

I'm about to respond when I feel Chase's heavy presence next to me.
He settles onto the bench to my left, close enough that his thigh rests
against mine, and he stretches his arm to rest on the bench behind me.

As we work through more conversation, my mind can't focus. Every so often, Chase will bump into me or poke my side to get me to answer an unheard question.

When Mom starts to drift, we say our goodbyes, wishing her a happy birthday and giving Dad a hug. He claps Chase on the back and it all just feels a little too...normal.

"What was that about, Liz?" Chase is on me before we even have our seatbelts on.

"I don't know what you're talking about."

"You were barely conscious for the last hour. What got into you? Did it really bother you that much that I was with you?"

"No, it's not that, it's just—"

When I don't answer, he stares at me for minutes, not starting the car.

"It's just what, Elizabeth?"

"I don't want to talk about it, okay?" I don't need him to think that I'm pathetic. I don't want to end what we have, whatever that may be, because he thinks I'm getting too attached, too involved, and will at some point expect something that he's been very clear he won't be giving.

How am I supposed to tell him that I got into my head because of what Mom said? That there is more there? How much more is what I've been wondering. And not just that, but if he truly feels more for me than he lets on.

I don't even want to let myself get to a place where I think he might develop strong enough feelings to give me more than just a great fuck. More than some nights together. Because I know the reality is that he won't get there, he doesn't want to, and if I let myself believe he will, I'll be the one who ends up hurt in the end.

This way, if we keep believing that we're just people who have ended up liking each other instead of hating each other while we fuck our brains out, then nobody gets hurt when it runs its course. Eventually, we'll stop sleeping together as much, and he'll get bored and be ready to move on.

It's something I keep in the back of my mind at all times so I can try to avoid developing any truer and deeper feelings.

Because if I let that part go, then I know I'm going to fall hard and fast.

Chapter 23

We're just getting back from work on Friday, and Chase has me trapped between him and the door as he struggles to unlock it while grinding his erection along my ass and kissing my neck.

"Hurry up." I giggle the words out.

Finally, the door opens, and we almost fall through it, but Chase catches me, flips me around, and pins me up against it. His hips press against mine, his palm running up my body, and his nose glides down my neck, when a throat clearing behind him makes all the silliness drain from my body as Chase freezes.

Briefly, he dips his forehead against mine, heaves a sigh, runs his hand through his hair, and turns around.

Without a second of hesitation, I step next to him to take in who's in his house. And I'm shocked when I see a stunning redhead with legs for days standing next to a rollaway carryon.

Without moving my head, I glance at Chase, and find recognition flooding him. "Janine. What are you doing here?"

She narrows her eyes, and her lips press together. "Can we talk alone?"

Chase looks at me, and then back to Janine. "Sure."

He places his hand on my lower back before walking away, putting that same hand hovering just behind the same spot on Janine and ushering her around the corner and out of sight.

All the air leaves my lungs, and my blood crystallizes. Who is that woman? They certainly seem to know each other. She has a key, for God's sake. I don't even have a key, and while I'm not entirely sure what to label Chase and I, even after months of practically living together, I feel like if anybody were to deserve a key, it's me.

Is she somebody who comes around when she's in town? She had a suitcase with her, so she probably is traveling. Maybe she's a flight attendant, only comes by when she lands here. Or maybe it's some pre-determined date he forgot about.

Why else would they need to talk out of earshot? She didn't look at all pleased to see me, almost angry. Surely, I interrupted whatever plans she had tonight.

Well, that goes both ways, honey.

Before I can dwell on it too much, Chase comes back into the room, adjusting his cufflinks, and walks right up to me, cupping my neck as he tips my head back and opens my mouth with his tongue.

He pulls away far too fast but keeps himself right in my bubble.

"Sorry about that."

"Who is she?" No reason to beat around the bush.

"My sister-in-law. I love my brother, and her, but I don't appreciate when they show up unannounced, especially now that I have a frequent visitor."

His sister-in-law? That's so much better than somebody who comes by just for sex. And I'd just been starting to plan my escape, which is difficult with no car, but thankfully, that's no longer needed.

"She seemed irritated I'm here."

"Surprised is more appropriate. She's never really seen me with another woman before, especially in my house. I told you, Liz, nobody besides my family and my cleaning lady have been here. She also said she was hoping to just have a quiet night. I guess she's here for an interview or something."

"I guess this means our plans for the evening are off?"

"Oh, not a chance, princess." He trails his fingertip down the side of my face, to my neck, and down my chest to land between my breasts.

"But she'll be down the hall."

"No, she'll be on the other side of the house." While that's better, I'm still not sure it's far enough.

"Chase, you have two spare rooms upstairs. It's a nice house, but it's not *that* big."

"All the time you've spent here, and you've never taken the time to explore the hall off the kitchen farther than the office. There's a room at the end of it. I made it far more enticing to use as a spare room than anything upstairs. I like my privacy, Liz. You, of all people, should know that."

"You think that distance is enough?"

"It will have to be. Or maybe tonight I gag you." With his words, his hand creeps up to my jaw, his thumb tracing my lips.

I'm not entirely sure how I feel about it, but part of me is enticed by the idea. Chase has this way of pulling me out of my head, getting me to try things I otherwise wouldn't even dare to entertain.

"Chase?" The voice comes from the general direction of the kitchen. It's deeper than I imagined.

With a low growl, Chase leaves a small peck against my collarbone before turning toward Janine, his arm looped around my waist and tugging me to his side while pocketing his other hand.

Janine has completely changed, now wearing loose pants, a tank top, her makeup gone, and her hair piled on her head in a bun.

"Mind if I make some dinner? I'm starving." She hooks a thumb over her shoulder and tilts one foot to the side. For some reason, she's asking permission, even though she let herself into the house.

"I can cook if you don't want to." Chase tips his face down but doesn't move either hand from their spots.

"I don't mind. I do it every day."

"Hence why maybe you'd like a day off?"

"Oh good, that actually sounds delightful. Plus, it will give me a chance to chat with your lady friend here." A wide smile spans her face, one that clearly screams gossip that I'm sure she'll be eager to bring home to her husband.

"Elizabeth," he answers gruffly. "Maybe I *do* want you to cook."

"Oh please, I'm harmless." She swats him against the chest as we make our way to the kitchen. He's already rolling his sleeves up in the sexy way he knows I love. I never knew a man's forearms could be such a turn on.

When he rolled them up in front of Colleen the other day, I nearly choked on my water, and then flooded with irritation when he smirked, immediately knowing he did it on purpose.

Janine steers me toward the couch, and I glance over my shoulder at Chase, whose green eyes are locked on mine.

As she flops onto the couch and puts her fuzzy socked feet up on the table, she pulls me down along with her. She's clearly at home here, comfortable in this space. But Chase said only he and his brother had been here. So either he was lying, which I doubt, because he doesn't pull that with me, or she's just comfortable with him. Which makes sense because he said his brother has been with her for over a decade. He probably just clumps the two of them together as one entity.

"So, Elizabeth. Tell me about yourself."

"Um, what would you like to know?" My back is ramrod straight, hands folded in my lap.

"Well, I guess the best place to start is how you and Chase know each other."

"Oh, we've worked together for years."

"Ah, so you're also a lawyer. Interesting." Her gaze raises over my head to the kitchen, and I know that Chase is looking at me. I can feel the burn of his eyes on my neck.

"I suppose."

"Dealing with what you do on the day to day, do you want to get married? Have a family?"

A sharp chop echoes from the kitchen, and I know that Chase is giving an unvoiced warning. Janine must know the same because she clears her throat and shakes her head, giving me a gentle smile and patting my hand.

"Are you from around here?" Quick subject change, so she definitely got the message, loud and clear.

"For the most part. About an hour away, give or take."

"And you didn't care to leave?" It's a question I get a lot. Why have I stayed in the general area I grew up? Don't I want to see more of the world? But my parents are here, and I'm exceptionally close with them. Moreso now that they're in the facility.

"I did for school, but I'm an only child and my mother has some health issues that I feel the need to be close by for."

Her eyes widen briefly, and I see her stuff it down. I'm not sure what she does for a living, but she knows how to reel in her emotions before they get the better of her.

"I'm so sorry to hear that. It can be tough when our family is ill." Once again, her gaze raises over my head toward Chase. This time, I don't feel his penetrating eyes, and from the way I've gotten to know him, I'm sure that he's not looking at anything but the food he's preparing, which smells heavenly.

"Well, no matter who you are or where you're from, you certainly seem to have captivated our Chase over there. I can't even remember the last time he had a girlfriend."

With that last word, Chase slams a door, drawing our rapt attention. "Dinner's ready, ladies."

While I know he's reacting to the word, a word we've never used or even discussed, it cuts a little deeper than I thought it would. Is it really so terrible? My parents have all but said the same thing, and I still have no idea what Dad and Chase discussed on their walk.

We take our seats at the table, and Chase's hand immediately finds my thigh. He and Janine seem to be having a silent conversation as he stabs at his chicken.

There's tension, and there doesn't need to be. I'm a big girl, and I'm fine.

"This is really good, Chase. Thank you for cooking." Trying to break the tension seems pointless the way these two are looking at each other.

When he doesn't respond, I cover his hand and squeeze. The response I get is a squeeze in return, and a tight smile. "You're welcome."

"What time is your interview tomorrow?" Maybe trying the other party will break some of the ice.

"Eleven. And I'll be leaving right from there for my plane home. Don't worry, I'll be out of your hair tomorrow." She shoots a very pointed look in Chase's direction.

"You know I don't mind having you Janine, I just wish you or Justin would have informed me so I didn't show up at home to company." His tone is frustrated, irritation dripping from his words as his fork hangs between his fingers. I can't blame him for being annoyed.

"He said it was fine to let myself in and that you likely wouldn't be here. You didn't inform us that you have been with somebody. Besides, it was incredibly last minute."

"Okay, well, now you know. So next time, please just give me a heads up."

Next time? Surely, he's just wanting them to be more respectful. He can't possibly mean with me.

While we're getting further and further into this thing with no conversation of an end date, we both know this can't go on forever. Or maybe Chase thinks I'm willing to sign up to be his never-ending plaything. That as long as we work together, I'm agreeing to be his sex toy.

It's not necessarily the worst thought or agreement, but I want more. He can't possibly know that since I've never really shared that with him. But I wonder if on some level he does.

Small things have come out here and there. Mentions of "when" I get married or have kids, not ifs but whens. He's always just glazed over it, and I let him, figuring he just didn't want to talk about it or face it.

But now, with his mention of them being more aware in the future, I wonder if he truly means with me.

If he does, either he plans to change, or we need to have an unwanted conversation.

Chapter 24

C hase stalks over to me and cups my cheek with one hand as the other rests on my lower back, pulling me flush against him as his mouth collides with mine. It catches me off guard, and it takes my body a second to respond. When it does, I wrap my arms around his neck and melt into him, my tongue seeking his.

Deepening the kiss, his hand slips under the back of my pants, squeezing my ass, before he slips a finger between my cheeks. When his finger circles my hole, I tense and pull away, eyes wide.

"I've, uh, I've never done...that." And I'm not entirely sure now is the time with his sister-in-law downstairs. Granted, she went to bed two hours ago and I can hear the TV from any spot downstairs.

"Really, Liz? That surprises me." The look on his face is a combination of surprise and admiration. He almost looks like a kid in a candy store. "Do you trust me?"

Pulling my lip between my teeth, I nod. At this point, how could I not? I've given him my body on a daily basis, and he's always treated me well. Yes, at one point, we hated each other, but now, I trust him implicitly. His mouth closes over mine again and his tongue sweeps in. Taking careful steps backward, he walks me over to the bed, slowly lowering me down and lying over me. My body is so accustomed to the pressure of him on top of me that it reacts as my panties soak and my nipples pebble.

His hand glides up my shirt as he continues to plunder my mouth. A large hand cups my breast, massaging and taking my nipple between his fingers. I sigh into his mouth, and he moans in response.

I bend one leg at the knee and wrap it around his waist. His hand pulls from my shirt and slides from my ankle and down my leg, under the hem of my shirt. I've already changed into one of Chase's shirts, and when I was downstairs, was also in a pair of his very large pants. The second we closed the bedroom door, the pants came off.

Fingertips brush along my skin, igniting little fires on their way before they dip under my panties and pull them off. He lowers himself with them, kissing his way down my body, through my shirt, until his lips hit bare skin.

Standing at the edge of the bed, he slowly, teasingly, removes his clothes, taking his damn sweet time, before he's straddling my legs. With a quick movement, he yanks me up by the wrist, and I fall against his chest. He pulls the shirt over my head, tossing it to the floor, and brushes my loose curls behind my shoulders, his hands following that path down my back.

"You're so beautiful, Liz. I'm not sure if I've told you that before, but you are."

My heart races, and I don't know how to answer him, besides clasping him behind the head and yanking his mouth to mine.

Carefully, he lies me back, his body hovering over mine as his palm cups my ass. I know it's a question he's asking, and I nod imperceptibly, deepening the kiss and pulling him closer to me.

There are many ways I've opened my mind and body to Chase, what's one more? If I'm going to do this with anybody, it's going to be him.

Understanding my gesture, he rolls us to our sides and slides his hand between us, two fingers slipping into my pussy while one goes gently into my ass. It's not the first time he's done this. He thinks I must not know, but I've never said or done anything about it because it hasn't bothered me. But a finger now and again is very different from his rather large and wide cock. And to say I'm nervous would be an understatement. But I trust Chase.

Parting from me, he reaches over my body, half leaning on me, to get a bottle of lube out of the nightstand drawer.

The reality of the situation has my heart fluttering, and I take a deep breath to try to calm myself. I know Chase would be fine if I were to say no, to stop this right now and not look back. He'd happily plunge into my pussy and not think twice about it.

But I don't stop him. Not as he lubes himself up, not as he moves around to be behind me. And not as he teases my hole with the tip of his cock.

When he inserts the tip, I clench around him.

"Relax for me, Liz. I won't hurt you. I promise to make this feel good for you, and if you want to stop, you just tell me, and I won't hesitate." His voice is low and deep in my ear.

Taking a deep breath, I focus on loosening my muscles. Ever so slowly, Chase pushes inside me. Every little bit I tighten, he freezes. There's the slightest burn with each deepening, but it's quickly erased.

Sliding a hand under my hip, he reaches forward, finding my clit with his finger. When he starts swirling around it, my head tips back into his shoulder, and I relax as he presses himself the rest of the way in.

"Holy fuck, Liz. Goddamn, this is incredible." He hasn't even moved yet, staying still while inside me, all the way to the hilt. Pulling my hair over my shoulder, he kisses along the exposed skin and up to my ear. "If you want me to stop, say the word."

I nod as he circles my clit again, using just the right amount of pressure, and he starts slowly pumping into me.

Looping my leg over his waist, his other hand slides up and cups my breast, taking my hardened nipple between his fingers.

He's thrusting in earnest now, my head tipping back toward him. It's such a different sensation and feeling of fullness. But I can't say it feels *bad*.

"Fuck, baby." The gravel in his voice is a sure sign he's thoroughly enjoying himself. It's not an infrequent sound, but it's more defined when he's overly pleased. Having him say 'baby' doesn't even phase me anymore.

I'm about to respond when the pressure in my clit rises and peaks before I realize it was threatening. Covering his hand on my breast, I cry out as my body shudders and tightens around him.

He practically chokes on the air in his lungs as a strangled sound eases from his mouth and he comes. Resting his forehead against my shoulder, he breathes heavily as he lays otherwise still around me.

Kissing the nape of my neck, he moves across my shoulder as he slowly pulls out from me. In a second, he's hopping over my body to lie in front of me.

Tucking some hair behind my ear, he looks at me intently. I rest my hand against his chest and lean toward him.

"How was it? Give me something, Liz." His eyes dart back and forth, searching mine.

"It was fine." There's not really more to say. It wasn't bad, but it wasn't earth shattering like our normal sex.

"Liz. At least tell me if I hurt you."

"It definitely didn't hurt."

"Can you give me more? Liz, I just want to know you're okay with everything." He's said my name three times now. That means he's borderline frantic.

"I'm good, Chase. It was...different. It didn't hurt. You were right, you made me feel good. Just not sure how I feel about it in general or for future experiences." I think I'd rather just stick to cock in pussy for now. But if he really loved it that much, it's something I'd be willing to consider doing again for him. Because I'm realizing that's where my feelings have grown to.

"That's fine, Liz. I'm happy you let me be the one you did that with. And while I fucking loved every second, I'll never push you to do it again if you don't want to."

"I know." Chase has always been good about not pressuring me. His bark is worse than his bite. Where he says a lot about each day, time, anything, if I were to say no, he'd stop immediately.

"Let's take a shower." He pulls me off the bed, hands on my waist as he stands so close to me that his chest brushes my back and walks us to the bathroom.

Once standing under the warm water, I let my head fall back as the water runs down my chest. Chase steps behind me, wrapping his arms around me and soaping up my front. He continues to soap me, taking a little too much time at my breasts, which results in me elbowing him in the ribs.

Watching the bubbles glide over his chiseled abs and the few pumps he gives his already hard again cock, my clit tingles and wetness pools between my thighs. Chase's eyes bore into mine as he soaps my back, sliding his finger between my ass cheeks before rinsing us both, never breaking his gaze.

Once the water runs clear, his mouth is crashing onto mine as he pushes me back against the wall. I wrap my legs around his waist as he lifts me.

"Again? Already?"

"I haven't filled you enough tonight, Liz."

I cry out as he impales me on his erection in one fell swoop. He pounds into me hard and fast as he supports me with one hand, the other leaning against the wall next to my head.

He's hurried and frenzied and sloppy, almost slipping more than once. But within minutes, we're both coming.

I'm not sure whose heart is beating faster and harder as I feel both begging for attention in my chest. My legs are still around his waist as I cling to him, too tired to do much more.

"Fuck, woman, you might kill me." He doesn't lower me to the ground, instead he turns and carries me back under the stream, which has gotten colder and causes me to scramble higher in his hold. Once he adjusts the water to be warm again, I can think of my rebuttal.

"Nobody says you have to fuck me every time an opportunity arises."

"My dick does. Goddamn, Liz, you may not know how hot you are, but my body certainly does. Anytime you're even in the same room, I'm dying to be inside of you."

"Then either tell it no or don't complain that I'm going to kill you. I'm not initiating these sessions."

"You could, you know. Every once in a while."

I'm about to refute that I did a few weeks ago at my house, but the thought dies in my mouth as I realize it's one of three times in nearly six months. "You don't even give me the opportunity. You pounce on me within seconds."

"I'm a man who knows what he wants. And I want you." He lowers me to the ground but keeps me close. His possessiveness is something I still find myself getting used to. As is his giving attitude in the bedroom. I absolutely expected Chase to be the way he is in the courtroom. In some ways, he is. He's demanding, ruthless, and makes his points exceptionally clear. But he's also so different. In the courtroom, Chase doesn't take no for answer; he tramples over people if he needs to, and everything is absolutely about him. His win, his client, his everything.

Yet when we're together, he puts my needs first. Yes, he's still demanding and tells me what to do and what he wants. But he makes sure I come first, always, literally and figuratively.

It used to throw my mind for a loop. Now I realize, it's just Chase.

Chapter 25

Mrs. Douglas pulls her lip between her teeth as Chase goes over some details of the trial and how it will work. It's unusual for us to actually stand in front of a judge for a trial in the case of divorce, but due to the high-profile nature and extreme funds of this one, that's exactly where it's heading.

I'm fiddling my pen between my fingers as I watch Chase as he leans back in his chair, confidence rolling off him in waves. I have to clench my thighs to quell the need settling in.

My phone buzzing draws my attention. Glancing at the number for my parents, I send it to voicemail, flipping my phone over.

When it buzzes two minutes later, and it's my parents again, my brow furrows as my lips purse. But I send it to voicemail again. I'll have to call as soon as we're done. I'm sure it's just because I haven't spoken to them in a few days.

When my eyes lift, I find Chase's on mine as he continues talking to Mrs. Douglas. If I didn't know better, I'd say there's concern in his gaze.

"Excuse me, everybody. Miss Prescott? There's an urgent call for you." Julie pokes her head into the conference room. I don't mind her, but she's not as good as Nancy. Of course, I'm biased since Nancy's been working for me for years.

"Oh, thank you. I'm sorry, Mrs. Douglas, I'll be right back." I glance at Chase and see his narrowed eyes, the corner of his mouth ticking downward. I hope he can't see that my heart is ready to beat out of my chest and my knees suddenly feel shaky.

I take a shuddering breath, shaking out my hands, as I take the six steps to Julie's desk, where the receiver sits face up. Leaning one hand on the top of the desk, I lift the phone with the other, staying standing to be able to head back to the meeting quickly. "Hello?"

"Miss Prescott? This is Trisha at Watering Pines. I'm very sorry to have to be the one to tell you this, but your father passed away this morning."

I collapse into the chair behind me, not able to hear anything coming out of the receiver before it falls into my lap, along with my hands. Staring at the carpet, I can't move, I can't think.

"Excuse me, Mrs. Douglas, I'll be right back."

I must be so attuned to him that I can pick up on his voice because I can't hear anything else around the whooshing in my ears and the hammering of my heart.

Chase kneels in front of me and hangs up the phone, linking his fingers with mine, bringing the pair to his mouth to kiss along my knuckles. His other hand cups my cheek, thumb brushing along my skin. "What happened?"

"My dad." It's all I can say. I can't get the rest of the words out. I can't even wrap my brain around them.

Pulling me to standing and immediately against him, looping an arm around my waist, Chase leads me to the conference room door. "I'm so sorry, Mrs. Douglas. Something urgent has come up, and we're going to have to reschedule. Please call me if there are any emergencies; otherwise, I'll have Julie call you to set up the next meeting."

He doesn't wait for her answer as he starts walking us toward his office. "No calls and no interruptions, please, Julie."

His secretary gives a curt nod as she eyes me with a mix of sadness and jealousy.

As we walk in, he closes and locks the door, sitting in his desk chair and pulling me into his lap. Sniffling, I fight it when he tries to lean me against his chest.

"I'll ruin your shirt."

Taking my face between his two hands, he turns it toward his. "I don't care about the damn shirt, Liz. Lay down." He doesn't give me much choice as he pushes my cheek to rest against his chest.

That's when the floodgates open. I grab at his shirt collar, gripping as tightly as I can, wanting to pull him as close to me as possible. There's too much space, too many clothes, too much separating us.

He keeps his arms wrapped tightly around my waist and every few minutes will lay a gentle kiss on my forehead. It's the sweetest he's ever been, and it makes my body rattle harder.

"You're okay, Liz. I've got you."

When I turn to him and start peppering kisses along his jaw, working my way to his lips, he leans into me, his mouth working against mine as his tongue seeks its companion. But when my hand cups his cheek, he pulls back, brow furrowed.

"What are you doing, Elizabeth?"

"You don't...want...to have sex?" My words have to work through ragged breaths.

"Not right now, Liz. Not right now. I just want to be here for you. I want to hold you for a little while, let you know you're okay because I'm here, and I've got you. Cry against me until you can't anymore because I'm not going anywhere. I'm not leaving this room or answering a single call until you're calmer. And then when you are, I'm driving you to your mom and staying with you until you're too tired to do anything but go to bed. At which time I will drive you home, put you in my bed, and hold you while you sleep."

The tears erupt again. Both at his words, his sentiment, and the loss of my dad. He holds me while the tears flow and my body shakes. His hands work over me, rubbing circles on my back, running down my hair, pulling curls straight as a finger grazes along my spine. He places tiny kisses on my forehead, taking my face and kissing away the tears. Nothing will make them stop except running out.

That finally happens what I assume is over an hour later. I gather the tissues that Chase routinely passed me and lean up in his lap. Concern laces his features, pooling in his striking eyes.

"Thank you."

"You're welcome." He tucks a curl behind my ear as he says it. "Ready to go see your mom?"

My head falls forward to hang over my lap. My mom. How am I supposed to see her at a time like this? What do I say? What do I do? I hate that she's been alone all this time, but I was in no position to go to her. That may be selfish of me, but I just couldn't. She won't remember anyway.

Unable to form words, I nod without making eye contact.

Easing me off his lap, Chase keeps an arm around my waist. To support my weakened knees, no doubt.

"Chase, I..."

He cuts me off with a kiss. "I know, baby. I know."

I don't question that he knows I need him right now. I don't question that he knows I'm more thankful than I can say.

Chase has been through this before. It's surely how he knew what happened without me having to put the words out there. The words I still can barely even think, let alone say.

We just saw Dad a few weeks ago and he was fine. Happy. What happened? How could this happen?

Chase keeps his fingers laced through mine, resting on my thigh as we make the drive to Mom. Though I'm worrying my lip with my fingertips and staring out the window, out of the corner of my eye I can see Chase glancing at me every few minutes.

I can't look at him, I can't say anything, and I'm glad he's not trying to get me to talk. The most he does with his mouth is kiss my knuckles every so often.

Everything is muted. The sounds, the sights, the colors. Feelings. All of it. It's all dimmed.

After Chase parks and shuts off the car, I can feel his eyes on me. Sighing, he gets out and walks around to my side. I make no move to open my door, so he does it for me, reaching in and pulling me out with a hand around my waist.

Once I'm standing, on what's only semi-solid ground, he cups my face and kisses me softly. Holding my gaze, his beautiful greens meet my blues.

"I'm right here, Liz. Okay? I'm here with you."

All I can do is nod in his grasp.

Sliding a hand down my arm, he links his fingers in mine and waits for me to take over and lead us to the building. But I can't. Not yet. Staring up at its immense size, I take a few deep breaths and steel my emotions. Mom's not going to remember why I'm crying, and I don't know that I'll be able to remind her repeatedly.

"Before we go in, you need to know, she's fairly far gone. She usually remembers me, and she'll remember my dad. But she probably won't remember that he's gone. I'm anticipating her asking repeatedly where he is. You can tell her who you are, but she'll forget within an hour."

"It's okay, Elizabeth. I remember from when we were here. I can handle this. Don't worry about me. Let me worry about you. I'm here for you."

Oh right, we had come together not too long ago. I almost forgot he'd been with me. It feels like another lifetime ago that we were here together. I meet his eyes and let my gaze linger on his intense one. Normally, my heart races when he looks at me like this. But right now, I'm lucky my heart's even still beating.

Dad and I were close. I'm the true definition of a daddy's girl. I mean, I bought him a house, for Pete's sake. How am I in this position? Having to go see Mom and tell her that he's gone, remind her he's gone when she forgets. With somebody who only recently stopped hating me, but I've been screwing for the better part of a year.

My eyes flutter shut as tears silently drip down my cheeks. Chase wipes them away with his thumb, running it over my bottom lip and squeezing my hand. He's with me, he's reminding me that he's here for support.

It'd be nice to be here with somebody I love, who loves me, but Chase is the closest thing I have to that. And on some level, I wonder if one of those boxes is, in fact, checked off. He doesn't love me, but I'm wondering if I love him.

Right now is not the time to dwell on that thought, and with a deep breath, I step into the building and toward impending doom.

Chapter 26

C hase and I are sitting on the couch in Mom's living room. In this moment, I'm so thankful he's such a broad and sturdy man because I'm sure he's holding me up as I lean into him.

It's quiet. I never noticed in recent months how much of the talking Dad did when I came to visit. It took until now for me to realize that as nobody else is talking.

A strong hand squeezes my knee, and I look up at Chase, his eyes on mine. It takes me a second to realize I'd been bouncing it incessantly.

"Sorry," I mumble quietly as I look all around the room, unable to focus on anything specific.

"It's okay, baby. Relax. Please." His voice is low and next to my ear.

"I can't." The words are barely a whisper. How does he expect me to relax when Mom's asked the same questions about a dozen times and Dad's just gone? He's not here.

It's hit harder and become more real that he's not in the apartment. It's like part of me thought it was a bad dream; that I'd get here and he'd be standing there with that smile on his face, calling me Lilla Bean.

All the air leaves my lungs, and it's like a punch in the gut when I realize I'll never hear that nickname again. My heart would absolutely break in two if it wasn't already in pieces all over the floor of the office.

"Who is this young man with you, Elizabeth?" The fact that she remembers me is a good thing. But she can't seem to hold on to anything else, even though I've had to tell her who Chase is and the fact that Dad's gone almost a dozen times already.

Irritation pulls at my mind, and I just don't have it in me to keep doing this. "Mom, I've already told you, Chase is—"

"It's okay," he says quietly to me. He must pick up on my frustration. "Mrs. Prescott, I'm Chase. I'm your daughter's boyfriend. Of about eight months now."

Boyfriend? He's never said that before. I'm sure it's just for Mom's benefit. I mean, we are holding hands and sitting pressed up against each other. But he knows she'd never remember. Why not just say friend? Coworker? Does he really consider himself my boyfriend? The sex aside, is that how he views this?

No, it can't possibly be. I'm sure it's just a show for Mom. He can say it one time to appease her, possibly even me, and then be done with it since she won't remember. That doesn't mean that I won't, but I'm sure he knows that I'm well aware he doesn't want anything serious.

"Oh. That's nice, dear. Where's John? He's not usually so impolite around visitors."

My heart sinks, and my body tries to fold in on itself at the mention of my father. Again. But Chase doesn't let me collapse, wrapping his arm tight around me and pulling my head against his shoulder as he kisses the top of my head.

By the time we're leaving, I'm physically and mentally drained. There's nothing left. Chase's arm around my waist is the only thing keeping me upright, and I'm sure it'd be easier if he just carried me. My whole body is sore, my eyes swollen.

Opening the car door, Chase helps me in, buckling my seat belt and adjusting me so I'm sitting comfortably in the car.

I take in nothing but passing lights as we make our way home.

Once we get there, Chase silently comes to get me out. He puts one arm under my knees and the other under my arms and carefully lifts me from the car.

"I've got you, Elizabeth. Come on. You'll feel better after some sleep."

I wrap one arm around his neck, sliding under the collar of his shirt, needing to feel his warm skin against mine. The other twists into the front of his shirt as I bury my face in the crook of his neck. Right now, he's all that's holding me together.

Once we're inside, I start to feel a little more myself. The comfort of this house, what's basically become my home in the past few months, starts to bring me back to the land of the living.

Settling on the couch, Chase sits, pulling me into his lap. I lean into him, not even trying to support my weight at all. He's rubbing big circles on my back. It feels nice, and listening to his heartbeat is helping to bring me back.

"Elizabeth, I think you should eat. You haven't eaten since breakfast."

Is he paying attention to that? "I can't."

"I know, baby, but you have to. Maybe just something small. Why don't I call Fusion and get you some sushi?"

All I can do is shrug.

I feel his sigh more than I hear it. Tilting his pelvis up, he pulls his phone from his pocket. Keeping me in his lap and continuing to rub my back, he places an order for delivery.

Once he hangs up, he takes my chin his fingers and tilts my face up to his.

His eyes are filled with concern, his brows knit together as creases line his forehead. Leaning down, he brushes his lips against mine briefly. As he starts to pull away, I push myself up, wrapping a hand around the back of his neck to connect with his mouth again.

He's hesitant with his body, slow with his mouth on mine, which is so unlike him. I wish he'd just be bossy and demanding.

Pulling myself closer to him, I increase the intensity of the kiss, moving my mouth firmer against his, pushing my tongue through his lips.

I can almost feel the chord holding him together snap as his hand flies to the back of my head and tangles in my hair, his mouth becoming more forceful on mine. His fingers slide up my leg, dipping under the hem of my skirt.

I've all but lost my surroundings, and I have to really think about why I'm in a tight skirt. I worked this morning. It feels like it was ages ago, not a mere twelve hours.

Adjusting in his lap, I turn to face him, hiking my skirt up so I can straddle him. His heated gaze bores into mine as his hands slide up my thighs. If I sit high on my knees, it gives me the slightest height edge and I feel like I have the tiniest bit of power. Power I don't normally have.

I can't get my brain to focus as I run my hands up his chest. I want everything and nothing at the same time. Tearing his clothes off and letting him fuck me into oblivion sounds amazing, but exhausting. Too exhausting after the longest day of my life.

But I need to drown it out. The pain, the ache, the emptiness. I need to feel full right now. It may be different, but I need to feel it.

"Take me upstairs."

Hooking his hands under my thighs, Chase stands, carrying me carefully through the house and up to his room. Instead of the usual toss to the bed, he gently sets me on the edge, unwrapping me from his body.

Instead of laying over me or even joining me, he walks into the closet as he unbuttons his shirt. I wait for him on the bed, not getting up or moving at all. Part of me wants to, but every bone in my body throbs with exhaustion.

I grip the edge of the mattress and let my head fall forward. There's a kink in my neck that I have no will to try to stretch out.

"Stand up, Elizabeth."

I didn't even hear Chase's return, didn't feel his presence that I've become so attuned to. But I do as he says, leaning into him as he puts an arm around my waist to support me.

He moves my hands to his shoulders as he unzips and pushes my skirt over my hips so it drops to the floor. His fingers start working the buttons on my shirt and let it fall away. My bra joins the pile and I'm standing in just my panties, hands still resting on his bare shoulders.

Raising my arms for me, Chase puts a t-shirt over my head and arms. It falls to mid-thigh and wraps me in the scent of Chase. It has my muscles loosening the slightest bit.

Pulling back the covers, Chase climbs onto the bed, wrapping his arm around me and tugging me to the top of the bed. He settles in next to me, lying on his side and looking at me intently.

When I slide against him, he stiffens. I press my mouth against his, resuming what we started downstairs.

His palm settles at the small of my back as his tongue seeks mine. A tiny moan eases from my throat, and he presses his pelvis to mine, his erection pushing into my stomach.

Intensifying the kiss, I loop my leg over his waist, my hand sliding up his chest to wrap behind his head.

Before my hand can settle, he grabs my wrist, stopping me.

"I thought you couldn't go a day without sex," I mutter against his lips.

"I can. I just don't want to. But I fucked you hard in the shower this morning." Oh, and what a fuck it was. The back of my head is still sore from rubbing against the tiles as I bobbed up and down on his cock.

"And that's enough for you?"

"It can be." But it doesn't have to be. He can do more, I know it, because most days, he fucks me at least twice, if not more.

"What about me? What if I need more?"

"I'm not sure you're in the right frame of mind to be deciding that, Elizabeth."

My head pulls back with a start. Who is he to be telling me what I can and can't decide right now. "I'm a big girl, Chase. I know what I can handle."

I give a press with my pelvis, trying to push him to his back, but it's no use. He's too strong for me, especially if he doesn't want to go, and right now, he doesn't.

"Please, Chase." The idea of begging feels so beneath me, so unnecessary and a little dirty. But I need him and don't know what else to do or how else to convince him.

He stares at me silently for a few minutes while I can barely breathe.

I'm ready to give up, to roll over and go to bed, when his hand closes around my hip and pulls me against him as his mouth crashes onto mine. Easing me to my back, he glides over me, cupping my breast and running his thumb over my hardened nipple.

Kissing down my neck, he moves to my breast, taking my pebbled skin between his teeth.

His hand glides down my body, under the hem of my shirt, and rubs over my panties. After the fourth pass, he pushes them to the side, sliding his finger along my wetness and giving my clit a firm swirl.

It feels like he's hurried, like he's trying to make sure I'm not going to change my mind. But I'm the one who started this, the one who wants it.

My panties are yanked from my body, my shirt slid up to just above my breasts. Chase kisses along my chest, giving each nipple a few flicks of his tongue, eyes locked on mine as I arch and moan.

He eases into me, but takes no time getting to it, pulling out to the tip before thrusting back into me. His movements are hard, fast, and exactly the mind erasing roughness that I thought I wanted. But it's not doing what I hoped it would.

"Chase. I need...mmm. I need..."

"Tell me what you need, baby."

"You."

He slows his pace, lowering himself to be right over me as his lips meld to mine in a slow and sensual kiss. His tongue glides along mine as he makes steady movements inside me.

Keeping things at a much more leisurely pace, Chase dips his hips lower so every thrust tips up, rubbing right against my most sensitive spot. Every time, my head arches back and I whine at the pure pleasure.

Kissing up my neck, he pulls my earlobe between his teeth as he groans, low and deep.

Sliding his hand down my body, he rests it between us, his thumb pressing against my clit. He starts making slow circles that match his thrusts. Every glide inside is a pressurized swirl, and every pull out relieves the pressure.

Within minutes, the pleasure is building and the pressure in my hips is increasing, and my body is starting to tremble.

"Come for me, baby."

My nails drag down his back as I garble out a moan.

Chase moves his hand from between us and quickens his pace for all of a minute before his breath stunts and he falls against me.

We breathe heavily for a minute as he runs his open lips along my damp skin. And what happens next both infuriates me and embarrasses me.

Tears spring from my eyes and drip down the sides of my face like an unleashed tidal wave. It came out of nowhere, and I'm taken by surprise.

Chase leans up to look at me, his brow pulled tight and his lips downturned as concern flashes through his eyes. I haven't even heaved a sob yet, so he either reads me that well, or he felt the tears.

Giving a tiny peck on my lips, he kisses along the tear tracks, first on the right, then the left, before landing on my mouth again. The saltiness of my tears resides on his lips and dances along my tongue.

Pulling away, he rolls to his side, turning me to mine and guiding me into his chest. This is the only time I wish he was wearing a shirt to bed. My fingers twitch, needing something to grab on to.

I loop a hand around his neck, my fingertips twisting into the wisps at his nape. He circles my waist with his strong arm, tightening so I'm right up against him, trapped to him.

"You're okay, Liz. I know it hurts right now, but I promise you'll be okay."

I can't answer him, sobs rattling me as he holds me closer. He shushes me, kissing the top of my head, smoothing my hair, rubbing my back. There's a tension settled in his body; I can feel the stiffness in his movements.

He's worried about me. If I could feel anything, I'm sure this would bring on some sort of emotion. But I can't. It's all quelled by the anguish tearing me apart from the inside out.

How is anything ever going to be okay again? He says it will be, and he's been through this, but he doesn't know my dad. He's met him once and he doesn't truly know a world where he exists and then now the one where he doesn't. How am I supposed to do this? How does one navigate this terrible loss?

It's my only hope that Chase will stick by me for long enough to help me understand this incredibly darkened world.

Chapter 27

I wake up in a daze. The bed next to me is cold, and my stomach is gnawing at itself. I fell asleep from sheer exhaustion before dinner showed up. If Chase ate, he didn't wake me.

Rolling to my side, I grab my phone off the nightstand. It's almost noon.

Sitting up and stretching, I have the faintest memory of Chase leaving and telling me to stay, that he called in for me. It was early, the sun barely shining through the large windows and my mind was hazy, eyes feeling too heavy to open more than a slit.

But the remembrance of how touched I felt that he called in for me is still residing in my chest.

I'm alone in Chase's house for the first time ever. But instead of feeling weird, I feel at home. Maybe I should have given more consideration to moving some things here.

Nope, *that* thought still feels weird.

While I feel hungry, the thought of eating makes my stomach roll. Instead, I start a fresh pot of coffee. There's a lot I have to plan and need the clarity of caffeine to help me. I decide to toss a few pieces of bread in the toaster for good measure.

I know Chase said to make myself feel at home, but I feel weird looking through his things without him here. I need a pad of paper, though, to make a list. I'm handling everything alone. There's just no way Mom could.

Padding down to the office, I open a few drawers in his desk. Chase is ridiculous about his desk, even at work. While the rest of his house is pristine, I know that's thanks to his housekeeper. His desk, though, that's all him. It's organized exactly how his work one is, the same pencil cup and everything.

While I don't spend a lot of time in here, it's my favorite room in the house, mostly because of the books. Okay, maybe solely because of the books.

Shaking my head, I pull open the top drawer, looking for paper, any paper. After going through every drawer, I come up short. Looking around for somewhere else he may scurry some away, my heart stops.

I hadn't noticed it as I came in, my mind set on my mission for paper. There's a large comfy chair in the far corner. On more than one occasion, I'd told Chase how nice a big chair would be so I could sit and read. His argument was that I shouldn't be reading in his house unless I'm doing it naked in his bed.

And yet, there sits a chair. It's big enough for me to curl up on, probably even big enough for us to both sit on. I feel a little ridiculous for not having seen it the second I strolled into the room. But there it is all the same.

When did he do this?

My mind immediately flashes back to two weeks ago. We were spending the night at my apartment to give Cheshire a little attention, something Chase did begrudgingly, but I told him the alternative was me staying alone because I needed to be home for one night. He was late coming over, said he had to do something at home besides just grabbing clothes.

This must be the something he was doing. I rarely have a reason to come in here. The last time was probably over three months ago when we were grabbing a specific law book for the case.

My body warms as tears spring to my eyes at this sweet gesture. One he didn't even feel a need to point out, even knowing it was a sure-fire way to get laid.

I'll have to reward him somehow. Naked me in the chair is probably sufficient.

Shaking my head, I get back to the task at hand. Paper.

Once I'm back in the kitchen, I add a little butter to my toast and pull down the biggest mug I can find.

Unlocking my phone, my thumb hovers over Chase's name. We never send each other messages. Even before all this started, if we ever needed to communicate, we usually went through other avenues, like other people or emails if we couldn't just talk in person.

I flick open the message, typing it out and hitting send before I can rethink it.

Me: *I need a pad of paper. Where can I find some?*

Leaning against the counter, I keep my eyes glued the phone while I chew my lip, cup in my other hand begging to be drank. I'm too focused on the three bubbles that are popping up and disappearing.

What's hard to answer? Was he expecting something different? Does he have more to say?

Chase: *Oh. Um. Try the closet in the laundry room. Don't ask, I didn't put them there. If there's none, I'll bring a pad home.*

Chase: *What do you need paper for?*

Me: *Have a funeral to plan. Need to make some lists and notes.*

My hands shake as I type out the word funeral. But right now, I don't have time to break down. Task-oriented Elizabeth is here, and she doesn't get distracted.

Finding a legal pad where Chase mentioned, I bring it back out to the kitchen. Sitting with a fresh cup of coffee and a heavy sigh, I start my list.

Yet, I find I don't know where to begin. I don't know what goes into this process. I'm sure there are a million people to contact. But who?

In all my years as a lawyer, never once have I had to dive into the estate side. Lost beyond measure, I tap the pen against the pad and stare off into space.

I startle as the door opens, my hand flying to my chest to try to contain my racing heart.

"Chase? What are you doing here?"

"I live here."

"Yeah, but it's the middle of the day. And your house is like a half hour from work. You can't possibly be taking lunch." Did he come back to check on me? No. He wouldn't do that.

"It's a long lunch." He juts his chin toward the pad. "How's the list coming?"

"Um, I'm not sure. I'll have to look at some articles online or something."

"Well, I *am* here to help, Liz."

My eyebrow arches as I look at him. I don't want to have to bring him into this, this personal level of hell. But leaning on him helps relieve some of the ache in my soul.

He groans and looks back over at me. "Hang on, I have something I need to...just...hang on a second." Disappearing back out the door, I'm even more confused than him being here in the middle of the day.

Walking back in, he's holding a carrying case and a meowing cat.

"Cheshire!" I'm on my feet and across the room in a few quick strides.

"I stole your keys this morning and swung by to get him. I thought he'd bring some comfort right now."

Bending in front of his cage, I set him free, and he loops around my feet, looking up at me with his emerald eyes and purring so loudly I'm surprised his body isn't vibrating.

After a quick scratch under his chin, he darts over to make figure eights around Chase's legs.

"Hey, little buddy. Consider this home for the next little while. But you scratch my furniture, you get put in the basement." He points a finger down at the cat as though he'd understand.

"I mean, I love that he's here, but he needs his stuff; his litter box, his food."

"Yeah, I'm aware. It's all in the car." He jerks a thumb over his shoulder toward the outside.

My eyebrows shoot to my hairline as my eyes widen. "They're...they're what?"

"In the car. I told you, Liz, I'm here for you. Right now? That means bringing you your cat. But I'm serious. If he scratches anything, he's getting locked in the basement."

I throw myself into Chase's arms as he wraps them around me and kisses the top of my head.

"I know what it's like to lose a parent, Liz. And you've basically lost two. But I need you to know you're not in this alone. I'm here for you, to help you and comfort you. And if that means bringing you your pesky feline, then I'll do it, even if you didn't ask."

My whole body warms at his sweetness. Every time I think he can't do anything sweeter or anything to surprise me more, he does, and it throws me for a loop every single time. "Hey, you like him."

"He's alright for a cat."

"Thank you." Looking around, I notice he's nowhere to be found. "I guess he's off exploring."

"Let me get the rest of his stuff in, and then we'll get to that list."

"Don't you have to go back to work?" I pull my lip between my teeth because as much as I don't want to admit that I need him, I know that I do, and I'm pretty sure he does too.

"Took a half day."

"You didn't have to do that for me."

"Who says I did?" He throws a wink in my direction.

My face tilts to the side as my lip turns down. Why can't he just admit that he did something nice for me? Would it kill him? Maybe he thinks it will.

"There's a lot to do in a short amount of time. So yes, I took a half day to help you with that. Mrs. Douglas is set to wait for a couple of days, all my other clients are set exactly as they are, and I had nothing to do there. I only even went in to grab a few contacts that I didn't have here."

"Contacts?"

"I have a good estate attorney. A buddy of mine works at the paper for the obit."

LOVE ME NOT 217

As I take a deep, shaky breath, Chase pulls me back against him. "It's a lot. And all at once and while you're in a not great place. That's why I need you to let me help you."

"Chase. It's just. Is that what we are now? Is that what this is?" It's the sort of thing that people do for each other when they're dating or spouses. They help each other in times of crisis and lean on each other.

"I don't know. I can't give you a definitive answer on that. But it doesn't change that I'm going to go through this with you." His voice is gentle, and he rubs his hands slowly up and down my arms.

I let Chase hold me in silence for a few minutes, just enjoying his nearness. I've given up denying that it brings me comfort, that it makes my heart beat erratically every time, right now being no exception. I don't even care anymore that I surely have stronger feelings for him than he does for me. But I'm going to revel in it and let it do its job.

Pushing me back slightly, he tucks some hair behind my ear. "I'm going to get Cheshire's stuff and change. Then I'll make some lunch and we'll get to that list."

I look at the ground and nod against his palm on my cheek.

After he's left, I walk back into the kitchen to refill my coffee, but end up with my hands tight on the counter as I try to get control of my breathing, suddenly unable to take a breath.

His behavior, his kindness, the sweet gestures...it's overwhelming my senses. It's overwhelming my ability to keep a lock on the feelings that want to erupt from inside me. Because I'm pretty sure at this point I'm way beyond just liking him, way beyond this being casual. And that's terrifying because Chase will never feel the same way.

I nearly shriek as his arm wraps around my waist. "You okay?" His voice is low and right in my ear and my body responds the way it usually does with my head tipping back against his shoulder and my panties wetting.

Inappropriate response, Elizabeth. Now is not the time.

It'd be easier to believe if his breathing didn't become heavier and he didn't start to harden in his pants. God, what a little relief could do for my brain right now. But I know if I fall into that trap, I'm never getting out, and I may just fuck him straight through what would be my dad's unplanned funeral.

"God, Liz, you have got to be the most intoxicating person I've ever met. All I can think about right now is popping you up onto the counter and fucking you until we're so exhausted, we can't move."

"And what's so bad about that?" I tilt my head slightly to look at him.

"I don't exactly think it's appropriate right now."

"What if I don't care? What if I want the same thing?"

"One of us has to be strong here, Liz. One of us has to do the right thing." But who's to say what the right thing is right now? Is getting lost in Chase really a terrible thing? Is taking some time to let him heal me bad?

I turn in his arms and press my pelvis against his as I kiss slowly along his jaw. I have to stand on my toes to reach as my fingers tangle into his hair. A little stress relief never hurt anybody. If we spend the whole day wound together, who cares. Everything will get done. This is something I need for me.

Pulling back, I lean into the counter, yanking him toward me so hard his hands land against the granite on either side of my hips.

"Liz."

"I need this, Chase. I need to clear my brain for a little while. You can stop it if you really want to, now, after one time, after three times. Or you can just let go and see what happens."

"The last time I let go with you, Elizabeth, we fucked all over this house." That was him letting go? Why doesn't he do it more often? It was by far one of the best nights of my life.

"Your point?"

"There are things you need to do." The tightness of his posture tells me he's holding back as much as he can.

"Will those things still be there later?" I ask right against his lips.

"Yes."

"Then why do I care if I get to them now when I have much more pressing matters on my mind?"

He stops hesitating, his hands grabbing my hips and lifting me onto the counter, stepping right between my legs as his palms run up my bare thighs and under the hem of my shirt.

"I don't know what you've done to me, Elizabeth."

"Mm...I think it's more what you've done to me. You're the one who was sex crazed."

"Not like this. Not like there can never be enough. And never did I imagine it'd be like this with you. But I'm so fucking glad it is."

I wrap my legs around his waist, hooking my ankles and gripping at his hair as I pull his mouth to mine. My actions are urgent. There are too many thoughts swirling in my head, too many emotions flying through my chest. If I don't get him inside me soon, I may fall to pieces.

All it takes is one grind against his erection for him to free himself and plunge into me. We moan in unison as our bodies connect.

Resting his head against my shoulder, he looks down at the places our bodies meet as he slides in and pulls out ever so slowly. It's agonizing yet tantalizing at the same time.

"Fuck." His voice is full of grit.

I open my mouth to respond, but I'm cut off as he grabs onto my hair and yanks my head back, biting his way up my neck and retracing the trail with his tongue, soothing the sting.

Keeping my head pulled back, he puts his other hand tight on my hip and increases his speed, slamming into me as his mouth stays against my neck.

The sound of our bodies smacking against each other echoes off the tile, surrounding us.

Releasing my hair, his hand drops to my breast, cupping it before running his thumb over my hardened nipple.

"Fuck, Chase."

With hooded eyes, he locks his gaze on mine and slides his hand between our bodies, his thumb swirling over my clit with exactly the right amount of pressure. It's a practiced move that I know he does as the added sensation that tips me right over the edge. He doesn't need to; he can make me come just by how he uses his cock and the way it fills me, but he likes to make my orgasms as intense as possible.

My body trembles, and a smirk pulls at Chase's lips as I tighten around him, hands twisting into his shirt, and I scream his name.

A few more hard thrusts, and he groans into my shoulder. Pulling me against his chest, he carries me over to the couch, lifting me slightly as he tucks himself back into his pants before sitting. He settles me right on his lap, in exactly the position I was in when he pulled me from the counter.

My head rests against his heaving chest as I let the tingles work their way out of my body, slumped into him as he rests his chin on my head and runs his fingers up and down my back.

As his breathing slows and my body feels normal again, I don't make a move to get up. When Chase adjusts beneath me, I wrap my arms around him and he freezes before settling back into the cushions.

"How about a bath?" His murmur is low, and I hear it in his chest more than from his mouth.

I just shake my head.

"I think you should. Come on, let's go."

I whine as he holds me under my thighs and carries me up the stairs. Setting me on the bathroom floor, he turns the water on and starts filling the tub, walking out as he pulls his shirt over his head.

Staring at the water, my mind is completely blank. Everything is muted.

Chase's fingers graze my skin as he removes my clothes. He holds the vase of bath bombs in front of me. "Pick one."

It takes me an extra moment to tear my gaze from the filling tub to look inside. The colors all seem dull. I grab the top one and toss it in.

Chase wraps his arms around my middle and kisses below my ear. "You'll be okay, Liz."

"I don't know how to live in a world where my dad isn't. What am I if I'm not a daddy's girl? And I barely have my mom. She's physically here, but she hasn't been mentally for a long time."

He tucks some hair behind my ear. "I know, baby. I know. But I'm here. And I get it."

Neither of us says more until we're sitting comfortably in the tub, my back pressed against Chase's chest.

"It's just...it feels like I shouldn't be leaning on you too much. I mean, I feel like it's very boyfriend/girlfriend. And we have so much other stuff going on that makes it seem that way that I just, I don't know. I like how things are, and I don't want to push you too far." Or lose what it is that we have, whatever that may be.

"Why do we have to label anything? Why can't we just enjoy each other's company? I know what I'm offering, Liz. If you'll remember, I also invited you to start leaving stuff here and to bring Cheshire. He's here now, which where the fuck is he? He better not be causing trouble."

"I'm sure he's fine. He's probably hiding somewhere." I raise one shoulder because he can't really get into too much trouble. I don't think.

"Anyway, Liz, this doesn't have to be some grand thing. We've established we don't hate each other, that we may like each other, and really love fucking, and enjoy each other's company. Is that not enough? Does it need to be more? Can I not also support you emotionally at what will assuredly be one of the worst times in your life without it being more?"

I swish my hand through the purple water. "I guess."

"Just relax. There's a lot coming down the pipe these next few weeks, Liz. It's going to be hard. You need support. You don't have your mom for that. But you have me, and you'll have Lydia. Have you called her yet?"

"No. I can't. I can't even say the words."

"Okay. We'll add it to the list then."

I groan at the mention of the list. The tickling of panic starts in my chest, but it's too far away to reach, too many other things burying it far beneath the surface. My head hangs forward, my hair draping into the water. Usually, I'm more careful, but not today.

Chase's hands close around my shoulders and start massaging the muscles that have been tight since that first phone call yesterday.

My tears take me by surprise as I thought I had a tighter lid on them, diving into 'do' mode versus 'feel' mode. Chase gives a squeeze to my shoulders and pulls me back against his chest as I shake with sobs.

Moving my hands to cover my face, Chase adjusts, pulling me up into his lap instead of between his legs, and turns me to my side. His arms wrap tightly around me as I rest my cheek against his chest, still hiding behind my palms.

When the water starts to chill, Chase stands, pulling me out with him and carrying me to the shower to rinse. He makes no move to put me down and I don't try, wrapping my arms around his neck.

Though in any other situation, one of us would be attacking the other and fucking under the shower stream, right now, I'm just enjoying the warmth of the water and Chase's embrace.

Setting me down, he wraps a towel around me, then himself, and scoops me back up. I'm thankful he's babying me a little. Normally, I wouldn't be, but today, today I'm more than okay with it.

It's not really something I'd expect from Chase. But after everything we've been through and everything that's been said, it doesn't really surprise me. He's always taken care of me; he's just stepping it up a notch.

After setting me on the bed and leaving a kiss on my head, I follow him with my gaze as he walks around the room, gathering clothes for us to wear. My routine outfit while here is a ratty t-shirt. I kind of prefer it to my own clothes at this point.

Pulling on a pair of gray sweatpants, which make me smirk the slightest bit, he walks over to the bed with a shirt. Standing in front of me, he raises an eyebrow at me, like I'm supposed to know what he wants.

"Arms up," he requests gently when I don't make a move.

"Chase, I can dress myself. I'm not a child, and I'm not depressed. I'm just really sad. But I can dress myself." I think. I'm actually not entirely sure I can move.

"Let me take care of you, Elizabeth."

"I am. But that doesn't have to mean getting me dressed."

"It's a damn t-shirt. Just put your arms up." Though his words are commanding, his tone is soft and gentle.

Sighing, I acquiesce. What's the harm?

As he lowers the shirt over my head and removes the towel, his fingers graze my breasts and warmth spirals through me, settling between my legs.

All I get is a quick kiss on the lips. I'm tempted to pull him against me, but I felt like I had to convince him in the kitchen, and I didn't like that.

"Lie down for a bit, Elizabeth."

"I'm not tired."

"It wasn't a request, Liz."

Grumbling to myself, I push up toward the pillows and lie down. "Happy now?"

"Elated." He climbs into the bed next to me and lies facing me, face propped on his hand.

I curl into him despite myself. Letting him take care of me is one thing, but I don't want him to know that I *need* him. Appreciating his help, letting him be here, is one thing.

From my vantage point of the top of my head resting just under his clavicle, I have an excellent view down his rippling muscles. His hips dip in at the top of his pants in that mouthwatering V that I've frequently thought about biting but have yet to do.

Chase is taking curls and twirling them in his fingers. Playing with my hair has become one of his favorite things to do, besides fucking, of course. I almost think he wanted to do it for a long time and held back. As things shifted between us, he started to do it every so often. When we said we didn't hate each other anymore, it became somewhat regular. Once we said we have feelings for each other, it's become almost constant.

"When does it stop hurting so much?"

He's quiet for so long, I'm not sure if he heard me. I know he can't be asleep because his hand is still moving in my hair.

I open my mouth to ask again when he hums.

"I'm not sure it ever really does. You just kind of learn how to deal with the pain. It becomes part of your daily life, part of you. Sometimes there are things that make it less, that dull it a bit more than other things. Certain days are better than others. But I'm not sure the pain ever really goes away. At least it hasn't for me yet."

We lie in bed together for what feels like hours. Maybe it is, as I feel like all concept of time has disappeared. All the minutes, hours, years with Dad feel so far behind me, distant memories. While years without him linger ahead of me.

I never got married, never had children. He won't be able to walk me down the aisle if it ever happens. I won't get to see him be the amazing grandparent I knew he would be.

He'll never get to see me move into the house. The one he loved almost as much as he loved me and Mom. He always said the next best thing to him living there was me.

At some point, Chase gets out of bed after leaving a long kiss on my temple. "I'm going to go make something to eat. Come down if you want; otherwise, I'll come get you when it's ready. Okay?"

I nod in response. I can't move from this spot.

The reality of what's going on between me and Chase is getting harder to deny. I'm well beyond just *liking* him. And while I almost can't admit it to myself, I fell for him a long time ago. All of this only helps solidify it. Dad had always wanted me to find somebody who treated me right, who took care of and prioritized me as he'd always done for Mom and then me. Dad always put me first, quickly followed by Mom, and then he put himself last. He said we were the two most important people in his entire universe, and if we were happy, so was he. That our happiness was enough for him.

The problem with all of this, my feelings for Chase, and his possible somewhat returned feelings for me, is that he doesn't want to get married. He doesn't want children.

Am I okay living this life forever? Or am I going to leave this comfort I've surrounded myself in hoping to find somebody else?

Before I can spend too much time dwelling on it, Cheshire jumps up on the bed with a meow and starts rubbing his head under my chin, purring loudly.

I can't help but smile.

"Well, there he is." Chase's deep voice sounds from the doorway.

"I knew he'd come out. New place for him, he's probably scared. But he always knows when I'm upset. It's like he can sense it."

"That's part of why I brought him. To help you through it. I made some food, come on down."

Giving Cheshire a scratch between the ears, I climb out of bed. He darts through the doorway ahead of me and down the stairs, skidding a bit as he turns the corner on the main floor.

"Is your cat possessed or something?"

"Nope, just excited. A lot more space to run around here. He's probably happy not to be so cooped up anymore."

Walking into the kitchen, I freeze as I take in what's in front of me. At the island, there are two plates of food and fresh coffee. Not that different from most mornings. But on the small table off to the side, that we sometimes eat at, is the pad I'd been using with a few different stacks laid out around it. Even from where I stand, just on the cusp of the room, I can see the page is filled.

Noticing my gaze, Chase rests a hand on my lower back. "Oh, I, uh, I hope it's okay, but I took the liberty of writing you a list. It's basically everything I had to do after my mom. There may be some things you don't need to do, but I figured it was best to be thorough."

Did he really *ask* if it was okay? Chase has never asked before.

"I, um. Yeah. It's uh. Thank you." I can barely put a sentence together. Honestly, I don't know what to say aside from thank you.

"I wasn't sure if you were going to be particular about doing it yourself so if you want, we can toss it. It's not a big deal so don't feel like you can't tell me."

Turning, I rest my hand on his forearm. "Chase, really. Thank you. It's a giant relief. A huge burden lifted off my shoulders. Not that I don't now have to *do* all those things, but I don't have to first figure out what those things are. It's incredibly helpful."

A wide smile spans his face. "I'm glad. Let's eat."

He takes a step away before I grab him and pull him back to me, flinging my arms around his neck as I push up on my toes and crash my mouth to his. He tenses for a second, taken off guard by my sudden assault on him, as it's usually the other way around. But when his body comes to life, his hands grab my ass before lifting me up as I wrap my legs around his waist.

Carrying me over to the island, he keeps his mouth moving against mine. Setting me in my chair, he pulls away, unwrapping my hands from behind his neck.

"I had a thought as well as to how we can get through the list." He slides into his seat next to me, picking up his fork to stab at his omelet.

"Oh, really? What's that?" With an eyebrow raised, I look over at him, coffee cup between my hands but not a bite of food taken. I'm still not sure if I can eat.

"You get an orgasm for every item you accomplish."

I nearly choke on a sip of coffee.

"Not a good incentive? Hm, I thought you'd jump at that."

"I, uh, I didn't say that. I was just surprised is all. Not quite what I was expecting." Not even a little. It does sound like an extremely enticing proposition, though.

"Really? That's interesting. I thought we knew each other better than that by now, Elizabeth." He bumps his shoulder into mine as he teases me.

"You sure you can keep up? That's a pretty long list of things to get through."

"I wouldn't have offered if I couldn't. Besides, they won't all be sex given."

I have to rub my thighs together as an ache settles in my clit. A smirk flashes across his face as he notes my reaction.

"I think those are some pretty lofty promises."

"I'm up for the challenge." His gaze rakes over my body.

"Alright. I'm game. What's first on the list?"

"Call Lydia."

My whole body crumples as my stomach plummets to the ground.

"I think it's the most important, Liz. There are probably a lot of other people who need to be called. Having somebody close to you to help, to maybe make some of those calls for you, it's a huge relief. You're dreading making this one call. Imagine having to make it one or two dozen times."

Taking in his words, I nod, understanding what he's trying to tell me. Lydia's been there for me through so much; I know she'll be understanding, supportive, and do anything and everything she can to help me. On some level, I think that's why I'm so hesitant to call her.

Mostly, it's because it makes it real. Voicing it, saying it aloud. Makes it all very, very real.

I can't believe it's only been one day. A little over twenty-four hours since my dad took his final breath. And I wasn't even there. It'd been weeks since I've even seen him.

The heavy weight of guilt settles over me and into every crevice of my body. It's not like I make the trip very often, seeing Mom is just too hard. Dad always understood that. But that doesn't alleviate the heaviness of not having seen him in weeks.

Falling into Chase didn't help. In fact, the last time he saw them was the last time I did. That was over a month ago.

His hand falls on my back and rubs big circles. "I know I promised an orgasm a task, but I want you to pace yourself. It's going to be a lot at once. The days are going to feel incredibly long and incredibly short at the same time. You'll have not enough time and far too much. When it gets to be too much, stop."

"It's already too much."

Putting his arm over my shoulders, he pulls me against him, kissing the top of my head. "I know, baby. Take your time. It only gets worse."

"Do you...do you have to go back to work tomorrow?" I feel ridiculous even asking him. Like some schoolgirl who needs her boyfriend around to feel comfortable.

Boyfriend. There's that word again. We never discussed what he said to Mom. It's probably better that we don't. I'm not sure I want to hear what he has to say.

"I don't. I took the day off."

Pulling away, I look up at him as his hand falls form my shoulder to my waist. "You did?"

"Absolutely, Liz. I told you, I'm here for you. I'm going to be here to support you and help you through this. It's not something I'd wish on my worst enemy, which happened to be you at some point, but definitely isn't anymore."

"Really? I was your worst enemy?" This makes my lips pull up a little.

"Of course. Wasn't I yours?"

"I suppose. Sometimes you still are." Leaning to the side, I bump my shoulder into him.

"I'll stop feeding you if you're going to be mean."

"Oh, come on. Let me have a little fun. Besides, I'm not really that hungry anyway."

"You need to eat, Elizabeth. At least a little."

When I do nothing, he stares at me with a cocked eyebrow.

"I meant now."

"Ugh, fine." I shovel down a few bites of food. "Happy?"

"Over the moon." He sighs as he shakes his head and takes a few angry bites of his own meal.

While our day-to-day back-and-forth has lost the scathing edge it used to have, we still have a need to dig our heels in. I'm not sure how long we have on this ride, but I have a feeling this is going to stick around. Not that I'm complaining; it keeps things fun, even if it's frustrating at times.

Chase clears the plates and shoos me over to the couch to make my phone call. I keep my phone between my hands, which rest in my lap. I can't seem to take a deep enough breath to prepare myself. It's a phone call, to my best friend of twenty years, but I can't even open my phone.

Flopping next to me, Chase puts his feet up on the coffee table, stretching one arm across the back of the couch behind me while the other runs along his mouth.

"Elizabeth. You have to call. It's the first step. I'm right here. You'll be okay."

Nodding, I try to fill my lungs with a shaky breath, looking up at the ceiling to stave off the tears threatening to fall. A quick nod of my head and I'm ready.

Chapter 28

"Liz! Hi, honey, how are you?" Lydia always has a sweet name for me. Honey, sugar, babe. It's just part of how she is and one thing I adore about her.

"Lyd." My tone is severe. And rarely do I not just jump into whatever the reason is for why I'm calling. We don't need pleasantries anymore.

"Oh no. What's wrong?"

"Lyd, I. My. Hm." I don't know how to get the words out. I nearly jump out of my seat when Chase's hand squeezes around my shoulder. Somehow, I've forgotten he's right next to me.

"Just get it out, Liz. It's the only way." His voice is low enough that only I can hear him.

"Lyd...my dad passed away. Yesterday morning."

"Oh, honey. Oh, I'm so sorry. What can I do? Tell me what you need. Should I come over? I can ditch this popsicle stand in ten minutes and bring the biggest coffees and tubs of ice cream to your apartment." In true Lydia fashion, she dives right into the crisis.

"No, no, that's okay. I'm with Chase." I turn to look at him as I say his name, receiving a light smile and back rub in return.

"Oh, of course. Duh, Lydia. I don't know why I didn't think of that. I guess I still think of him as you used to. Okay, so what can I do? Please let me do something, anything."

Standing, I walk away. There's too much rolling around in me that I need to be on the move. It's a million emotions, sadness, anxiety, nervous energy, I just need to give it a place to go.

"Actually, if you could contact people for me? Friends, other family. You know Uncle Gene like he's your own uncle. I'm sure he'd love to hear from you. And the cousins. I actually think you talk to Pearl more than I do." Lydia's been around so long she knows my entire family, distant cousins and all.

As kids, we spent so much time together that we practically lived at one another's houses, but she came from a very tiny family and used mine as a surrogate.

"Of course, sweetie. I'll set up a whole call tree and make sure we get the family. I'm assuming work is handled?"

"Yeah, work is handled. If they didn't see my breakdown at the office, then I'm sure Chase either already handled it or will." Turning back to Chase, he nods resolutely. I haven't even had a chance to think about my breakdown and Chase comforting me. That show of affection in the middle of the office surely didn't go unnoticed and was far more than just a coworker comforting a coworker.

"Alright, anything else I can do? I know Chase is there, but if you need anything, if you want me to send food or alcohol or anything, let me know. Oh! Cheshire. Do you need me to check in on him for you?"

"Uh, no, actually. Chase brought him here."

Silence meets me, and I have to look at the phone to make sure we're still connected.

"Lyd?"

"I'm sorry. I just...I'm shocked. You better hang on to that, Lizzie."

Heat rushes my face as I look away, staring at my foot on the rung of the barstool in the kitchen. I have to lower my voice so Chase doesn't hear as much. "It's not like that, Lyd. You know that."

"I don't know, Liz. You say that, but you're always together. When was the last time we saw each other? You're always with him, you practically live with him. Hell, he asked you to bring clothes over. And now your pesky feline lives there?"

"One, he's not pesky. He's...spirited. Two, he doesn't *live* here. He's here for emotional support. It's temporary." My voice drops another octave. "It's all temporary."

"Alright, Liz, if that's really what you want to believe. But excuse me if I don't agree with you. Maybe you can't see it right now, but there's more going on there."

I can't think about any of this right now. "Time will tell."

"You let me know if there's anything else I can do for you. And I want to see you so I can give you a big hug. Keep me posted on all the dates and things. I'll update you on the call tree, but I'll make sure everybody is reached. I have a pretty solid idea of everybody who would need or want to know, but send me a message if there's anybody who I maybe wouldn't think of."

"I think just family and the few friends we still chat with is plenty. And they'll likely do the rest. There's the family in Nebraska we haven't spoken to in years, but I think Pearl is in touch with them."

"Okay, sweetie. Let me know what else I can do. And let that man take care of you. I love you."

"I love you too, Lyd. Thanks."

Clicking the line dead, I hold my forehead in my hand as I exhale a heavy breath.

"You okay?"

Nodding and turning to him, tight-lipped, I walk over to the table where the list is and cross off the first thing.

"You want your prize?" I can tell by his tone he thinks that I don't actually want it. And he's right. This whole process is utterly exhausting.

"No. Not right now. It's a nice idea, but I have a feeling I won't want to cash in."

Wrapping an arm around my waist as he appears behind me, he nuzzles his nose into the slope of my neck. "That's the point, Liz. It will make you feel better, even if just for a few minutes."

"I know. I'm just not into it right now." Getting my brain to work with my body is something I don't think I'm capable of at the moment.

"You let me know if you change your mind."

"I will. What's next?" While I'm rolling, I'd rather just keep going with it, get as much over and done with as possible. If I'm already in this world of hurt and pain, I'd rather just stay in misery a little while longer.

"Well, we can call my attorney together. The funeral information is hard. Did your dad have a will or anything? Any directives of what he wants?"

"Oh, I'm not sure. I probably should know that, right?" That seems like the sort of thing a daughter should know, especially after his heart attack, but I always refused to talk about it, not wanting to face this. Now I realize I should have at least had some idea, especially with Mom's memory loss.

"Not really. My mom had planned it all out and had extensive conversations with both myself and Justin. But she knew it was coming. Did your dad do anything after his heart attack? Considering your mom's condition." Sometimes I'm convinced Chase can read my mind.

"Uh, I want to say yes, but I really don't know. We talked about it briefly, but no specifics."

"Maybe Whispering Pines knows something."

"Yeah, I'll have to call them, I guess."

"That might be a good first step. They may have some more information. You trust them, right?" It's not the worst question to ask. There are so many issues with retirement and care facilities on a regular basis that making sure my parents are in a place I trust is a worthwhile question.

"Yeah. I mean, I think they'd be crazy to mess with a lawyer's parents. I know things happen anywhere and everywhere, but they've always been good to my parents and me."

"I think that's where to go from here. You'll need a lot of the information to start doing the rest. Would your dad want any sort of religious affiliation?" The fact that Chase knows all the questions to ask, the process to go through, makes my heart ache even more, but for him. He's had to do this before, and was mostly alone, save for his brother.

"No. That I can be sure of. But I'll have to host a wake or something, right? For people to give their respects?" So many people are going to want to come. My parents are beloved in their facility and were in their neighborhood before they moved. There are still people in town who ask about them should I ever run into them. Not to mention, all the family that will surely come to town for the funeral.

"I mean, you don't *have* to do anything. But yes, that's customary."

"Ugh, my apartment is too small to host a lot of people. Maybe if I hire somebody, I can get the house ready. But it's the opposite direction from them. I'll have to find a place." Just another thing to add to the list.

"Elizabeth. You are welcome to host that here." He puts a little emphasis on the word 'here' and shock crawls through my brain at the suggestion.

"Here? I thought you didn't like people in your house." Anybody. Sometimes I'm still surprised he lets me in his house.

"I don't."

"Then why—"

"This is obviously an extenuating circumstance. And it's for you."

Looking up, I meet his eyes. He hasn't released his hold on me, and I haven't moved away. All these things he does for me, it's making me fall harder and harder. Which is difficult, because I know that's never going to be reciprocated.

I stuff it down; I can't deal with that reality right now. I have too much going on to think about an end to something that probably never should have started. An ending that will surely break my heart.

"You okay? You have this far off look in your eyes." A hand waves in front of my face, and I know he's trying to get my attention back.

"Huh? Oh, yeah, just a lot, you know."

"I do, and that's not the look on your face right now. What's going on?" Dammit. Why does he have to know me so well? It's part of what makes me feel more for him. He pays attention to me and learns things about me constantly. It's not just a quick fuck and a nap anymore.

"Nothing. I don't want to talk about it right now."

"Is it nothing, or do you not want to talk about it?" And of course, he caught that quick change.

"I don't want to talk about it." Now or ever if at all possible.

He narrows his eyes at me, but he doesn't press. That's something Chase doesn't do often. He doesn't press me. Not if he knows I've put my foot down, and he can likely tell this is a situation that's just that.

I'm already wallowing in self-misery, I don't need to add to it by telling Chase that I'm pretty sure I'm falling in love with him, if I haven't already fallen, and for him to tell me that he doesn't feel the same way.

I wouldn't be able to handle my heart breaking twice in one day. So instead, I'll just keep it to myself...for now.

Chapter 29

S omehow, over the course of the week, I manage to get everything crossed off my list, many with Chase's help and even Lydia's. I wouldn't be able to stand today without the two of them supporting me, both literally and figuratively.

Lydia had her arm hooked through mine while Chase had his arm around my waist while I leaned into him as we stood at my father's gravesite. The way he held me was protective and possessive. The whole firm showed up, and if anybody had questions about our relationship after my meltdown, they certainly don't anymore. Thankfully, interoffice relations aren't exactly against company policy, and we just need to fill out a form.

They may not know the intricacies of it, hell, even I don't know what to call it, but they certainly know we're together in some capacity.

Chase hasn't left my side since people arrived. The whole day, really. He's basically been my shadow. If I move, he follows. His hand on my back is the only thing holding me together right now.

"How are you, Liz?" his deep voice rumbles low in my ear. I keep the fake smile plastered on my face while more people come through, everyone giving a quick handshake and condolences before grabbing some of the catered food and drinks.

"Fine." It comes out a huff.

"Don't lie to me, Liz. It doesn't benefit you."

"What does it matter? What can I do? I have to be here." Right here, in this spot I basically haven't moved from in over an hour. Lydia's tried to get me to eat, bringing food repeatedly, but I just can't, leaving plates filled on the counter behind me.

"Take a few minutes. Go take a short nap, go lock yourself in the office for a bit. Go scream in the woods. If you need a break, take a break."

"What about all the people?" Technically, though I'm the one grieving the most, I'm also the one entertaining.

"Look around. Everybody's fine. And if somebody comes looking for you, I can handle it."

I turn to him with wide eyes. "You'd stay?"

"You want me to come with you?" One of his brows arches, but I'm not sure why he's confused by that. He's been my rock for the past week.

I start chewing the corner of my lip. Maybe I shouldn't? But yes, I definitely want him to come with me.

"Yeah?"

"Okay, baby. If that's what you want." He tucks a curl behind my ear as his gaze roams my face. These tender moments make my heart race and my mouth run arid. "I'm sure Lydia can handle things. If you're comfortable with that?"

I nod while I take a big swallow. It hurts around the lump building in my throat. The one I've been able to keep down for the better part of today. At the funeral, I was nothing but stoic, but if I started crying, I wouldn't have stopped all day long.

Standing on my toes, hand resting on Chase's forearm, I try to search through the throng to find Lydia.

But she appears in front of me as if summoned.

"Hey, sweetie. How you holding up?" She runs her hand up and down my bicep. The reintroduction between her and Chase held less fanfare than I was worried about. She's known him for years, having met him at some event or another hosted by the firm where I brought her with me. But I was worried she wouldn't be able to contain herself now that we're...whatever we are. Thankfully, she did.

"Um, I'm alright. Actually, I could kind of use a break. Any chance you could—"

"Say no more. I got this. You disappear for a bit. I'll handle everything." Taking my shoulders, she turns me around and practically pushes me away.

"Thanks, Lyd."

"Go, go. Shoo." She waves her hands at me as she takes my place. Most people are milling about, talking, eating. I'm sure things will be fine without me.

"Come on, Liz." Chase's hand is on my lower back, pulling me from the spot I've been stationed at and off toward the hallway away from the kitchen.

I let him lead me into the office, shutting and locking the door behind us. Once the lock is flipped, I collapse against him. My head rests against his shoulder, my hands balled between our chests.

Encircling me in his arms, he squeezes tight. "This is the hardest day, Liz. Tomorrow, we'll lounge all day. I'll let you sleep as late as you want."

I lean back in his arms to meet his eyes. "Really? As late as I want?"

"Really."

He never lets me sleep past eight. "Will I wake up alone, though?" That would be a terrible feeling. I don't typically mind, but I need his comfort more than anything else. Cheshire has taken to sleeping curled up at the foot of the bed, sometimes on Chase's feet. But I don't need Cheshire as much as I do Chase.

"Not if you don't want to." The green of his irises is soft and gentle as he cups my cheek.

"What will you do while I sleep?"

"I'm fairly confident I can get my workout and a shower in at five and have you still be asleep when I'm done, since I do that just about every other morning. But I'm pretty resourceful."

Removing an arm from behind my back, tightening his grip with the other, he gestures to the shelves around us. "I do like to read from time to time, Liz."

Nodding, I lean back into him as I twist my fingers into his shirt. I'd been momentarily distracted by promises of sleeping in, but now that that's resolved, the burn returns behind my eyes.

A sob rattles my body before a single tear falls, but once it does, there's no stopping the torrent.

Shuffling me backward, Chase keeps his arms around me and turns us around as he sits in the chair he bought me, pulling me down in his lap.

We sit in silence as the tears flow. When I can finally take a steady breath, I fill my lungs slowly and release, trying to calm myself and put myself back together to see people.

Pushing myself up from Chase's chest, I find two large wet marks with black smudged in, the corner of my mouth tugging down.

He hands me the tissue box and I start to clean my face as I continue to take in the damage.

"I ruined your shirt."

"Why do you care so much about that? I don't. It's just a shirt, Elizabeth. I have plenty more and can replace it easily. Please stop worrying about crying in front of me, about letting me comfort you, about my damn shirts."

Looking down at the balled-up tissues between my hands, I nod.

Taking my chin in his hand, Chase tilts my face to his. "I only care about you right now. You can ruin every shirt I own if you need to. They're not important, they don't matter. Understand?"

I nod again, unable to form words.

"You ready to go back out yet?"

I take a deep breath, filling my lungs to capacity, and hold it. I hold it until they burn and feel like they're going to burst before releasing it slowly out of my mouth. "Yes."

As we stand, Chase pulls me to his chest, cupping my face and closing his mouth over mine. It takes me by surprise, and I remain stiff for a moment before melting against him.

His tongue gliding across mine, hand sliding to my hip, I forget all about the people outside, the pain in my heart, the emptiness in my soul. But the second Chase pulls away, it all comes slamming back into me, and my whole body aches like I got hit by a bus.

I almost wish I had been. Maybe it would hurt less.

"Come on. Not too much longer and then we'll be alone."

"Thank you for my chair. I appreciate it. Really." Though it's been over a week, the time to mention it hasn't come up, but now feels as good as any.

"You're welcome. I had a feeling you'd like it."

"I do. I really do."

With a squeeze of my hand, he leads me back to the open space of the living room and kitchen.

"You okay now?" Lydia takes my hands in hers when we get back to her.

I nod without being able to talk, the lump back in its home.

"Okay. I'll go circle. But it seems like some people are starting to leave or at least thinking about it. Almost over, sweetie." With a tight smile, she walks back into the group.

"You haven't eaten yet today, have you?"

He knows the answer, since he didn't *really* ask, but I answer anyway. "No."

Reaching behind us, he grabs a plate of fruit and shoves it into my hands. "I want to see an empty plate, Elizabeth." Bossy Chase is in the building and telling me to eat. I know better than to defy him, but I'm just not hungry. "You're going to eat, because you need to. I know you don't feel hungry, but you are. Please, Liz. For me."

He's never asked me to do anything for him before. He's demanded sure, but not like this. This is practically pleading, and I can tell by his expression that he's overly concerned about me.

Slowly, I nibble at the cantaloupe. The second it hits my stomach, a rumble roars through me. I'm utterly starving and end up devouring the rest of the plate and then another of crackers that he hands me.

"Feel better now?"

"My stomach isn't trying to eat itself if that's what you mean."

Before he can answer, a large group comes up to say their goodbyes, quickly followed by another, and then half the office. I'm shocked they all took so much time off today. That's one thing I do appreciate about where I work; we're a solid team and there for each other in times of crisis.

It's not long until there are just a few stragglers left who realize they're the last ones and quickly say their goodbyes and give their final condolences as well.

By four o'clock, the house is cleared of everyone except Lydia, Chase, and me.

"Can I help you guys clean up?" Lydia looks between us and the thought of having to now take care of this mess has my shoulders slumping.

"Thank you for the offer, but I scheduled my cleaning lady to make an extra trip. She'll be here around six." I silently thank him by squeezing his hand. I know he won't let me touch a single thing and while he'll throw away much of the garbage, he'll leave a lot of it for Greta to take care of.

"Alright, well, then I guess I'll get out of your hair if you don't need anything. Make sure she eats please." I roll my eyes at Lydia acting like Mom. She's always done that, always looked out for me.

"Already on it."

"Thank you for being here, Lyd. Really, it means so much to me."

"Like I'd be anywhere else." She wraps me in a tight hug and sways me from side to side. "I'm just a call away if you need anything."

"I know."

When she lets me go, she turns to leave, her coat flung over her arm. But she looks back at us and wags a finger between Chase and me. "You know, you two would make some gorgeous blonde-haired babies."

Despite the wide eyes I shoot in her direction, she smiles and wiggles her fingers as she leaves.

Once she's shut the door, I turn to Chase, a hand on his forearm. "I'm so sorry about her. At no point have I even insinuated that we're dating or a couple or anything more than what we are. In fact, I've been very adamant about the opposite."

"It's fine, Liz." He practically laughs the words out, and I'm not sure if it's at what I said, how frantically I said it, or at the thought itself.

But the fact that he says it's fine and doesn't press or go against her is a little unsettling. That's not typical Chase, and I know it's not something he wants, so why isn't he jumping on it and stating that fact?

Instead of dwelling on it and giving it a thought that I don't really have the mental capacity for, I let him lead me up the stairs, very much looking forward to a long night of sleep.

Chapter 30

The next morning is exactly what Chase promised it would be, but I can't sleep later than eight-thirty. Despite being awake, I can't bring myself to get out of bed.

With a raised eyebrow, Chase looks down at me from where he's sitting up, leaning against the headboard, his perfectly chiseled chest taut as I snuggle further into the bed.

He doesn't make a sound as he turns back to his book, and I roll toward the window. It's a bright, sunny day, but that doesn't feel right, it shouldn't be possible. How can the world be so bright when inside I'm so dark?

The whole world should be dark, having lost one of the brightest lights.

"Liz, it gets easier. I'm here for you, lean on me."

It's impossible to turn toward him, even when my eyes spill over. Chase closes his hand over mine where they lay clasped on the blanket at my chest. It's one of the first mornings I've woken up clothed. In some ways, it feels wrong, but in so many, it feels right.

Giving myself over to Chase now, letting him into this lowest part of my life, will only enhance my already strong feelings.

Regardless, I shift closer to him as he lies down next to me, rolling to face him and letting him pull me against his chest.

The tenderness he exudes as he kisses along my shoulder, linking his fingers through mine at my stomach, sends warmth sprawling through my otherwise cold and numb body. There's no urgency behind them, no need or desire to do anything besides kiss me, heal me.

But he can't, nobody can. I know he knows that, and I appreciate his effort, but it's causing the war within me to increase.

The feelings I have are growing stronger every day, and I know I'm in love with him. Despite how hard I tried not to fall, how hard I tried to hold on to even the tiniest thread of hatred for him, I couldn't. All my strings have been severed, being retied in a new shape and forming something far more intense than the loathing.

Part of me wants to tell him to see what he does, how he handles it. Will he not care and keep me around anyway because he enjoys the sex that much? Or will he push me away because it's more than he wants to take on?

It's why I can't tell him.

In the grand scheme of things, of life, that barely matters with what else I have going on right now, but it's easier to think about that, the potential of what will happen, than the ache and pain in my heart.

The loss of Chase will hurt, but nothing could ever hurt as much as losing Dad. As much as I hate to admit it, even losing Mom won't hurt this badly. Part of that is probably because I've slowly been losing her for years, so I've had time to become accustomed to the idea, to mourn things, mourn her. But Dad was ripped from this earth in one swift movement.

The coroner said it was a heart attack. Not that I had any other thoughts. His heart had already tried to fail once; I knew in the end it would be what took him away from me.

While I don't know what Chase and Dad talked about during the visit we had, I do know that Chase is the kind of guy Dad would have wanted me to end up with. Everything Dad always talked about wanting for me in a man is what Chase represents. The bedroom aspects are for me and me alone, but he takes care of me, protects me, is possessive over me. I'm his and his only. While he's never said the words explicitly, it's clear with some of his body movements and the way he holds me around other people.

He has a good job which he loves and makes good money at. Not that I need somebody to take care of me financially, but Chase could. And from what I've learned of him in our time together, he would.

It's a shame the last man Dad saw me with was Chase, somebody who doesn't want a wife and kids, the things Dad wanted for me.

That and moving into the house. The thought seems impossible now with Dad gone. How do I move into the house he so desperately wanted and not only never got to live in, but never got to see me live in? I can't let somebody else be there either. There's no right choice, except for the fact that deep down, I know it has to be me.

"If I make breakfast, will you eat?" Chase has a way of pulling me from the darkest depths of my mind.

"Maybe."

"Let me rephrase. I'm going to make some food, and you're going to come down and eat something."

I'm still tucked into Chase's chest and buried under the covers. No part of me wants to leave this safe haven I've found myself in. But I know he's going to get up, and I know that if I don't join him soon, he'll come up here and carry me downstairs.

"Fine."

With a lasting kiss on the top of my head, he climbs out of bed and leaves me alone with my thoughts again.

That's not a safe thing for me right now. There are too many thoughts whirling around, sad and scary. I can't be alone.

So, with a stretch that makes my body scream in pain from being curled and tense and tight, I get out of bed and follow Chase downstairs.

He doesn't seem surprised to see me climbing onto what's become my barstool and slides a cup of coffee across to me.

"I meant what I said yesterday, Liz. You may not have slept in, but we're just relaxing today. Reading, a bath, a shower, a nap. Whatever you want for the day, we'll do."

As I take a sip of the scalding liquid, barely feeling it as it surely burns its way down my throat, I nod.

I wonder if he'd let me just get lost in his body all day or help me get lost. Past experience tells me he would, but this situation is different. This is one where I need to feel the feelings and they won't be gone once the euphoria is over.

"What if I want to spend all day in bed?"

"Then we spend all day in bed."

"Naked?" It's a challenge, and there's some snark to my tone that isn't necessary, but I can't help it. "Whatever you want, Liz." His voice is gentle and he's trying to be soothing. I'm taking my feelings out on him in anger, and it's not fair because none of this is his fault, and he's been nothing but understanding.

We eat our omelets in silence, but he keeps his hand on my thigh the entire time. He's being patient with me, and I appreciate it.

Once we get back upstairs, I strip my shirt and panties off and climb into bed. I'm too exhausted to really make a move but hope Chase will once the clothes are off.

But he scoots under the covers with his pants on.

"Um, excuse me. No clothes party. You agreed." I push up to sit, the sheet draped over my chest.

"You didn't make it clear that was your expectation. But okay."

"Well, it is." The snark is next level, something I haven't heard out of my mouth since Chase and I were hating each other almost a year ago.

Which explains why as he gets back on the bed, naked and utterly delicious, he grabs my hair and yanks it back so I'm looking up at him. "Watch your tone, Liz. I've been nothing but sweet and patient with you, but I can be back to my asshole self if that's what you want."

"It is. Right now, it definitely is."

Without another word, he licks up my neck, biting just below my ear and throwing me backward so my shoulders hit the pillow. His hands rest by my shoulders as he moves over me, his knees on either side of my hips as his cock hardens between us.

I need him to take control of me, to do whatever he wants with me, because it means I don't have to think. I can lose myself in the sensations of his body and the bliss he brings me.

He takes both of my wrists in one of his hands and his muscles tense as he holds them firmly against the mattress, far above my head.

His other hand glides down my body, stopping to give my breast a squeeze and my nipple a twirl of his finger.

"Do you want me to touch you, Liz?"

"Yes." It comes out utterly breathless because just the mere thought has me soaking.

"Where?"

"Everywhere." Anywhere. As long as he touches me.

"No, no. Be more specific. Tell me what you want."

"I want whatever you want." I don't want to think. I don't want to have to tell him. I know this is for me, to make me feel good, but what he doesn't realize yet is that it *all* feels incredible, and he can do whatever he wants with me right now. I'm a ragdoll he can toss around and fulfill his wildest fantasies with.

"Well, in that case..." He kisses down my body and settles between my thighs. One lick up my pussy and I'm already a goner. He keeps my wrists against the mattress as his tongue circles my clit a few times before spearing into me.

My back arches, and I wriggle my hands, trying to get them free so I can twist them into his hair, but it only makes him hold tighter as his lips curl around my clit and he sucks hard. His tongue moves quickly and firmly, and when he slides two fingers into me and starts stroking immediately, I'm undone. I wrap my legs around his shoulders, keeping him close to me while I tighten against his fingers and come on his tongue.

As he moves his body over mine, he eases into me, taking it excruciatingly slow. My legs are still around him, having slid down to his waist, but when he starts thrusting fast, I let them fall apart so he can move deeper and harder.

He groans at the change just as I whine, and his free hand wraps around my hip, pressing it into the bed.

Before long, he pulls out, letting my now sore wrists go and flipping me around so I'm on my stomach. He hikes my ass into the air and pulls my stomach up so I'm resting on my hands.

With one large thrust, he's all the way inside me, and my head tips back with a long, loud moan. One of his hands holds my waist while the other grips the top of the bedframe. He uses it as leverage as he thrusts into me with abandon, the bed creaking and groaning with each and every movement.

The sounds are mixing with his skin slapping against mine and every whine that flies from my lips with every slam into me. My curls are swaying around me and over my shoulders.

The whole experience is helping my mind go hazy, and I can't focus on anything except the amazing feel of Chase inside me and the way he's grunting as he fucks me so hard it almost hurts.

He pistons into me with such force, it's almost like he's trying to punish me with his cock, but he can't possibly because it feels absolutely incredible. My legs and arms tremble with my impending orgasm, and as Chase grips tighter around my hip and pounds into me, I come hard on his cock.

But thankfully, he's not done yet, pulling out of me while I'm still coming down from the haze of an orgasm. He moves below me, sitting with his back against the headboard, and lowers me down on top of him.

His hands slide up and down my sides, his thumbs twirling along my nipples, before settling around my waist as he rocks me forward and back. Then he adds lifting me every few movements. It's not until we have a good momentum going, me practically putty in his grasp, my fingers barely grasping onto his shoulders, that he holds me above him and thrusts up into me.

My head tips back with a moan, and he licks up along my neck, biting the tract of skin from my neck to shoulder. He nibbles my earlobe as he groans something about how amazing it feels.

His words barely register; nothing is registering but the fullness of his cock in my pussy, the way he glides in and out so smoothly yet forcefully. My mind is hazy, a swirling nothingness of pleasure and ecstasy.

I'm practically exhausted from the physical drain on top of the mental and emotional stress I've had over the past several days that the pressure builds and crests in a matter of seconds as I tighten around his perfect cock and whine loudly as I come. He groans and slams his head back against the headboard as he joins me in bliss.

His chest heaves as I collapse against him and he wraps his arms around me, hugging me tightly to him.

My eyes are barely open as I shift with his deep breaths, our skin slick, and I slide the slightest bit with every breath.

Kisses pepper along the top of my head and he brushes away my curls, pulling the long strands off my back and separating them from the moisture.

As the post-orgasmic feeling starts to dissipate, reality and pain settle back into my bones.

Dad's gone.

For a very brief moment, I was able to forget about the ache in my chest, the one that's been created from the gaping hole of him being ripped from my life.

I turn my face into Chase's chest, and he wraps his arms around me, squeezing tight. It's like he understands what the sentiment is all about and why I'm suddenly in this turmoil again.

"Bath time." He shifts from where we're sitting and throws his legs off the edge of the bed, putting his arms underneath me and walking into the bathroom. One arm stays around me as he turns the water on and tosses the top bath bomb into the water.

"Are you starting to like those?"

"Not a chance, but you do, and I know it soothes you. That's what you need right now, Liz. Soothing. Mental, physical, emotional, sexual. Whatever I can give you and do for you, I'm going to."

I'm not sure if it's the emotional state I'm in, where everything hurts and I'm looking for a salve, something to put over the pain to make it stop, or if it's just how Chase is, but through all of this, I find myself falling further in love with him.

To a point where I'm going to sink into such a deepness that I won't be able to find my way out.

Chapter 31

Somehow, I manage to take another two weeks off. I'm not really sure how exactly, and the days pass by in the blink of an eye.

We have a routine. Chase wakes up and leaves at his normal hour, barely waking me in the process, and I sleep until I can't anymore. At that time, I make my way downstairs to brew some coffee, have something to eat, and feed Cheshire.

Chase has been running the case without me, taking it in front of the judge and everything. Yet I can't seem to get myself to care. The promotion I've been gunning for is on the line, but none of it seems to matter anymore.

Why did it ever even matter in the first place? I'm not sure I can say.

After Chase gets home at night when I've filled my time doing random things like reading or watching mind-numbing television, he'll make dinner for us and then we'll find a time and place to fuck.

Thankfully, it hasn't lost its magical ability to take me away from the pain in my soul, even if just for a little while. I'm able to be transported to a place where nothing matters but me and Chase and our bodies coming together. But it's always over far too quickly.

On the weekends, Chase will indulge me, and we'll spend the whole time in bed, naked. Not that he's complaining, as it's probably his favorite thing to do too.

I know I have to go back to work, back to the life I've built. But I just can't seem to find my focus, my drive anymore. Part of me is sure that it died with Dad, and the farmhouse looks more and more appealing every day. The only loose end is Chase.

I'm in love with him, enough that I'd stay here and probably go back to a job I no longer love and no longer want to be the only part of my life that matters, just so I can continue to be closer to him.

One of the afternoons near the end of my stint at home, Chase comes in early. "We won."

"What?"

"We won! The case, it's over. We won." He scoops me in his arms and spins me around. "Everything she asked for, Liz. Everything. She got it all. Even the custody."

In the end, Colleen had chosen to go for sole custody of her kids, claiming that their father would be too busy with his new girlfriend and career to give them the proper attention they need.

"Congratulations, Chase. I knew you could do it."

"*We* did it. It was a joint effort, Elizabeth. You may not have been there at the end, but everything at the beginning and keeping Colleen's faith in us, that was all you."

I should feel proud, happy, excited, anything. But there's nothing.

The change in his face lets me know that he reads me, my lack of enthusiasm. One corner of his mouth tips down, and he pulls me into his chest, kissing the top of my head. He's been incredibly patient with me and my horrible mood.

"You won't feel like this forever. I promise. Today is a good day for us. Try to let it sink in." For us. I know he just means in a job sense, that he means our careers took a good move today, but it just makes my heart hurt because he doesn't mean us as a couple.

"Nothing is the same anymore." He doesn't have to know that I mean between us as well.

"I know, baby. It gets better." A hand runs down my curls as he keeps me locked against his body. Sometimes I find it hard to imagine that Chase *doesn't* love me with the way he treats me, but then I know better.

"I just don't see how. Everything makes me think of him, of what I've lost with him. There are things for my future that I want, and he won't ever get to see them."

"I know you wanted him to see you in the house, but he knows you planned to move in, right? So that was a big part of it for him, even if he never actually got to witness it. He knows you, Elizabeth, so he knows you were going to make good on your word to move in and love that home like you would have wanted him to." Instead of correcting him and letting him know about my other wants, I keep my mouth shut.

It's stupid of me, and childish and cowardly. But I can't bear for him to leave me right now. And knowing that I want more than he'll ever give me will be a surefire end to this immediately.

Him letting me go right now, both physically and emotionally, would destroy the fibers of being I have left.

"Think you can hold yourself together to go out to dinner?"

Though I'm truly unsure, I can't let him know that and need to show some happiness for him because this is a big day. It was a huge case, and he deserved to win. And while I'm hurting, I can feel the tingling of pride deep down inside, wanting to break free.

"Of course. We need to celebrate your big win."

"*Our* big win, Elizabeth. This wasn't solo." The only reason he's giving me credit is because of our relationship, whatever strange sort of one it may be. Old Chase never would have given a lick of it if I'd missed a few days of work or the trial itself. But this Chase, he wants me to see the positives, especially now when I'm so down.

"You're right. So yes, let's celebrate." While it's one of the last things I feel like doing, I can put on a happy face for Chase. And pretend that it is in fact our win when it really only feels like his.

And somehow, I'm okay with that. I never thought I would be okay giving Chase credit for anything, but he deserves it.

It takes me no time at all to change with Chase helping me pick my outfit, his favorite jeans and a low-cut top. While I haven't technically brought clothes here, I have a few things that have taken up residence since I wear them frequently and every now and again need *something* other than Chase's clothes.

They weren't my choice to get. Chase swung by one day after work and collected a few things, mostly his favorites. I was fine not changing out of his shirts and pants for, well, the foreseeable future. But he felt it was important for me to have a few articles of my own clothing, that it would help me feel more like myself.

But what he doesn't understand is that his clothes have become just as much a part of me and myself as my own.

Chase looks over at me repeatedly as we drive toward Gianni's, a local Italian restaurant we like. It's probably because I'm not saying anything and though his hand is over mine, my gaze stays stuck out the window. It's strange how trees full of leaves can look so glum. There are no vibrant colors as they start to change. The cars that whizz past are surely full of others who are going on with their lives, but I don't understand how they can be when everything else has stood still because of the greatest loss I've ever known. The world has experienced a great loss too. How can they not be aware and carry on like nothing has happened?

A warm softness against the back of my hand draws my attention as Chase lowers my hand from his mouth.

"I know you're hurting still, Liz. That's okay and expected. But trust me when I tell you, it gets better and that I'm here for you. Lean on me. Don't be afraid to."

"I'm not. I just don't know how you can help. It all feels so...personal and internal. They're my thoughts and feelings and they're just dark and sad right now. I'm not sure how you can help with that besides being here, which I know you are." Not just because he tells me, but he shows me regularly.

"How about after dinner, we go home and take a bath?" It makes my heart flutter every time Chase refers to his house as *home* in reference to both of us. I guess for now it is.

"We've been taking a lot of baths lately."

"Yeah, you like them, and they soothe you. It's something I'm willing to do for you." He runs his fingers along his mouth. "Besides, I get to have you naked and slick and sitting between my legs while I fondle you until I'm ready to plunge inside."

I swing a hand out to smack against his chest, but a light laugh settles in my own.

"There she is." A wide smile sits on Chase's face. Probably because it's the first time I've laughed since Dad died. "Slowly but surely, Liz. We'll get through this."

Though I nod, I look back toward the window, because dread has settled in my stomach. I'm not sure anything can get me through this, and even if he does, I'm going to have to face my real feelings for him, facing the repercussions head on.

Chapter 32

I t took me a total of three weeks at Chase's, but I managed to make it back to work. The chaos that had been part of my daily routine before Dad died has quieted down tremendously.

My caseload wasn't too strenuous before and those clients were beyond understanding and able to wait until my return.

I spend most of my day making phone calls to check in and get things back on track to hopefully finalize some of the divorces I have pending and adjust a custody that has been requested in my absence.

Chase spends a fair amount of time checking in on me. It's always something random; a quick pop in to say hi, bringing me coffee, handing me a paper. Things he'd never normally do, but I know he's concerned about me.

It's not until after lunch—which Chase and I eat together—that the day takes a turn.

Mister Lions calls us into his office, and the second we're sitting, he jumps right down to business.

"Based off recent performance, and absence, we've chosen to give Chase the promotion." I get a very pointed look at the mention of an absence.

Biting the inside of my lip, I nod resolutely. It's not really a surprise. They were calling me to come back the day after the funeral, already displeased with the time I'd taken. They nearly lost their marbles when I said I needed a week, then two, and then negotiated to get three.

Chase's face is tilted toward the table, but his gaze is fixed on me.

"I quit." Wait, that wasn't what I was going to say. I was going to say that I understand, that I wish things were different, but I know that Chase will do a great job, because he will.

But it did feel pretty damn incredible. "Yeah, yeah, I quit."

Chancing a look at Chase, his mouth hangs open, and his eyes are wide, his pen dangling from his fingers.

With nothing left to say, I push up from the table and walk out of the room. I've given this company years of my life, sacrificed a family due to the time I've invested in my career, and lost vital final days with Dad to be reprimanded for taking some time off to plan his funeral and mourn my loss. Yet I've never once taken so much as a vacation or sick day.

A hand wraps around my upper arm, and I know it's Chase before he even spins me around. It's not just because of his scent, or his very presence that I've come to recognize in a packed room. It's because I knew he would chase after me. While it wasn't my intention, it's still nice that he cares enough.

"Elizabeth, what are you doing?" Shock is wrapped around his words and sprinkled across his face.

"I quit."

"I know. I heard you, we both heard you. You can't be serious though, Liz."

"I am. I quit." For some reason, I can't stop saying it.

Gritting his teeth, he looks around the common room before dragging me to his office, closing and locking the door behind both of us. I'm not really in the mood to get frisky, but it has been a while since we've done it at work.

Taking a step forward, I reach for his belt, but he pushes my hands off. "Elizabeth, what is wrong with you right now?"

"Isn't this why you brought me in here?" My eyes narrow, and my head tilts to the side.

"What? No." Putting his hands on my shoulders, he takes a step closer so we're practically chest to chest. When he's this close, when I can breathe in nothing but the scent of his cologne and feel nothing but his warmth, it's incredibly intoxicating. "Elizabeth, what is going on? Why did you quit? Is it because I got the promotion, and you didn't?"

"Of course not. I'm happy for you, Chase, and I know you're going to do amazing. I'm incredibly proud of you. But I can't stay here." I twist my fingers into the sides of his shirt, the part that poofs out the slightest bit where it tucks into his pants. "It wasn't what I meant to say, but when I did, it just felt...right. And I realized why. There's all the stuff about my dad and how they reacted with my time off, but really, I can't work with you anymore."

His brows pull together, and his fingers tighten in my shoulders. "Why? Have I done something to upset you? I know we used to be enemies and go at each other, but I thought we were past that."

Meeting his intent gaze, I make mine strong and unwavering. "I'm in love with you." Damn his poker face; he gives away nothing. "And I know you don't feel the same way, that you won't. But I can't keep doing this with you feeling how I do. I can't work here and not be with you now after everything. I'm sorry because it's my fault. I knew you were never going to love me, and I tried, Chase, I tried so hard not to love you. But it was impossible."

Swallowing around the lump forming in my throat is nearly impossible. "Tell me I'm wrong, Chase. Tell me you love me, could love me, and I'll walk into Lions' office and tell him I made a mistake, that I was emotional about them choosing you and I didn't mean it."

Silence fills the office as we stare at each other, neither of us losing our resolve. When Chase's fingers loosen against my shoulders and his chin drops to his chest, I know I have my answer.

Moving out of his grasp, I take one last look at the man I love but who will never reciprocate my feelings. "Goodbye, Chase."

Walking out of his office, I don't even stop into mine. Nor do I turn around or say goodbye to anybody else. I walk straight to my car, getting in and leaning my head back against the seat, struggling to catch my breath.

"I can't breathe." There's nobody in particular to say it to, except maybe myself. "What am I going to do?"

A knock on the window draws my attention. It should probably frighten me, but it's hard to focus on anything but catching my breath and silencing the pounding in my head.

It's Nancy.

I open the door to talk to her, but I can't move my body to get out. "I thought you might need your purse. I grabbed your phone and keys from your desk. I saw you leave but knew you wouldn't be able to get far without this." She's probably heard the news. Our office has a strong rumor mill, and I wouldn't be surprised if the whole office already knows that I won't be working there anymore.

And surely there are stories to go with it about *why* I quit, likely revolving around Chase and possibly our relationship. But none of that matters and none of it bothers me. Because the simple fact is that I quit for me, I quit because I needed to. A change is necessary and that's the only way to get one.

"Thank you, Nancy. You've been a great assistant. I quit today, and I won't be back." The need to tell her myself is strong. Just in case one of the rumors is that I got fired instead of quitting.

"Oh. I'm sorry to hear that. It's been a pleasure working with you, Miss Prescott." With a small bow, she walks away, and I watch as she disappears into the building I no longer have any right to be at.

I've always liked Nancy. She remembers my birthday, brings my favorite coffee after trials and what look to be late nights. Plus, she's quiet.

Starting the car, I take one last look up at my office. Then I glance at Chase's. Maybe some part of me expects to see him standing there, looking out the window at me. Maybe that's why defeat shrinks my shoulders when I don't spot his frame.

With a heavy sigh, I leave the only job I've ever known.

Arriving at Chase's alone has me slumping. We're together constantly now, but since I returned to work, we started to drive separately again. I needed that little bit of extra alone time to prepare myself for the day ahead and to listen to music that Chase has deemed dreadful.

Cheshire greets me at the door. Chase had started joking that sometimes he's more of a dog than cat. I can't really argue most of the time. "Hi, buddy. We're going back home today."

Packing my clothes in the suitcases they came in is such a menial task it takes no brain power, which is good because I'm not sure I have any. I'm trying to look around as little as possible. In the past few months, this house has become my home, as much as I fought being here at the beginning.

I'm certainly going to miss my wake-up view. After throwing the bags and Cheshire's things in the trunk, I take a final look around the house, my heart stuttering in the office when my eyes land on my chair. I hope he keeps it.

Finding Cheshire in the bedroom, I scoot him into his cage and close it, my heart breaking even more at his tiny meows. Eyes welling, I take my key off the ring and lay it gently on the pillow that's become mine. Cupping my mouth to try to contain the sob, I double over and try to breathe.

I have nobody to blame but myself. Chase was never going to love me. I'm not sure he's capable. This was supposed to fun, just sex, and I let it get messy, complicated.

Only I can fix that. By leaving.

Chapter 33

"Hey, Lyd." My tone is defeated.

"Liz, honey, what's wrong? Why are you calling me in the middle of the day?" She knows I went back to work and that I don't make personal calls during my work hours.

"I quit."

"Hold up. You *quit*? *You*? Why?" She can barely get the words out and I know she's beyond stunned.

"Chase."

"What about him? Oh, honey, did he break up with you?" The note of sadness and pity in her voice disgusts me and makes me feel weak.

"No, Lyd. He got the promotion, which is fine, and I'm happy for him. But you're right. I'm in love with him. I can't work there when I know he doesn't love me back. I can't keep doing what we're doing if he'll never love me." There are too many strings now, too many things that wind us and bind us together, and I can't stay with somebody knowing he won't love me back.

Sometimes I feel like a child, picking the petals off a daisy, asking it if he'll love me or love me not.

"So, what's your plan?" This is why I love her. She'd never convince me to stay, never convince me that he's worth it. Instead, she'll tell me I'm strong and can be a single, independent woman.

"I can't stay here, Lydia. I'm going to the house. I'm halfway there."

"Liz. You have nothing there. No clothes, no food. No furniture!"

"I'll get it all. I have pent-up energy and a broken heart. Let me put it into something productive and get the house up and running."

"What do you need?" Yet another pang in my chest for my best friend and how much she does for me.

"I need you to bring me my stuff. Clothes, Cheshire's stuff. I have what was at Chase's, but there's more at home. My books." Everything. She needs to bring me anything she can fit in her car.

"What about furniture and food? Do you even have electricity?" She's never been up to the house herself to truly see it the way Chase did. Though I feel like his was more of an inspection than just checking it out.

"Of course I do, Lydia. I already called the utility company to get it turned on all the way instead of partially. It may be pretty country, but it's still town water. After I get Cheshire settled, I'm going to go to the grocery store and then I'll swing out to one of the furniture stores." Extra money can bring faster delivery, and if I have to, I can swing into Target and get something temporary for a night or two. A futon even, so I have a couch and a bed all in one.

"Liz, is the house even safe to inhabit?" Though it sounds like she's doubting me, I know she's only worried about my safety.

"Safe enough."

"I don't like that answer."

"Lydia, I have to do this."

"I'll call Paulie and get him out there today. At the very least, he can assess what's safe and what's not." Paulie is her regular maintenance guy who she calls for her clients at her realtor firm. She may sleep with him every so often to get a few added perks. I may owe her big after this.

"You're the best."

"And I'll give Nina a call at Sofas and More to get you some stuff by tonight."

"I can handle it, Lydia." Any furniture store will suffice, and I can grease hands on my own. "I know you can. But let me do this. At least a couch."

"Fine."

Silence fills the phone for a few moments.

"Liz. Are you okay?" Her voice is gentle and soft, full of compassion. It takes me a minute to think, to reach deep down into myself to take inventory. "No. Not really."

"You will be." Her tone is resolute, and I know she believes it.

"Yeah." I'm not so sure I do.

"I know you have a lot going on all at once with now leaving work and Chase and not that far from your dad, but you are a strong woman, Liz. You never took crap before, and you won't start now. Besides, you have me as your bestie. Together, we can do anything, including fixing up this monstrous house." She may be over an hour away now, but I can feel her positivity and support pouring through the phone.

"Thanks, Lyd. You always know what I need to hear."

"Anytime, sweetie. You know I'm just a call away, and once you have at least a couch, I'll come see you, bring some food."

"Sounds like a plan."

In true Lydia fashion, she rushes a loved goodbye and hangs up before my answer.

Once I arrive at the house, I peek through the windshield up at the large structure I've owned for years but have never inhabited.

Getting out of the car, planting my hands on my hips, I blow a curl out of my face. Part of me wishes I had the forethought to swing by my apartment to grab some comfy shoes. My feet are killing me, and there's no chance in hell I'll be walking barefoot in there. Not yet.

Taking Cheshire's carrier out of the car, I hold him close to my face as we look at the house. "This was Dad's dream, Chesh. Now it's ours, and we're going to fix it up and make it what we want it to be, what Dad would have wanted."

The frightened meow he responds with gives me little hope. I'm not entirely sure he's safe to run around. I don't think there are any nails anywhere, since I was just here with Chase not that long ago, but I haven't done a thorough walk through.

And I'm sure I'm going to find out if he's a good mouser or not. I'll probably have to add mousetraps and an exterminator to the list.

With a deep breath, I walk up to the front door and let myself in.

Though it's a bit dusty, it's not terribly dirty. But I will be calling a cleaning lady as well. Right now, it's all temporary. A trip to Target is high on my list, as I can grab some slippers to walk around in. And maybe some blinds or curtains, since there aren't any down here, and I do plan to be staying in the downstairs for now.

I bend down and open the cage. "This is home now, Chesh. Go explore, but be careful." He figure-eights between my legs and purrs loudly. "I know it's not where we've been, but we can't live there anymore. This is it."

Walking through the house, I take a mental inventory of what needs to be done now and what can be a waited upgrade. The fixtures in the bathrooms and kitchen are newer and all work well so those can wait. The carpets all need to be torn up and replaced as soon as possible. The kitchen and bathrooms, while a little outdated, are in good shape and clean, so while I'll be upgrading, they too can wait.

The priority is furniture and floors, or at least any carpets. They're threadbare and stained. I wonder if I can get a company in tomorrow. Regardless, they're on the top of my list too.

When my stomach rumbles, reminding me I haven't eaten all day, I grab my purse and keys, leaving Cheshire to explore his new home and to go grab some essentials and lunch.

This is exactly what I need for a fresh start.

Chapter 34

A lmost four months into living in the house and things are really coming along. Lydia, of course, came through on not just the furniture, but a contractor as well.

All of the floors are brand new, including in the kitchen and bathrooms. Honey oak hardwood floors span most of the downstairs and the hallway in the upstairs, while gray carpets sit in every bedroom.

At the moment, I have a crew finishing up putting the new cabinets up in my kitchen.

While most people wait a while to get things done, Lydia was able to pull a few strings to get me at the top of the list so my house could be fully upgraded and completely livable within a matter of weeks.

I'm not sure how she did it or how many favors she had to call in, but I'm eternally grateful and can never repay her.

Though I don't have a job anymore, I saved for years and never had many expenses, so blowing through cash left and right on the house isn't a problem. I still have a pretty nest egg to get me through.

At some point, I'll need to find something to do with myself during the days, but right now, overseeing the house has taken up all of my time. Enough so that I've barely thought about Chase. I wish I could say the same about Dad, but at every turn I find myself asking what he'd want for the house. What kind of flooring, what color cabinets and countertops and paint, what he'd leave because it has a certain charm.

Chase only comes to my mind in the quiet hours of the night, especially when Cheshire curls up at my feet. Those are the times my mind wanders, and I miss him in bed next to me. Even after all this time, my heart still hurts.

I haven't heard a word from him since I walked out that day, so clearly the feelings were one-sided.

I can't say I blame him for not reaching out. I dropped a bomb on him, one that he probably never expected, and left without another word. His whole world turned upside down in a day and he started a new, demanding job the next.

What room does he have for me and my needy self?

It's not like I can expect him to give everything up for me and change what he wants. So instead, I'm here, trying my best to distract myself.

Dating seems like such a hard and foreign concept to me, and I'm not quite healed enough yet to jump into the pool, despite Lydia's begging. But I made it clear I need a little more time to heal, both from Chase and Dad. Emotionally, I'm just not in a place to let somebody new in, but I promised I'd let her know as soon as that changes.

The banging in my kitchen is enough of a headache, I don't need to add dating and blind dates and apps to that right now.

While Austin, my contractor, is kind of cute and has definitely been flirting, I can't get myself to go there, not even to flirt back. The house is becoming more of a home with my updates and furniture. I was lucky and able to get top quality everything. I officially moved out of my apartment two months ago. It took me three weeks to move everything here and make this place fairly comfortable, which really meant tearing up the old carpets and getting the new floors installed.

Living here is very different than apartment life. Not just that, but city life. It takes longer to get everywhere, and my neighbors aren't in my face. In fact, without the construction, I may not talk to another soul all day because the houses aren't on top of each other.

It's kind of peaceful, kind of lonely. It's a nice house for a family, but for now it's just me. And of course, Cheshire. He's a great listener, but not the best conversationalist.

No, it's a rather quiet life, save for the construction. Which finishes around two in the afternoon, leaving me in peace for the foreseeable future since I have no other projects in the works.

Which is why I'm shocked by a knock at the door at four in the afternoon.

When I swing the door open, my jaw hits the floor, along with my heart.

"Hey, Princess. Can we talk?"

Chapter 35

S hock renders me speechless for minute as my mouth hangs open and my heart skips a beat before it starts racing.

"What is there to say? I get it, Chase. You have no feelings for me. Your radio silence has made that abundantly clear. Now get off my front porch and leave me alone." I start to close the door when his strong hand stops it.

"God, you're so fucking stubborn. Why the fuck do you think I'm here, Liz? Because I felt like a two-hour drive to the fucking country? To take in some scenery?"

"So, what, you want one last hate fuck? 'Cause guess what, Chase? Even though you let me split, without a word, might I add, I still don't hate you. I can't." I'm not sure where this anger came from. It's like the second I saw his face with that damn smug smirk, the rage started to boil below my skin and is erupting out of me even though all I want is to invite him in and have him hold me.

"It's kind of hard to hate fuck somebody you love."

"Okay, well, that's great, but you—" I stop talking as what he said finally registers with me. "Wait, what did you just say?"

Taking a step closer, one of his hands closes around my waist while the other brushes down my cheek. "I said I love you."

Not trusting myself, or him, really, I narrow my eyes as I look up in his emerald ones. They've always taken my breath away.

"How do I know you're not just saying what you need to say to get my pants off?"

"When have you ever known me to placate you? At work, in the bedroom, anywhere?"

Never. He's never given me an inch.

"Please, Liz. I miss you. And not just your body."

"You hurt me, Chase. A lot. I'm sorry if I'm not so willing to just let you back in." It's one thing I've never admitted, barely even to myself. Him not saying a word and merely backing away, it hurt. Even though I expected it, even though I knew he was unlikely to feel the same, it nearly broke me the rest of the way.

"I'm willing to work for it."

"Good. You'll have to."

"Can I start now?" I haven't left the comfort of his hold on me. The hand at my waist has tightened while the one that had been on my cheek has rounded to cup the back of my neck, his thumb resting against my jaw.

"What exactly did you have in mind? And no, throwing me over your shoulder and taking me to the closest surface isn't going to work." It might. But I don't want him to try it, thinking just sex is enough to win me back.

"What if I scoop you in my arms and carry you instead?" The corner of his mouth tics up as he finds this amusing.

No smile breaks my face. He thinks sex can solve anything. But not this.

"Alright, I get it, not funny. What if instead I start by telling you all the things I love about you that have absolutely nothing to do with your incredibly sexy body?"

"You mean the two things you've noticed?"

"Oh, Elizabeth. There are far more than just two things." The glint in his eyes as he looks down at me makes my heart flutter.

As he slowly closes the gap between us, I pull back a little. I don't know that I'm ready to let him kiss me, knowing it always makes my knees weak and resolve disappear.

But when he leans in again, I don't move away. The hammering of my heart starts the second his lips brush mine. Pulling me flush against him, my mouth parts for his as his tongue seeks mine.

His hand drops from the back of my neck to rest over my chest. "This beats for me, Liz. You can't deny that." Taking my hand, he puts it against his chest, above his heart, hand pressing tightly against mine. "Just like mine beats for you."

And with those words, all resolve is gone. All promises I made myself to hate him forever, to never let him in again, albeit weak ones, flow out of body and seep through the floor beneath me.

I throw my arms around his neck and practically climb his body as my mouth collides with his. Wrapping one arm firmly around my waist, he walks into my house, closing the door behind him as his tongue skims the seam of my lips.

Granting him entrance, a low moan rises from my chest that draws me back and I lower my feet, pushing away from him.

"Dammit, Chase!" Spinning to face the wall, one of my hands settles on my waist while the other rubs my forehead. I can't think when I look at him.

"What the hell just happened?"

Flipping back to him, I find a furrowed brow, his hands still in the air as he holds nothing.

"What just happened is me being weak and giving in to the first nice thing you said to me. I should have learned last time that it doesn't mean shit."

"Telling you I love you doesn't mean shit to you?" His eyes narrow, and his face distorts in a grimace.

"That's not what I said. You were going to tell me all the reasons you love me, yet instead all you did was tell me my heart beats for you and yours for me and while that's very sweet and poetic and Romcom swoon-worthy, in real life, I need a little more." The last part comes out on the tail end of an overrun breath. I spoke quickly, frantically, needing to get it all out before I lost my resolve and jumped at him again.

Chase's mouth sets in a hard line. When he takes a step closer to me, I take a step back, palm out to stop him.

Running his hand down his face, he looks harried. Like this one task of telling me where his feelings emanate from is utterly exhausting.

"I can't tell you if you won't let me close to you, Elizabeth."

"Why?"

"Because I need to hold you when I go over the many reasons I'm unapologetically and unabashedly over the moon in love with you." I falter on my feet, wanting to run to him, but I need to be hesitant.

"I don't know that I can trust you not to hurt me again, Chase. I need to guard my heart because the last time I gave it to you, you completely shut me out. How do I trust you won't do that again?" He didn't just shut me out. He shut down. We went from seeing each other and fucking every day, practically living together, to not even communicating at all.

"I'm here, aren't I?"

"You are. And it could be for one last hate fuck." While he said it wasn't, who knows what to believe. My mind is in a tizzy, and I can't keep track of what's what anymore.

"You really think I'd drive all the way out here just for that?"

"Did you or did you not once tell me I was the best lay you'd ever had."

"I absolutely did. And it's true. But I wouldn't come all the way out to middle of fuckoff nowhere just for that. I'm here because I'm irrevocably in love with you." He takes a small step closer to me. Instead of retreating this time, I stand my ground.

"Why?" I need to hear him say it.

Sighing, he puts his hands in his pockets, taking another small step forward. "You're incredibly frustrating sometimes. Do you know that?"

"I've been told a time or two." By him. A smirk plays on his lips, making my stomach flip. "And no getting cute and trying to quote a literary work or Shakespeare or some sappy movie. Especially because I'll know."

"I know you will, Liz. That's the thing. For years, we were rivals who hated each other. But love and hate are just two sides of the same coin. That first time we got together, we flipped it. Even in those years of hate, of competition, of distrust and anger, I was paying attention to you. At the time, I thought it was to know my enemy better. Now I know I was preparing for something bigger."

He's taken imperceptible steps closer to where he's now only an arm's reach away from touching me. How did I not notice that? He's a good attorney for a reason; he fully captivated me with his words as he made his move.

"You always have a book with you, even on trial days. It used to annoy me. I'd always wonder why you had a book in your bag when we had a full day of examining witnesses or were drowning in paperwork or really any reason at work at all. But every so often, I'd catch you at lunch, reading while you twirled a lock of your hair around your finger." As he says this, he reaches out and touches the very curl I twist when I get engrossed in a book.

A flutter settles in my chest as it sinks in that he paid enough attention to notice that, even when he hated me.

"After a little while, it stopped irritating me, and I started paying more attention. You're well read, it's clear from the way you speak and use language, despite your filthy mouth. In any given week, I'd see you with anywhere from two to four new titles. Weeks with fewer could easily be attributed to heavy caseload weeks, long trial days, or even sheer thickness of the text in front of you."

He hasn't released my hair, now twisting it around his own finger, and I find myself moving an inch closer.

"That's an awful lot to notice in somebody you hate."

"I agree. And it frustrated me at first that it became a part of my routine at lunch to glance at the title of the novel you had situated in front of you."

"What else?" I need to know more.

"You know your craft very well. While I've known this for years, I'd never have been able to admit it before. But you're one of the best lawyers I've ever known or worked with. Better than me, at times. I'm

not ashamed to admit that because it makes me damn proud of you."
While this isn't exactly an overly romantic declaration, it still makes my
heart ping.

"While I could spend hours talking about how gorgeous you are and
all the various parts of your body that I love and why, I'm not going to
because it's not a big factor in why I love you. It's an added perk, for
sure." Glancing over my face quickly, he cups my cheek and leans in to
my ear. "Besides, I'd rather show you what parts of your body I love by
kissing my adoration onto every square inch of you."

Resetting himself in front of me, he continues, "I love the little 'mm'
that escapes your lips with your first sip of fresh coffee."

"I don't do that."

"You absolutely do. And it's adorable and sexy. It's not that different
from the noise you make when I pull your pebbled nipple between my
lips." He runs a fingertip over his mouth, as though he's thinking of the
feeling and sensation and sound all at once.

I allow myself one heave of my chest before I steel myself again. But
he's a lawyer, who apparently pays very close attention to me, and his eyes
turn predatory. Taking a slight step backward, he follows my movement,
stepping with me but slightly farther so I have to move even farther back.

Shaking away the lusty haze settling in my mind, I push him to continue. "What else?"

His lips curl at the corners as he gently brushes his hand down my side
to rest at my hip, thumb tucking under the waistband of my jeans. As
warmth races through my body from the slightest bit of skin on skin, I
chew the inside of my cheek to keep myself in check.

"There's also the way you come driving into the parking lot. Windows
down when it's warm enough, but music always blaring. Not a care in
the world, a bit of a wild child rocking in her car. But the second you

step out of the car and shut that door, it's professional-faced Elizabeth Prescott. Who is rarely rattled by anything or anyone." As he says this, he steps forward again, pushing me backward.

"I may find your taste in music questionable, but your ability to be unabashedly yourself is a major turn on." Cupping my cheek with the hand not on my hip, he takes one more step toward me and my back connects with the wall. Closing the slight space, his hips press against mine as he boxes me in, towering over me so I have to tip my head up to look at him.

His eyes, those piercing green eyes. I fell in love with them long before I fell in love with the man behind them. I could swim in their aquamarine pools forever.

As we stand here pressed together, our breaths mingling in the slight space that still exists between us, I want to give in so desperately. But I'm scared.

He must sense my hesitation. "I love you, Elizabeth. I didn't come here for anything except to let you know and hope you still love me back."

"I do." I sidestep and turn us around slightly so I have an escape route if I need one.

"I didn't put my dick in anybody else, Liz, if that's what you're worried about."

Shock pulls my eyebrows high on my face. I wasn't concerned about it, but it's still a surprising notion, considering how frequently we were together in just a given week, let alone a few months. When I left, I was pretty sure he'd sink into the first warm body, quickly followed by many others, but I wasn't worried about it.

But I notice he's wincing, which causes me to pull back. His arm tightens around me, preventing me from getting away.

"I'm not lying. I just...I'm trying to say things a little less crass for you. But I haven't even looked at another woman, Elizabeth. Not more than on a professional level for work."

"Why?"

"You want me to tell you how I've always loved you? Because here's the thing, Liz, I've realized that I have. That coin flipped for me a long time ago, well before I took you in my office that night. The moment I pressed inside of you, I knew it. I knew it for certain. And I spent all that time avoiding it, trying to push it away, but I couldn't keep myself from you. Not just because you were by far the best sex I've ever had, but because I wanted you, all of you." His tone is borderline angry, like he's frustrated he's having to convince me that he loves me. Part of it is likely because he just came to terms with it himself.

"When you told me you loved me, that scared the shit out of me. It confronted me with my very own emotions. There couldn't be any more hiding. I didn't feel ready. I still don't. But I can't live without you a second longer." He wraps his hands around my biceps and pulls me closer to him. His eyes are frantic, and I know right now he feels like he's losing me by having to convince me of his feelings.

"I want more than you do, Chase. I want to get married, I want to have children. I'm getting older, and it will be more difficult. I can't waste time on somebody who doesn't want those things." I can't be with somebody I love just because I love them. I need more, I need it all.

"I *do* want those things, Liz. I didn't before. But I do, with you. I'd be lying if I didn't say I'm scared shitless. My father was a terrible father and husband. I'm scared that one day I'll slip up, that I'll hurt you. It's what I was always scared of. But the way I feel for you, it's new and different, and while I'm still scared, I truly feel that you're more than enough for me, in every way."

Though I'm glaring at him with narrowed eyes, I feel my resolve dripping away.

"So, you want to be with me, no matter what? What does that look like? Do we pick up right where we left off?"

"Whatever you want, Liz. I can't imagine not being with you. But if you want to go slower, I'll come visit on weekends, or Saturdays, or whatever you want. Because I'd move in with you right now, I'd marry you tomorrow." Desperation doesn't look good on Chase, but it does make my heart beat faster because I *know* he means it.

"Wait, are you *proposing*?" While I'd say yes, it seems a little fast and very un-Chase-like.

"Yes? No? I don't know. All I know is that I want it, Liz. I want it all with you, and I don't want to wait any longer. I know you've never said it out loud, at least not to me, but I know you're worried about having kids. So I don't want to wait, I don't see a reason to. I'm ready to start that with you now, I'm ready to marry you now, I'm ready to...I'm just...ready."

We stand in silence for a few minutes, eyes locked on each other.

"I don't care about a big fancy wedding, Elizabeth. I just want to be with you. If you want one for your mom, that's fine. But I'd just as soon have Lydia and my brother and go to town hall. He'd fly out tomorrow. Hell, he'd find a plane ticket tonight if I asked him to. But I'll do bigger if that's what you want. Whatever you want, Liz, I'll do."

Wow, he's really serious. And I don't quite know how to take it or what to make of it.

"I don't need anything big. My mom won't even remember, though I would maybe like her there anyway. It still seems like something she should be present for."

"Are you saying yes?" A wide smile breaks his face, but I can see the nerves in his eyes.

"You haven't exactly asked me, Chase."

He runs a hand through his hair. "Fuck, I wasn't expecting this. I don't have a ring. I should have a ring." The slightly panicked look and tone makes me want to laugh, but I bite it down.

"Chase." He flicks his eyes up to mine, softening and relaxing. "If you're serious, really, truly serious, then I don't care about a ring."

I'm in his arms so fast, my head spins, and the air leaves my lungs with a whoosh as he yanks me against his body. "I've never been more serious about anything in my life, Elizabeth. I have to be with you."

"What if you came all the way here, said all of this, and I said no? It's been months, Chase." Not many, not several, but enough.

"I guess maybe it was a leap of faith, a trial of the soul. I'll do whatever I have to, Elizabeth. Anything. I didn't drive out here to tell you I love you and disappear. I came out because I'm miserable without you. I came out here to get you back. Whatever that takes, whatever it means. Maybe I'm not proposing officially, maybe I'm just stating my intentions. Because you deserve the best, Liz. A full-on, romantic, down on one knee, best ring money can buy proposal."

Tears burn at the rims of my eyes. Chase has never been so sweet. While it might throw me, might be the least expected thing I've ever encountered, it somehow feels like everything is finally falling into place.

Chapter 36

We spend a few moments in one another's embrace, and I'm taking a minute to enjoy the sound of his heart thumping in my ear again. It's been too long since I've heard it, and my muscles all loosen as the sound penetrates through any defenses I have left.

"I want you to ride me, Liz." The words rumble through my body and throw me for a bit of a loop.

"What?"

"You, on top, in control." While he's not expressly clearer on his intentions, they become crystal clear anyway. I don't need to ask what he means because it clicks into place.

He wants to seal whatever it is we just agreed on with a fuck.

"Why?"

"I've never really let you before. I always take over."

"And you won't this time?" Disbelief pulls up one of my eyebrows.

"Nope."

"Okay." I drag the word out. I'm not so sure about this. Not only because it's a little awkward that we're talking about how we're going to have sex while standing on the side of my living room, but we just got back together, only sort of officially.

Chase has never once asked me to actually be his girlfriend or be exclusive, but I suppose practically proposing is the best I'm going to get.

With one knuckle under my chin, he tips my face up, his green irises flickering with lust. His lips brush mine in a question that I need to be the one to answer.

Throwing my arms around his shoulders, I pull him down, crashing his mouth to mine. With careful steps backward, he walks us to the couch, lowering himself and tugging me down into his lap.

My legs straddle his while my hands cup his face, and our tongues collide in a heated battle. I drag my pussy over his hardening cock, and we both moan at the same time.

His hands slide up my blouse, cupping my breasts and pinching at my nipples. When my head tips back, his mouth latches onto my neck, sucking and biting and licking his way up and down and across my shoulder.

I feel the moment our shared composure snaps and our hands start flying around each other's bodies, removing articles of clothing, touching and playing with body parts. My shirt and bra end up across the room, his hanging off a lamp.

There's no room while I'm on his lap, so I stand and shimmy out of my pants and panties while he frees his erection.

Slowly, I climb back over him, tucking a curl behind my ear as I do so.

Gently, I lower myself onto him. His head tips back with a groan, and I suck in a breath, hanging my forehead against his chest as I need a moment.

"Fuck, baby. I missed how you feel around me." Sliding his hands up my back, he cups my chin and tilts my head to look at him. "Are you okay?"

I nod before I can even speak. "Mhm. Just been a while. Takes a minute to readjust."

Once I have my bearings, I move myself forward and back, grinding on his lap, my clit rubbing against his tight abs.

My hands rest on Chase's shoulders, tightening as I lift and lower myself while still shifting forward and backward. His fingers are clasped behind his head, and his eyes are all pupil as he watches the show, clearly enjoying himself by the groans and grunts he keeps making.

Every so often, his tongue will dart out and wet his lips while he takes in my body.

But as I get closer and closer to coming, there's something I need. More than what I can give myself. "Chase. Mmmm. Chase. I want you to fuck me."

"I am, Liz."

"No. I want you to flip me over and fuck me hard. Like only you can." And really, only he can. Nobody has every fucked me like Chase, and I'm sure nobody could ever measure up. I was prepared to live with that before he came back.

"Are you sure?"

"Yes. Please."

He doesn't hesitate to respond, wrapping his hands around my waist and lifting me off of him. Sliding out from under me, he moves to be behind me. A heavy hand presses between my shoulder blades as my chest collides with the couch. I can't help the smile that graces my lips.

Here's the man I've missed horribly for months. The man I tried to forget. The man who broke my heart. But still the only man who could ever dominate me. And of course, the only one I'd ever *let* dominate me. *Want* to dominate me.

When I'm sufficiently in the position he likes, he presses into me, quickly and fully. I gasp at the sensation, so different than it was just moments ago. Sliding a hand over my ass and up my back, he wraps my hair around it and tugs, causing me to rise to my hands.

His other hand grabs my ass and then a loud crack fills the air, my body jutting forward at the contact of his palm on my bare skin. It causes my hair to pull in the most glorious way.

"Fuck, Liz." Chase still hasn't even moved an inch, pressed inside me to the hilt, stilling as he takes in my body.

A growl from behind me resounds in my ears, making me wriggle against him, suddenly needing movement to ease the throbbing in my clit.

The hold on my hair tightens as his free hand slides up my body to close around my throat, pulling me up so my fingertips barely graze the couch.

Chase leans forward and runs his tongue up the side of my neck and along my ear. I swear if he doesn't start fucking me soon, I'm going to lose it.

"Chase. Please."

"You switched the roles, Elizabeth. I was happy to let you do it your way. You asked for this. It's been too long since I've enjoyed your body. I'm going to savor every single second."

There's nothing I can do. He has too strong of a hold on me, and nothing I can say will make a difference. While the wait is tantalizing, the need is stronger.

Just as I'm about to start begging, he pulls me up straighter, into his chest, as he slowly pulls out of me. Leaving just the tip, he hesitates, before slamming back into me. I yelp at the sensation.

He does it again, just as slow to pull out and just as hard to ram in. After less than ten thrusts, all exactly the same, I'm panting and deliriously happy.

Without notice, he picks up his speed, pushing me back into the couch, and my body jerks forward with every thrust. It makes my scalp sting and my breaths harder to come by. But fuck if it isn't exactly the reunion we need.

My fingers grip into the couch, but it isn't what I want. Reaching a hand behind me, I try to make contact with any part of Chase's body I can.

"Chase. I need to touch you. Please." Every word comes out on a jagged breath as he pounds into me.

When he does nothing, I think he's going to ignore me. But his hands release from my throat and hair, one gripping my hip while the other latches on my forearm, so I can turn mine back in a similar hold.

My head tips forward and blond curls fall over my shoulders. Chase's hand slips along my hip and a bead of sweat lands on my back. We're both slick, and the rawness and urgency of it all is so heady, it feels like the room is spinning.

"Mmm, Chase. Chase."

"Fuck, Liz."

I tremble, my walls clenching around him as I scream, coming hard. Chase groans behind me, and I feel him pulsate inside me as he makes small, tight bucks into me and pumps through his orgasm.

My arms give out, and my chest connects with the couch as I try to catch my breath. It's made harder when Chase collapses on top of me, our skin sliding.

"God, Liz. Your body is so damn amazing. I love you."

"Only for my body?" I ask, needing to tease him.

"Don't do that shit right now, Liz. Bust my balls later, but not right now." He rests his forehead against the back of my head, his nose nuzzling into my hair before he gently moves it to the side and lays tender kisses along the nape of my neck. "I missed you." The deep timber of his voice rattles through me.

Trying to turn my head toward him is futile, but Chase pushes up on his arms so I can shift slightly and meet his eyes. I run a hand along his cheek, the familiar scratch of his beard on my palm sending a shock straight up my arm and into my heart. "I missed you too."

My lip finds its way between my teeth. Because something has been bothering me. If he missed me so much, loves me so much, why did it take him *months* to come to me. He had to know where I'd go once I vacated my apartment.

"I have your things from your office." He speaks before I have a chance to ask.

"You do? You kept them all this time?"

"Of course I did, Liz. I planned to come sooner, but I needed a plan first. I knew you were here, where else would you go? But I didn't want to come with nothing to say besides that I loved you. This needed to be a grand gesture."

Does he think that coming and fucking me like that is a grand gesture? Or that professing his love is enough?

"I gave my notice at the firm. Months ago. I told them I would stay on until they found a replacement. It took just two weeks of working there without you to realize that I needed you back. First, I stepped down as a partner, then I gave my notice and said I'd wait until they found a replacement. While they clearly dragged their feet on finding one, they finally have."

I stare at him and blink repeatedly as shock steals my words.

"I have to be there a few more weeks to get this person up to par and introduce them to my clients and whatnot, but I'm free of them, Liz. I needed to have my life ready for you. And I have a realtor set up to sell the house as soon as you're ready for that. I'm serious about it all, but I'll go on your schedule.

"I mean what I said before. I'll come just on the weekends if that's what you want at first. But everything on my end is prepared for me to be here with you full time. Starting now. I even have a bag in the car in the event you tell me I can stay."

Words elude me, and I have no idea what to say. This sweet man of mine planned everything. He wants a life with me, a real one.

I rest my hand on his cheek, finally recognizing the somewhat strange position we're in, bent over the couch and butt naked, but it's us, so it fits.

"You can move in whenever you're ready. I love you, and I've missed you, and I want you here with me."

The smile that crosses his face nearly makes my heart explode.

"I was hoping you'd say that. Will you come with me the few days I need to be back at the office to get things situated? I just got you back; I don't want to have to be without you again."

"Of course. I miss your house. We can even bring some things from your house. I have guestrooms I haven't really furnished yet."

Standing up straight, he starts gathering and pulling on his clothes while looking around the downstairs. "It looks really great in here, Liz. You've done a lot."

"Yeah, well, I had some time."

He extends his hand to me, and I take it, letting him pull me up and handing me my clothes.

"I'd like to see the rest. Especially the bed and the shower. And please tell me there's a tub."

"A big one." I step next to him and press my lips to his ears. "And bath bombs."

As I walk past him to gather the rest of my clothes, he smacks my ass. Something has shifted, it's almost tangible. It's like everything feels right.

"So, we're two unemployed lawyers. What are we going to do for money, because while we both made a good amount, it will run out eventually."

"I agreed to consult for the firm. But I can do that from home mostly. And if I need to be in town, I can get a hotel."

"You don't want to keep your house?" I did come to love his house.

"I'd love to, but don't see a reason to, Princess. It's a great house, but we don't need two. Any consulting will pay well but won't be frequent or long enough for me to keep it. Unless you want a place near the city for us. I'll happily keep it if you want to." He seems excited that I may say yes. And honestly, it seems worth it.

"Let's look at finances. If we can swing it, I say yes. I know you love your house, and it grew on me. I'd hate to sell it and stay at a hotel. Besides, it has some special meaning to me." It's the place Chase and I really fell in love.

Before he can answer, Cheshire comes running out and starts looping around Chase's legs, meowing loudly.

"Well, hey, little buddy. Looks like I'm back now. But I was thinking, if your mom agrees, maybe we'll get you a canine friend?" He looks up from where he's squatting and scratching Cheshire's head. He almost looks like a child the way he's staring up at me, lip pushed out slightly.

With a roll of my eyes, I pull him up and to me, throwing my arms around his neck. "We can discuss the dog too. But only for you. I love you and want you to be happy here; you're giving up a lot to be here with me."

His hands land under my thighs, and as he lifts me up, I wrap my legs around his waist. "I'll be happy no matter what, Liz. Because I'll be with you. And that's enough for me."

I'm glad he said that, because having him is all I need to be happy.

Epilogue

Strong hands on my waist cause me to shriek as they lift me into the air. Chase sets me on his shoulders and takes a step toward the tree, allowing me to reach the apples that otherwise would have gone unpicked.

Once he sets me down, I put the apples in the basket and smack his chest. "You know I hate when you do that!"

"I was only trying to help, Elizabeth."

I drink him in. He's embraced the farm lifestyle, opting for a lot of flannel. At first it was a joke, but he quickly found it to be something he preferred. I do too. All the gardening and planting we do keeps him in good shape. He's taken to chopping wood for the fire pit by hand too.

Right now, his rolled-up sleeves, showing off strong forearms, has me pulling my lip between my teeth and wondering if we can even make it to the house.

"Flannel looks good on you."

He quirks an eyebrow and wraps an arm around my waist, yanking me against him. "Oh, really? Better than a suit?"

Running my hands up his chest, I consider. "Hmm. Different. In a *very* good way."

Grabbing me under my thighs, he lifts me up, and I wrap my legs around his waist. "I love you, Elizabeth."

"I love you too, Chase." Hearing him tell me he loves me, saying it back, or first, it never gets old. It was shocking for a very short while. The element of hatred had long since faded, but it was weird to hear him tell me.

Setting me down, Chase keeps an arm looped around my waist as he keeps me snug against him. "How are you today?" He presses his palm against my chest and locks his emerald eyes on mine.

"I'm okay." Things were hard after Dad died. The emotional turmoil became too much after I left. Instead of dealing with it, I blocked it all out and put all my focus into making the house livable. When Chase showed up, and quickly moved in, things became nearly impossible. His presence threw a wrench into my routine, my way of living, my ways of ignoring. His support, while incredibly welcome, made it harder to push out the feelings that wanted to crush me.

And at times, they did. But Chase was always there to pick me up and put me back together. It was no different when Mom died almost a year ago. He's always by my side, ready to pick me up when I'm down, ready to scoop me off the floor—which he had to do a few times—and do what he can to cheer me up.

The gold of his ring glints in the sunlight and pulls my attention back to the present. Mister "never going to get married or have kids" was an emotional mess on our wedding day six months ago and has been hounding me for a baby since a month before that.

"Come on, let me make us some breakfast." Chase slides his hand down my arm, linking our fingers together and heading off toward the house.

The quiet hours of the early morning are some of my favorites to get gardening done. It's peaceful with the sun rising, the dew fresh on the grass. Sleeping late used to be something I did daily. Now I'm up with Chase every day, coming out to check on the garden I planted in memory of Dad. He'd always said the house was perfect for fields and gardens for tending.

As Chase pulls open the door, Cheshire and our golden retriever, Atticus, both go barreling out the door, almost running into us. "Damn animals," he mutters under his breath.

"You wanted to get a dog." I have to remind him of this regularly.

"I didn't realize that it wouldn't scare away your crazy fucking cat. That he'd only make the cat worse."

"Oh stop, you love Cheshire." I playfully smack him in the chest with the back of my hand.

"No. I love you. I tolerate the cat."

"Whatever you say. But I saw you cuddled up with him reading two nights ago. You big softy." I pat his chest as I walk past him, getting a firm pat on the ass in return.

It's kind of amazing how much this house has become *our* home. In so many ways, it's everything Dad had always wanted for me. Never in a million years could I have dreamed of being happily married to Chase, of all people, but our life together is perfect.

With neither of us working, except for the occasional consultation he does, we're free to spend all of our time together, which I actually love. And having no close neighbors means we spend most of it naked.

That's a big reason why I'm not ready for kids just yet. I want to enjoy this time together, enjoy being able to fuck the day away in any room we want, on any surface that supports us, and even some that don't.

We learned the hard way that the coffee table was not strong enough.

Chase's utter adoration for me is new too. And I want to have the spotlight on me just a little longer. I know the second a baby enters our lives, that tiny being will consume both of us, and I'm not ready to lose his undivided attention.

Atticus was a compromise. Something for him to baby while we wait for me to be ready. Some of it is the emotional aspect too. How am I supposed to bring a baby into this world without my parents' help? Without their advice or having them to turn to?

Justin and Janine have been nothing short of amazing, very involved, loving, and extremely welcoming to me. But it's not quite the same as motherly advice. It's not the same as calling my mother and asking about something and having her tell me it would be alright and that I did the same thing.

Until the ache that resides in my chest every time I think about it subsides, I can't even begin to talk about it. Chase knows, he understands, and I love his eagerness to want to start a family with me.

And if I'm honest with myself, I am wavering. I am losing that resolve. Especially because I may encounter some of the same fertility issues Mom did.

Chase steps behind me, pressing his chest to my back, looping his arms around my waist, and resting his chin on my shoulder. "Where's your head at, baby?"

With his hands like this, so close to my lower belly, I can see it. I can picture it. The way he'd take care of me, the way he'd hold me, just like this, hands splayed on a swollen belly. Taking one of his large hands in mine, I lower it a bit and press, then turn in his hold.

"I think I might be almost ready. Not yet, I need more time just us, to have fun and do what we want, where we want. But I feel myself getting closer."

"Don't push yourself for me."

"I'm not."

The look he gives me informs me that he knows there's more. "Chase, I want to have a family with you. I've always wanted a family, and then we had our whirlwind. But part of me is worried I won't be able to give you children. And then you'll leave me."

"Elizabeth. I don't want children because I've suddenly changed and want to be a father. I want children because of *you*. If we can't have them, then so be it." He's quiet for a moment, but I know he's not finished. "I told you once early on that I didn't want to get married because of the statistics. I don't want to be one of them. So, marrying you, proposing...that was all with the intention that this is forever. No contingencies, no back-out plans, nothing."

"You'd really be okay just us? Forever?"

"Of course I would. Because that means I get to fuck you whenever and wherever I want. Forever." The thought is certainly enticing and a little bit of an argument to *not* have kids.

But I know they'd make our lives more whole. It's something I've always wanted, and it's just my loss that's holding me back right now. But I'll be over it, and soon.

As I walk through the house that we've turned into a home, I head to the office to grab a new book. A smile spans my face when I see my chair, the one Chase got for me as a surprise over two years ago.

It's still my favorite piece of furniture.

Chase was right years ago. When he said we'd been learning each other for years, he knew something then that neither of us could put a finger on. Until now.

One thing that has maybe always been true finally became apparent. Chase and I were meant to be together. Our story may have started out with us being enemies, but sometimes enemies make for the best lovers.

The End

COMING September 2023

The following is an unedited preview and subject to change.

C hapter 1

Liv

The lunch rush is always my favorite time of day. People bustling in to get their midday caffeine fix or a quick lunch, usually both. The hustle keeps me going, gives me life.

That's why the lull we're in right now is droll. People watching is a favorite past time of mine, and no better place than the large windows in the front of the shop. This time of day provides some good entertainment. It's not busy, but I can take more in, truly observe my sleepy town of Juniper Grove, that I both love to hate, and hate to love.

"Anything good today?" Alina bumps her hip into mine as she rests her forearms on the counter.

"Mrs. Henderson just walked into the pharmacy." I don't take my eyes from the picture window as I answer her.

"Ah so we have about ten minutes until the shouting begins."

"Roughly." Pulling my attention from the world outside our quaint little shop, I turn to my sister. "You look tired, Leen."

"I'm fine. Early mornings and all that." She waves me off like it's nothing but I know she hasn't been sleeping well. She thinks I can't hear her when a nightmare wakes her up screaming at three in the morning. My room is only down the hall from hers, I don't know what she expects.

"Leen, stop lying to me. You're having nightmares again. You promised me next time you'd see somebody." It's not just the middle of the night screaming that tips me off. It's the fact that she's been staying at my house at all. We have our own houses, and yet she insists on staying with me most nights lately, claiming she wants more sisterly bonding time.

Stiffening and taking a step back, she wipes her hands on her apron, which I'm sure only gets them more covered with flour. "I'm fine."

"You're *not*. Please, for me." Reaching out to touch her shoulder only makes her shrug me off.

"I'll think about it. I'm going back to the kitchen. Any requests for the afternoon?"

Huffing out a breath, I move on. I know it won't make a lick of difference what I say or do. We've been here at least a dozen times in just the past two years.

"Some of those mixed berry muffins would be great." Defeat hangs off my words and slumps my shoulders as I try to give a fake smile.

The smile she plasters to her face makes it all worth it. "You got it."

Grabbing a rag, I start wiping down a few tables, gathering the few tips left behind from the rush that I had yet to clear.

While focusing on the last table, scrubbing at something sticky that the cute, but loud, blond toddler left on the table, the bell chimes.

A boisterous voice fills the otherwise silent café, and immediately I'm put on alert.

"I don't know what kind of backwards, one horse town I landed in this morning but this is going to be a long trip. No, the motel is horrendous."

Glancing over I see a grade-A prick, in what is clearly a very expensive suit with it's sharp lines and the way it's tailor fit to his body. There's a phone plastered to his ear. Despite overhearing his conversation, I'd peg him as a visitor from the first second. Aside from never having seen him before, and knowing everybody in this Godforsaken town, he sticks out like a sore thumb. We're not a suit and dress type of town.

Hands spread in front of me, I stand behind the counter and plaster a smile on my face, ready to take on this suit.

"Yeah, I'm going to go, see if I can get at least a halfway decent cup of coffee here." He hangs up without so much as a goodbye.

"Hi, how can I help you today?" The smile stretching my lips couldn't be more fake but it's all about impressing the customers. That's what my other sister, Mazie always says at least, when she reminds me that I'm the face of the store. Whose brilliant idea that was, I have no idea.

A curt smile is returned to me. "I'll have an espresso macchiato with three shots of espresso. You know how to make that sweetheart? It requires the fancy machine over there." He points to the espresso machine, like I've never seen one before as opposed to the fact that I've been working here for over three years and read the handbook cover to cover. Twice.

"Oh, you mean this thing? Here?" I walk over to the espresso machine like it's a foreign object. "Hm, it sure does have a lot of buttons and levers. I'm not sure. Maybe you can order something else? Like a plain coffee. I think I can make that just fine." I use my most innocent and naive sounding voice, letting him think I'm just some stupid bimbo.

"Maybe they should hire somebody who knows how to use the machinery, somebody smart enough to figure it out," he grumbles.

I suck my teeth and grab a large cup, bigger than he asked for, but I'll throw in the extra for what I'm about to do. Scribbling on the cup I turn my back and set to making his drink. My focus makes sure it's the best damn one I've ever made.

I feel his eyes on me and glance over my shoulder, just enough to catch him staring at my ass. Rolling my eyes, I give my head a shake. We have a pretty busy tourist business here, I'm used to newbies coming in, hanging out, chatting me up. But this guy? He screams asshole.

Sliding the cup over the counter toward him, I bend forward, squeezing my chest a touch so my cleavage is on point. When his eyes drop, I all but jump up and down. Teasing rich assholes is something I excel at. It gets me free drinks at the bars in Pineville City, only a half hour away, all the time.

"I hope it's to your liking." I put on the sugariest voice and smile I can muster. "Oh, and also, it's not polite to check out your barista."

"Excuse me?"

"Please, I saw you, checking out my ass, looking down my shirt."

"Maybe don't throw yourself across the counter and I won't look down your shirt. Or dress more professionally in your place of business."

Standing in front of the register I quickly ring him up. "That'll be three seventy five. Unless there's anything else?"

His eyes roam the clear case to the right. "A muffin."

The mixed berry aren't out yet, though I can smell that they're almost done. Good thing, this guy doesn't deserve one. Instead, I grab a coffee crumb and put it in a bag.

"Five sixty."

"Does this place even take credit?"

"Of course we do. All major companies." The sweetness in my voice is wavering.

As he lifts his cup to take the first sip, I watch as his eyes drift to the two letters I scribbled at the top. "DB?"

"Yeah, for Douchebag. That is your name, isn't it?" My eyebrows perch high on my forehead.

His lips press into a line as his eyes narrow. "I'd like to speak to your manager."

Tapping my fingers on the counter, I step back and point briefly at him. "Sure thing, I'll go get her."

As I walk away, pride swells in my chest as I hear the faintest "mm" from him. Whipping off my apron as I walk through the door of the kitchen, I toss it on the table in the middle of the room.

"Tough customer?"

"Oh, you know, just another guy who thinks he's hot shit."

"You got it?"

"You know it."

Squaring my shoulders, I walk back out, a Mazie smile plastered on my face.

"Hello, sir, I heard you'd like to speak to a manager. What can I help you with?"

"You have got to be fucking kidding me. There's no way you're a manager here. You're what, twelve?" His gaze tracks down and back up my body.

"I'm twenty-three thank you very much. See that Three Sticks on the sign? I'm one of the three. My sisters and I own the café and bakery. I'd be happy to get one of them for you if my service is not to your liking."

Grumbling incoherently, he spins on his heels and walks towards the door.

Resting one elbow on the counter, I wiggle my fingers. "Thank you for your patronage. Please come again."

When he walks out, I bang my head against the wood in front of me. I love our shop, I love my sisters, but I hate this job.

The warm scent of lemon zest wafts into my nose and I turn my face just enough to see a fresh-out-of-the-oven mixed berry muffin in front of me.

"Your favorite Sibby."

Taking a big bite I don't even try to stifle the moan. My sister is an amazing chef. "You know I hate that name," I mumble around a mouthful of food.

"I know. But I love it." Alina is only two years older than I am. When we were little she couldn't quite say 'baby sister' and it came out as 'sibby'. The nickname has stuck around for twenty-four years, and at this rate, I'm sure I'll never be rid of it.

"Only for you Leen." I tilt my head to the side to rest my head against hers. While I may have the crazy colored hair and fashion flair—as Mazie likes to put it—Alina and I aren't all that different. Both a little more independent, both a little more on the wild side, but both fiercely family oriented.

Acknowledgments

What an amazing journey it's been to get here. With that, comes many thanks.

To my amazing husband and children:

Book number eight. I can't believe it. I still cannot begin to truly show or explain my gratitude for all that you do and all the ways you continue to support me on this incredible journey.

I truly could not do a single aspect of this without you. Having you by my side every step of the way means so much to me.

I love you!

To my amazing duo; AK, RL:

You two are my rock solid team. There for any question, any confusion, any help I need, I know you're there. It's amazing to have found not just great writing partners, but friends.

To my awesome PA, Jennifer Webb:
Thank you for being my biggest cheerleader! I could not do this without your constant support!

To my incredible street team:
Thank you all for you continued support of me and my work. It's amazing to have readers who enjoy my work enough to want to promote it for others to read. I'm truly thankful for you all.

To my amazing editors Mackenzie and Beth:
This book would not be what it is without you and your input. Thank you for helping me learn how to be a better writer, adjusting my words, and most importantly, keeping my voice my own. And especially for your beautiful words as you read through it.

Thank you to the amazing **Fine's Fine Designs** for my stunning cover!

To my ARC team: Your time and effort does not go unnoticed. Thank you for reading my novel before it hit the public and for your gracious reviews. I know it's not always easy to find the words, but it's all so appreciated.

And most importantly, to the readers:

Thank you for taking a chance on a small author like myself. I know it can be difficult to see a new name and say "hey let me try that" but it is so beyond appreciated, I cannot begin to find the words. I write because it's my passion, but I publish because I want to share my words with all of you. I hope you enjoyed reading it, as much as I enjoyed writing it.

About the Author

Shayna Astor is a romance author who loves writing sweet love stories, with a lot of spice. When she's not writing, she's probably watching The Office with a cup of coffee, spending time with her kids, or playing video games with her husband.

Stalk me for all the latest updates, teasers for upcoming novels, giveaways, and all the goods on what's coming next!
Instagram @shayna.astor.author
TikTok @shayna.astor.author
Facebook Group Shayna's Coffee Corner
Sign up for my newsletter www.shaynaastor.com

Made in the USA
Monee, IL
02 September 2024